Yet in the Land of the Living

Also, by Nancy Avery Dafoe
Fiction
Socrates is Dead Again
Naimah and Ajmal on Newton's Mountain
Vena Goodwin Series:
You Enter a Room
Both End in Speculation
Murder on Ponte Vecchio

Nonfiction
Unstuck in Time, A Memoir and Mystery on Loss and Love
An Iceberg in Paradise, A Passage Through Alzheimer's
The Misdirection of Education Policy
Writing Creatively
Breaking Open the Box

Poetry
Got Some River in Us
When Mine Canaries Stop Singing
The House Was Quiet But the Mind Was Anxious
Innermost Sea
Poets Diving in the Night

Yet in the Land of the Living

Nancy Avery Dafoe

Pen Women Press

ISBN: 978-1-950251-24-7 (print)

First edition, Kansas: WingsePress, Inc., 2024 (out of print, no longer operating)
Second edition, Washington, D.C.: NLAPW, Pen Women Press, 2026
Printed in the United States of America

BISAC: FICTION/Literary; FICTION/Metaphysical;
FICTION/Historical/General; Fiction/Multiple Timelines;
FICTION/Historical/19th Century/American Civil War Era;
FICTION / War & Military; FICTION/Women; FICTION/General

This is a work of fiction. Names, characters, places, and incidents are
the product of the author's imagination or are used fictitiously. Any
resemblance to actual persons, living or dead, is coincidental. The
letters in this story, however, are the actual letters of the author's
great-great-grandfather and given to her by her aunt.

Published in the United States by
the National League of American Pen Women, Inc.
PEN WOMEN PRESS

Founded in 1897,
National League of American Pen Women, Inc.
is a nonprofit dedicated to promoting the arts.
1300 17th Street NW
Washington, D.C. 20036-1973
www.nlapw.org

"This is to let you know that I am yet in the land of the living, and that I'm feeling tolerable well."
Lafayette Cross,
1st Veteran New York Cavalry, Union Army

Author's Notes

The epigraph, chapter titles, and letters in *Yet in the Land of the Living* are the words of my ancestor Lafayette Cross who first served in the Union cavalry and then the Union infantry during the American Civil War. Misspellings and grammatical errors were common and authentic to his voice and time. His letters were kept by his wife and passed down through generations to me from my aunt Loretta Avery. While the poetic language in the soldier's letters is his, this story, all the characters, and their names are entirely a work of fiction.

This novel was originally published by WingsePress, Inc., Kansas, 2024. This publisher is no longer in operation.

*Yet in the Land
of the Living*

ONE

How uncertain are the calculations of man

Rumblings of an approaching train unnerved Grace Storey for reasons beyond the physical. Percussive sound and its effects took her to another time, one not from memory but history.

A long line of cars carrying men coming home from the war was felt before she could see their outlines crowded inside the rail car. Her cottage on the lake betrayed the contemporary train's disturbance: painted teacups agitated on hooks on the wall, uncertainty accompanied stirring in the ground beneath her, acknowledging the train's weight on the iron rails. Only when she heard its air whistle, long and mournful, was Grace displaced from her 21st century cottage home to another era; her imaginings took shape.

She was riding the rails with her great-great-grandfather heading North on a rail car behind the locomotive—a steam engine hissing its arrival at a depot after the great Civil War. Her eyes were not looking out windows but inside the train car. Scenes changed—not with movement but, rather, fixed on her distant ancestor Ezra Cross near an aisle at the entrance to a passenger car. Overcrowded with men who still had the look of weary soldiers even in their new civilian clothes, the locomotive pulled away slowly at first and then with increasing speed. Ezra held the bearing of a man who led other men in battle, yet he continued to stand, as if for the first time uncertain of his direction, before tucking a cloth covered bundle inside his jacket, his mustering out pay from his service. Black wool overcoat fit him well, perhaps the first new coat he had ever owned, and it squared his shoulders, otherwise bent from burdens.

Waiting for Ezra to make a move, Grace, too, was unsure. The man, who was quite young but had the look of one in the middle of life, stood balancing himself during the jolting movement of the train.

*

Another long blast of the air whistle landed Grace squarely in the present. She must have grown impatient, unable to hold onto that vision of her ancestor, leaving the steam engine locomotive without passengers' notice. It was the last time Ezra Cross would be seen alive.

As a budding historian and former English teacher, she understood the importance of those steam locomotives during and after the Civil War, later termed the "railroad war." But she had stopped riding history for a moment. Only after pulling back, did she begin to feel the effects, not quite panic nor fear exactly. How would she find her Civil War ancestor again? How would she discover the mystery of what happened to him? Those insights were not easy to come by without more evidence. Something told her she needed to see this through, attempt to answer this unsolved puzzle in order to find peace in her life. The thought propelled her, and she turned from imaginings about her distant relative to her volunteer work at the VA hospital for the day, thinking about a young, disabled Iraq War vet.

*

Below his blackened knees, there was nothing. His hands opened slowly to twisted and impossible fingers, one missing on his right hand, skin scarred from extensive burns. Lifting her eyes to the young man's head, Grace saw one side of his face looked familiar like her neighbor who played baseball in the nearby field on Saturdays, but the other half was distended, bulging from the base of his forehead to the place where part of his skull had once been. No longer rounded out, the shape was deformed, right eyebrow gone, eye below it seemingly lost in a deepening socket that could only be filled with questions covered over with a large gauze patch where his wound was hidden. Cheekbone on his left side was hollow, his face haunting.

From the hospital doorway, Grace took in the patient's mother, a tall, Nordic-looking woman, doing her best not to cry in front of her son, and, yet, the mother of this grievously maimed soldier—back from Iraq and one of the direct costs of war—still believed in his recovery. The young soldier Tim does not, Grace knew. He had already told his visitor part of him was forever gone—more than the aspect of his face, but he put up a front for his parents, especially his mother. His father showed the stoicism of a man who had known war himself.

When his parents left, Tim would think about ways to die and if he would need help in carrying out his plan. Even this last thought he shared with Grace because she had the advantage of not being family.

If Tim had been a solider in the Civil War with his injuries— instead of in the 21st century, Grace considered, he would not have breathed this long. Such is the state of our technology, she nearly said out loud before setting down a tray with a pot of coffee and cups of water and Ginger Ale. The sameness of wars is the terrible damage they do directly and indirectly, the extent to which the mangled might yet continue in the "land of the living," the line that had stuck in Grace's head since reading her great-great-grandfather's Civil War letters to his wife Susa. Tim was in this modern technological world, however, yet still struggling, and Grace could not help but be moved by his Herculean efforts not to show his pain or sorrow in front of his mother. Grace brought the tray for the parents, as well as for the wounded young man.

Offering water first, Grace poured coffee for them when Tim shook his head at the water. She set a cup next to Tim's mother who was holding her son's hand. Mother had tried reading to her son but stumbled over words, her voice pitchy with emotion she was working to control. Tim's mother had practiced holding back in front of her son and pushing past her sadness. Volunteer Grace set a second cup on a stand next to the bed, one intended for his father, a former Marine, who looked out the hospital window, pulling the blinds all the way up to let more light into a room that was already too severe. The father's gaze never moved in the direction of his son or wife. Tim looked up at Grace, seeming to plead. Their eyes met. Grace smiled, but she noticed the nearly imperceptible shiver run through the man.

She left the family momentarily and returned with a warming blanket which she wrapped around him. The nurses were only too glad to have a volunteer help out. The young man was grateful but said nothing, only blinked or maybe winked at her. Yes, he winked. His mother's head was bent as if in prayer, and she did not notice her son's expression change on seeing Grace. Although surprised by their instant connection, Grace returned the quiet gesture of recognition before leaving the room a second time, turning away from an almost unbearable sight. She would come back to this room many times. Tim's courage and plight pulled her gently but powerfully away from her own life.

All the way back from the VA, Grace recounted why she initially had decided to volunteer, justifying to herself actions which sometimes seemed desperate or self-serving. The catalogue was preparation for her inevitable attempt to explain what she was doing with her volunteer work to her husband's questions. It was as if an imagined foe was asking her motives when it was the man to whom she had long been married. Wanting to be honest, she listed legitimate reasons out loud as she drove home: *helping others who are struggling—because I am struggling, too*? She really did want to make a meaningful contribution to those who had given far more than she to her country. Yet, it bothered her that the effort did not feel selfless, actions allowing her to gain perspective on her own considerable losses. Nor would her husband Bill understand why she wanted to leave a secure high school teaching job to launch herself into a teaching position in another discipline. She could almost hear him asking, "why history now?" It was not so much the field of study, however, as the necessity of immersion, the desire to sink herself into another realm, to work really hard at something new—that was her prescription for sorrowing.

If she and Bill had been on better terms—the way they used to talk about everything—then she would have asked him what he thought about motivations and when were we being selfish in our carefully constructed selflessness? Bill, however, was now far away, even when next to her. Grace held close her layers of hurt. With all of her pain, however, she knew the melancholy she felt could not compare to what had been experienced by the badly injured young man who lay on a VA hospital bed he would never leave.

It would be several more trips to the VA hospital before she could look at the young man without feeling only pity and the slightest hint of revulsion, an emotion she fought against upon first entering his room. Looking at Tim was like looking into death.

"I was at the VA today. He is struggling so much." Here, she stopped, wondering if this was the wrong choice of words but then ventured ahead.

"The VA again?" Bill Storey moved his right hand but not his eyes which were fixed on the newspaper's sports section. He always sat in the same chair at the table even when she moved her seat, she noted, as if his habit was something to add to her file of things annoying her about her husband.

"There is a wounded young man I visit. I've told you about him. Tim Fitzgerald."

"You've mentioned him, I think. What's the reason?"

Misunderstanding her husband's question, Grace answered, "I don't know how to describe Tim in a way that does him justice. His legs have been blown off. I feel so sorry for him, but I doubt he wants my pity. He has given everything for his country."

"Umm," said Bill. "Yes," already losing interest.

Grace looked at her husband. His reaction seemed awful to her. Shaking her head, she turned from him to wash their dishes. She dropped a dish into the hot water, and it cracked at the sudden collision with the ceramic sink. The blue sweater she wore suddenly felt too hot, and she pushed up her sleeves as far as they would go.

Although far off in thought, Bill pulled back and realized his error might give him away. "Oh. Did you break something there?"

"Yes, careless of me."

"You were saying something about your Iraq vet? It's terrible, of course, and expensive."

"Expensive?"

"An expensive war, I mean."

Moving back toward her husband, Grace sat at the table again. She hoped she had misinterpreted his comment about the cost of war being expensive, believing he was commenting on metaphysical costs. "It's so unfair. He's so young, not much older than our son, yet he will never walk again even if he survives his terrible injuries, and his face." Her voice trailed off for an instant.

Bill looked directly at her for the first time all evening, perhaps because she had mentioned their son. He studied her demeanor, then said, "Remember, those soldiers were all volunteers. They knew what they were getting into."

"Did they really?"

"They were trained and prepared. Grace, I'm not sure what help you can possibly be to them, to him?"

"'They knew what they were getting into?' How would they know they were going to have their arms and legs ripped off, their faces caved in, their lovers leave them?" Grace got up and poured more soap into the now lukewarm dishwater, loading the sink again, so she would not have to look at her husband. Why was he so distracted recently, indifferent to others' pain, indifferent to hers?

Bill's head jerked up. He sighed and studied his wife's straight back, covered by her long dark hair, before speaking. Realizing he was missing something that might be important later, he asked, "Did you say, 'Their lovers leave them?'" His heart was beating faster, and he hoped she wouldn't notice. "How do you know—this soldier's girlfriend or lover or whatever left him? Didn't you just start volunteering there?"

Turning again, Grace said, "I don't know his full history, but I know Tim's fiancée left him after she saw how horribly disfigured he is. He told his mother about her while I was in the room."

"What were you doing in there again? When the man's parents were with him?"

"Bringing them drinks and a warming blanket for him. I wasn't eavesdropping, but he was talking about his girl after I entered."

"Bringing drinks? That's what you do there? You sound like their maid or a waitress." Bill recognized he had slipped again but was relieved his wife did not seem to be indicating she knew anything about his current affair. The "lovers leaving" comment had nothing to do with him, after all. He would have to tell Grace at some point soon, but it was so much easier just to let things fall away naturally.

Grace looked at her husband in the way Tim's father had looked at his son when he mentioned his girlfriend's abandonment. "What did you just say? Their maid?"

"Oh, Grace, Gracie. You don't have to take offense at everything. Really, you're being much too dramatic. Just wondering what you hope to accomplish?"

"Dramatic?" Grace realized she kept repeating his words but was incredulous at his casual cruelty. "That's what you have to say? And I'm too dramatic about feeling something?"

"Look, I'm sorry this young man was injured, and you've had a tough time there and more recently with your mother's death and your brother's illness. But why torture yourself with more unhappiness? Why exactly is it you go? I'm sure there are plenty of other people who can volunteer. You have a teaching job and plenty to do around here." Bill picked up his paper again as if the conversation between them was over. He flipped pages, fully aware he was using the newspaper as a shield.

Grace pursed her lips, studied the man as if he were a complete stranger, looked at the top of his head, his thick, dark hair. He was still a handsome man, but she no longer saw him in the same way she once had, realizing she was not attracted to him anymore and wondered when the break happened.

Neither did he compliment has wife any longer—her youthful appearance, her long brown hair with scarcely a strand of gray, and her intelligent eyes. What had broken between them?

She stood across from him, silent for several moments, then began again. "Do you recognize the moment when everything turns to the right or left and becomes something different or changes, grows into a shape with a face, a sarcastic smile, or this transcendent expression? This soldier, he is horribly injured, but his face is somehow spiritual as if he has already left all the troubles of this world behind. His parents bring him back to our earthly problems. Bill, I go because I want to help, but there is something else I realize I am looking for there." Grace glanced down at the neatly pressed *Provence* cloth her mother had given her, running her fingers across the wrinkled surface to smooth it. The tablecloth made her think of her mother which was why she washed and still pressed it. "This young man, barely more than a boy, makes me feel needed, and in his presence, I feel—I feel the presence of grace."

"What was that? Sorry, the damn Sox winning again. Listen, dinner, the dinner was; it was good." There, he thought, a compliment. It should help. Now to make my exit.

"Did you hear anything I just said?"

"Of course, you're upset about that young man in the hospital, but there are lots of them. War is endless and wasteful, and, really, what are you going to do about any of it? He is beyond your help certainly. You'll worry yourself sick about some patient you don't really know. It seems like you have enough to worry about as it is."

She knew he was talking about her mourning the death of her mother. "I already feel I know Tim." For an instant, she almost stuttered like the young soldier.

"Maybe you shouldn't get so attached so quickly. Grace, I've got to get back to the office tonight. Need to finish up a few things before my client meeting tomorrow. I will be late."

"Again?"

"There's no need for you to wait for me tonight." With his abrupt announcement, Bill pushed away from the table, grabbed his coat hanging on a rack near the front door and was on his way.

How did they get to that point? Grace wondered. Certainly, the two high school sweethearts seemed once as passionate as Romeo and Juliet, but something happened along their paths, many somethings really. Grace was angry at her husband's inadvertent cruelty, remembering her soldier, not yet beginning her ill-defined search or discovered awareness of the sudden change of direction already in motion for them all.

When Bill opened their door sometime after 2:00 a.m., Grace was pretending to sleep, and he dropped his clothes on the floor, scents of the evening on his skin and in the air. There was only the faintest hint of perfume and a mild note of alcohol making a sudden appearance in the bedroom before he left to sleep in their guest room. In those moments, she knew everything about the night yet did not want to know.

She made the decision not to live in their house any longer. In the morning, she would pack a few clothes, notes, books, and head for her mother's and father's cabin. Although neither husband nor wife had said it yet, she knew their marriage had come to its end. If it had only been infidelity, she might have weathered the damage.

*

At the top of the hill, white windmills distended air like a flock of colossal gulls, surprising Grace with their presence. She had never taken this route in Upstate New York before, but her inquiry into historical records of her Civil War soldier ancestor led her down this road to the unexpected. Bouncing slightly in her seat, Grace acknowledged the beaten and exhausted vehicle told her its springs were broken. Grace pulled over to a wider section of paved shoulder and parked. Promising herself a new car at the earliest opportunity, she stretched her legs, shook her arms, hands, and fingers, walking around to fully waken to the moment.

As she looked up at the rows of those 400-foot wind turbines, she was struck by two associations: the powerful whooshing of their white metal wings seemed to match a god's labored breathing, and the symmetry of those windmills stretched out across the hillsides reminded her of the graveyards of soldiers with white crosses. Beneath those colossal blades, Grace felt her own heartbeat in sync with white noise. In the muffled but incessant pounding, she was comforted and felt her fears and imaginings about approaching death come down to relief.

TWO

————

I am not entirely well

My wheel is in the dark, Grace said aloud, reading again the Emily Dickinson poem title and line. How perfectly the words expressed grief, she wanted to say to the poet Emily, as if she were sitting in the room with her before returning to her own writing. Only recently, Grace had taken to talking to herself. "God-awful, pretentious," cursed Grace to no one as she tossed her first papers into a rattan wastebasket near her bare feet: much better to have been born before post-Modernism's doubt, self-reflection, self-absorption. It was history, not fiction, she was attempting to write, she reminded herself. But where were the facts compiled? Whose voices were recorded and preserved in a white patriarchy?

She glanced at her polished toenails, noted chips exposing flesh tones—the color was called Shakespeare she remembered—having chosen it because she loved the fact a color had been named after the Bard, not for the hue itself—then shuffled papers on the floor. All of this effort was in the beginning stages, and she stroked the notes with the tips of her toes. She had never polished her toenails when she was married to Bill. It was a small rebellion from her old self, and she realized she rather liked looking at her feet now because of that fact. Bill was gone from her life, and she was trying to rediscover her ancestors' stories, as well as her own.

After a moment, she forced herself back to the task at hand. A soldier's letters were all that remained of Ezra Cross and his unsolved mystery. Wives and daughters, then sisters and aunts wrapped the papers, now brittle with age and repeated readings, in ribbons or white string, and stored in cedar blanket chests, so, nearly 150 years later, the thoughts of a man going out on picket would be known and not lost forever. Grace inherited the letters of one of those soldiers—her great-great-grandfather, and she was attempting to treat these artifacts with respect, but she was also not reverential.

Caught between her love of fictional narrative and pursuit of trying to record and accurately uncover history, she realized the division would either constrain her or cause a schism. For some time, she had not felt like herself, even discerned her mind was struggling with something not entirely within her control. I am not entirely well, she nearly said out loud, then remembered a line from her great-great grandfather's letter. She was listening to him even when she walked away from those letters spread across the cottage floor.

Ezra and Susa were now living with her. She needed to show some methodology, Grace decided, as she turned away from her computer. Becoming a chronicler of history would take a different type of discipline than she was used to practicing.

The awkward historian leaned down and picked up a laminated copy of her soldier's letter which had been shoved under a favorite reading chair. A glancing survey of the room took in a tapestry ragged at the edges from chewing by a pup long ago grown into a sedate, gentle soul that had rested at her feet until very recently. She missed Riley, gone nearly a year now—so much loss all together. Her mother's death and brother's illness, then her husband leaving. Their old dog had been a daily comfort, but now, Riley was gone, too.

Recalling a scene with her dog, she thought of those moments walking the big black dog after an overnight surface hoar—ice cover complete. Riley nosed tall weeds in the fields and flakes of frost fell from the grasses onto him, and he was nearly blanketed in white, feathery crystals until he shook himself, creating a mini-snowstorm. The image made her smile.

Allowing herself only a moment to reflect on her dog before returning to history, Grace remembered Jason wanted her to buy another pup for company. She told him she was done with that phase of her life. Her son didn't believe her. The wayward letter under the chair was returned to its position.

Grace surveyed the map of Ezra Cross's letters for a few minutes before sitting with her computer in front of her. The desk was almost too cluttered to work, its surface buried beneath textbooks, stacks of papers, a file folder with bills, and a few novels opened to particular scenes, one with its spine broken and the pages partially askew. How would she get to the bottom of any of this? How would she make sense of it all? She briefly considered the idea she did not have the disposition for a recorder of history.

Even if she discovered every last letter from the Civil War, knew every date, and placed every event in its time frame, Grace knew there would be missing information from her ancestor, critical absences which would echo in her marrow. From the point at which she was told her great-great grandfather had disappeared from the factual record at the end of the Civil War, she considered him the answer to the intangible. What the record held was a gaping hole in which possibilities bubbled up as she read his lines, his amazingly graceful handwriting running across the page, created in the light of a campfire or oil lamp so very long ago. She could almost see him composing at last light.

*

Ezra Cross pulled out government notes from the bulging pocket of his unfamiliar civilian clothes. Out of uniform, he was redefining himself as he counted the currency quickly, glancing up just once to make sure no one was around. He steadied his angular tall frame on the train, legs astride, one calloused hand extended and pressed against warm metal of the railcar. He was going home, not a rich man but now, finally, a man of some means who could better provide for Susa, the boys, and his little girl. He would purchase a piece of land— land that would need working after all this time—or perhaps he would open a feed store. For once in his life, he had options. Susa had written she wanted to live in town. It was all new to him—this idea of being with his family again seemed almost foreign, returning to become a part of a community, part of a family and a place which no longer felt like home.

For the first time in his life, he moved like a wealthy man. There were possibilities he had not yet allowed himself to consider, grasping the greenbacks in his right hand with his twice broken index finger; he glanced at his grotesquely enlarged joint and wondered if Susa would notice his small scars. There were stories to tell her—ones too long and complicated for letters but would he tell her? There was much he had left out of their brief written exchanges. The paper money gave him a sense of freedom, and it was gratifying but oddly confusing. He could buy his wife a new dress, and he imagined her startled look when he tossed the currency triumphantly on their table. It suddenly occurred to him she might have moved the furniture around. No, she would have sold the table given to him by his grandmother when the money he sent never arrived. Nothing would be in the places he remembered. Of course, his wife was not even living in the same house. What had he been thinking? Times had been hard, and she had complained of not receiving his pay. Mails were too slow or unreliable. And he had mistakenly trusted a fellow soldier returning home.

He considered even her face would feel unfamiliar, and the children? How could he know them? They would most likely not recognize him. Certainly, the young one would not know him at all.

What would Susannah say when she saw him after all this time? She would throw her arms around his neck and cover his bearded face with kisses. Perhaps, he would splurge on a barber before anything, getting all the hairs along his neck, too. Any town's barber would do. I will cut a fine figure, he told himself. Susa was never one to be demonstrative, but surely, she would show him how much she missed him after the war. Yet, it occurred to him they might both feel like strangers to one another, at least for a time, but he had no doubt their affections would return.

Would his sons come running up to greet him? No, the older boy would hold out his hand to shake his father's. George certainly would offer a hand like the young man he was growing up to be. The girl was no longer a baby, Ezra reflected, recognizing his children's responses might be those of someone else's children. Susa might instruct them on how to greet him, but he could envision them standing back shyly. He then decided his sons would not be timid. They would wrestle and tumble with him, and Susa and little Jennie would give him a proper, respectful kiss. His children would be dutiful; Susa would have seen to that. When they were finally alone, Susa would show him her love again.

*

It was this exhilarating scene of respect, gratitude, and love that Ezra imagined when a blow to the back of his head ended all thoughts. There were no witnesses. There was no time for regret or panic or sorrow. His limp body was indifferently shoved off the railcar near the back of the train, body tumbling over, breaking like dry tree limbs, and landing unceremoniously in thick brush, caught by spines of thorn bushes. It was several weeks before a conductor in a passing train that could not stop spotted his corpse and notified an Army corporal at the next depot. Unfortunately, animals had dragged his body back to the tracks, and train wheels had run over the body, separating his head from his shoulders. The head was missing. Vagrants, like vultures, had lifted the money from the torn clothing.

The victim's identity was uncertain. Animals had eaten at his face and fingers before they had reached him even when they were able to retrieve parts of him. This was a broken and mutilated corpse. However, the body was eventually identified as Ezra Cross who carried a letter of discharge in his pocket but not a single government note in payment for his years of loyal service in the Union Army. This was all the information they gave a waiting Susannah Cross.

THREE

I had about given up

With a bit of elastic, Grace pulled back her hair and twisted it, securing the long strands, finally clearing her line of vision. It was impossible to get down to serious work with hair dangling across her line of sight. How was it women in the movies always had their hair sensuously falling and curving across their faces, their eyes half hidden, suggesting mystery? None of those women could ever have been doing any serious work, she reasoned.

Returning from her digression, Grace stared at the letters again, saved the document where she had begun researching clothing worn by soldiers in the Union Army, although she was unsure how the research she undertook would be used in her paper, and so she turned off the computer, leaving her words for a time hanging not in balance but suspended in darkness because they did not resonate in the way her soldier's letters home to his wife did. The quiet rhythm of her fingers on the keys stopped, and the cabin fell silent.

A chronological reading of letters offered no conclusions, only speculations. Chronology was all she learned of history when she was young; the pedagogy of the time suggested timelines and memorization leading to certainty about time and events and causal, traceable succession of which we are no longer so certain. Even time itself is no longer considered linear, Grace thought, knowing just enough about string theory to make her feel curious but discomforted.

Trying another methodology antithetical to historical research, Grace began picking up letters in random order, hopeful layers of this history would somehow reveal themselves coherently. Perhaps, she would stumble across something, a word, a phrase, she hadn't noticed before. Within this phrase, she would find an authentic glimpse into their lives, revealed like an opening act when the curtain was pulled back and live actors walked across the stage.

She was still forming her ideas about what she was looking for, but she hadn't read very many of Ezra Cross' letters before she began to think more about his wife, the woman to whom he wrote all those letters from the field. Susa survived the war, another woman without a historical voice, but whose progeny and resilience allowed the continuation of life, her own existence found in her children and successive generations.

Picking up a letter, she wondered about the reductive formality of address, Ezra writing "Wife" instead of Susa.

*

Tuesday
October 20th/'63
Dear Wife

I again will try to write you a few lines to let you know that I am well and I hope those few lines will find you and the children enjoying the same great blessings of God.

The Regt. left here yesterday for Washington instead of NY and I am left here in charge of men that have not been mustered yet. I expect to have them mustered Saturday and if I do the probability is next Monday I shall leave hear for Washington. So, you see how

uncertain are the calculations of man for but a few days again I expected to get my pay and come home before I went to Washington but in that I am disappointed and a great disappointment it is to me I assure you but what cant bee cured must be endured the saying is so I suppose I must submit to my lot.

I heard about you by Wm Whitcomb. He said he saw you at the depot and that you told him that you and the children were well. I was glad to hear it. I believe I shall get a furlow as soon as I get to Washington and get my pay. I have not time to write anymore.

This from your affectionate husband
Ezra Cross

*

This man, this nearly forgotten ancestor of Grace's, had some tendency to wax poetic, she considered, typing his phrase on her computer, "how uncertain are the calculations of man," intending to use it later. Perhaps his line would become a chapter heading in her paper. Yes, she thought, despite our best planning, life is nothing if not uncertain. His words had not only a poetic ring but an authenticity. For his time, Ezra would have been considered an educated man, having gone on to and completed high school. Although his spelling was weak—as was the spelling of most people at the time, his vocabulary was excellent, she noted. He was an intelligent man, her great-great grandfather. Her great-great-grandmother must have endured many disappointments, the ones referred to in the letter only an inkling. How much could she discern of Susa from Ezra's responses?

Grace scanned war letters neatly set out across her library floor, one well etched by chairs dragged carelessly over it, as well as

21

damaged by Riley's claws when he raced to get to the door or from a lamp which had fallen, gouging the wood, a second after Jason tossed a ball across the room. This cottage room had been Jason's grandfather's fishing camp; the old, heart pine revealing lives of those who had once lived there. Even the wood took on the odors of history, her history.

Another letter, dated October 20th/ '63, jumped out at her with the word "Wife." Grace stopped again at the notion of this formal title and the idea "Wife" had never suited her even years ago, let alone now, but she had accepted it by custom—the wife of Bill Storey. Well, she would never be a wife again, she thought without rancor, perhaps some sadness and perhaps some relief the tensions between them had disappeared with their liberation. As much as she tried not to think about Bill, he kept appearing in her thoughts, and her questions as to why he left. Yet her name no longer felt like her own. Grace Storey had lilt to it, but only now did she think about ridding herself of her adopted surname.

*

Then, he was standing there again, at 18, with thick, curly hair the color deeper than the ink in a well; she could touch it with her mind as she stared at the back of his head in trigonometry class. It was his fault, she knew at the time, as well as in reflection, she had trouble passing the math class. Bill called her for a homework assignment they both knew he had already completed. He was the last person she was to tutor in the intricacies of mathematics.

Romantic love, forbidden love, and lustful love, Grace moved through the Brontë sisters to D.H. Lawrence with the "mystery of the dark mountain of blood, reeking in homage, in lust, in rage, and passive with everlasting patience." Bill was responsible for her diving deeper into literature, she decided, and for that, she would always thank him, and, of course, most importantly, for Jason their child. As a young girl,

Grace left novels and dove into poetry, composing with Lawrence's rhythms echoing in her head and on paper.

Seventeen-year-old Grace writing to Bill: "It was you who gave her a first kiss and told her not to be afraid of the world," with Bill never knowing she had stolen those lines from Lawrence. Her first kiss occurring much earlier, unexpectedly, as she sat on the steps of the public library when a boy she hardly knew came up and sat beside her, talking about nothing for a moment, then swiftly but sweetly putting his lips gently to hers. Stephen thanked her for the kiss, but she never dated him or wished to do so.

In her backyard, underneath the wintering bushes and late at night, Grace made love to a young Bill in the cold, with matted leaves and twigs pressed against her back; she was profoundly sad for reasons she couldn't explain and profoundly grateful. No one had to tell her she was in love. She recognized it from the ache when she woke in the morning and the ache when she could not see him or touch him. She stood just far enough out of his reach for him to want to leap across chasms. The smell of new earth was in her hair and on her clothes after she lay down with her boy.

"Geese breaking the film of blue sky" was her metaphor for sex in a poem she wrote for him. Lawrence had his elephants slow to mate. Grace started writing poetry, lines at once sanctuary and celebration for the acts of love and discovery of sexuality. She fell in love with Bill and D.H. Lawrence at the same time. They were children—lustful, raging hormonal teens, but those two young people had disappeared into past. Then past imploded into present.

Nights when they were two thousand miles apart, she brought them together with a poem written after 3:00 in the morning with sounds on campus: drunken teens stumbling in and hitting their feet against unexpected rises, cursing in the dark, and slamming doors, toilets heard flushing, and water running. Two thousand miles away, she could feel Bill's warm hand running along the base of her thigh, her heart pounding so loudly she was sure it would wake her sleeping roommate who had only come in fifteen minutes earlier and was already making a soft blowing noise that wasn't quite a snore. Grace imagined herself to be smarter at night, writing across the great gap of the Midwest separating the college lovers. She imagined Bill reading her letters and poems and sensing her suffering. Although she would not admit it, she was looking for suffering from him, too, a trembling of the hands, a pressure in the chest, and an uncertain glance around the room before giving into sorrow. If she could make her young man ache, she would know he loved her as well, and so she composed into the night, scratching out words, writing in margins, checking her spelling, before carefully, in her best calligraphy, rewriting poems on ivory colored stationery.

*

Almost smiling in this understanding and misunderstanding, she felt the lump in her throat again. Bill was not the same man, and she was no longer an innocent, girlish Grace. How many years ago had Bill ceased to be the person she thought he was? He could, of course, say the same about her. It would be fair if he asked her why she had become so internal, so brooding. She knew he had grown weary of her mourning. His lack of empathy was astounding, she thought, after she had lost her father, mother, and worry for her brother. Bill was gone just before Aunt Evelyn died. A sense of belonging, of being part of her origin family, had vanished like a soldier never come home from the war.

Grace turned to Ezra's letters again out of self-preservation, snapped back further into the past with the mind's winds. Susannah remained a wife throughout her long life. Was it possible to determine anything about her—this soldier's wife and so much more—from Ezra's letters? How likely was it more was known about the soldier who never returned from the war than the steadfast woman who persevered?

Having made laminated copies of the original, now fragile papers which were locked away in her new, safe deposit box—the prospect of having secretly stored and protected documents was still foreign to her, but advised by her attorney in a divorce proceeding—Grace shuffled these analogues around at will, sticking colored arrows on lines she found irresistible either as a scholar or simply as a woman descended from the man who never came home. Although related by blood, she still felt those connections to this Civil War era were a stranger.

Yet there was mystery and an answer to this puzzle contained somewhere in these words, and she would find it if she were not in a rush. If she was methodical and meticulous. Methodology was what her graduate school history professor had told her was critical. "Be patient." The problem? She was never very patient, even ripping out seams of a dress she had nearly finished once because the whole project was taking too damn long. Patience was some ancient virtue or another person's grail, absent from her experience, but persistence still counted for something, she reminded herself.

Air in the cabin grew stale and heavy with waning summer heat. Getting up to open windows, Grace struggled with one above the desk where white paint had been carelessly slathered on in too many layers, making the opening stick like cement. Old paint suggested yellowed glue. She lightly tapped the frame with a globe paperweight and tried again, cracking the paint, and finally, successfully managing to gain some breathing space. The metal fans at both ends of the room were plugged in and turned on, and air circulated, humming along indifferently, so she could work again.

Examining a second letter, Grace's eye caught the Christmas reference first. For an agonizing instant, she considered how radically altered her own holiday season would be. Would her son choose to stay with her for Christmas or go with his father and Beth? The idea should not have been so repulsive to her, and she was trying to think of her son's wants and happiness, not her own. Still, she could not bear the idea of Jason sitting on a rug near Beth's feet. She wouldn't get a tree this year, but, no, if she didn't, then Jason would be unhappy. Why was she worrying about buying Christmas trees in early September heat? Of course, she would get a tree. Or perhaps she would set out the little, silver artificial tree her mother had purchased the year before her death. Grace kept her mother's tree stored at the cabin because she held onto nearly everything her mother left. At some point, she knew she would have to give things away or stay buried in artifacts of the dead.

She called her son at his college. "Jason, do you want a real tree or an artificial one for Christmas this year?"

"What?" Her son sounded as if he had just woken even though it was late in the morning. He was on freshman dorm time.

"I found Grandma's silver tree, and I thought I might use it this year."

"Whatever you want, Mom." She could almost see the exasperation on her son's face through his tone. "I don't care. I mean, whatever you pick is fine."

"I just want you to be happy and enjoy your Christmas vacation. Sorry if I woke you."

Jason laughed. "You didn't wake me. Okay, sure. Gram's old tree works for me. Listen, I've got to get to class. Talk to you about Christmas later."

She could hear the hint of impatience in his voice. "Of course. Have a good day, honey."

"You, too, Mom." He hung up.

Imagining his relief at being free of her, she chastised herself for relying too much on her son since Bill had walked out. Although she never thought she would lose her son, her responses to him had turned needy, and she hated this neediness about herself. Traditions would have to change whether she liked the idea or not. How had her life turned upside down, like Eliot's "Upside down Towers?" She wondered what kind of historian couldn't keep her mind on topics without falling off into worries about small, insignificant decisions months away.

Grace recognized this idea of digging into the past as in some comforting process even if for no other reason than it kept her mind occupied and engaged in lives other than her own. Perhaps it was nothing more than distraction—the movement away from examination of self toward others. She hoped it was more. The soldier's letters were welcomed like old friends. "Come in," she invited them. "Distract me."

*

Camp Stoneman
Friday   December 26th/ '63
Dear Wife

This is to let you no that I am yet in the land of the living and that I am feeling tolerable well for me yet I am not entirely well. I have tried everything that I could get to cure my diarhea but havent fully succeeded altho at times it has seemed to dry up only to breake out and this morning nothing but blood passed my bowels but I believe I shall come out all right. I don't want you to bee alarmed for I feel perfectly confident that I shall come home all right I had a very plesant Christmas for I took gallop out in the country about 5 miles and I enjoyd the ride and seanry verry much there was but one
thing liking to make me happy that was my wife and children had they

been with me my joy would have been complete. we expect to leave hear in about a month or at leaste that is the report heare among the officers and should we go you probably will not see me again until my three years is up. I had thought if we stayd hear this winter that I would have you and little Jimmie come down and stay with me until spring and if I find out that we shall lay hear until March or April. I shall have you come but Susa I have learned not to count my chickens before they are hatched.

I hope this will find you and the children well. You have herde it said by some that the soldiers did not get enough to eate but it is not so for they get more than they can eat. I wish you could see the bread and meat we are obliged to throw away. You would not ask for any better provisions we throw away enough every day to keep a small family fed.

Susa, I wish you could have seen me mend my socks the other day you would have laughed I no but I don it as well as I knew how but it looked like cane.

I must now close by askin you to excuse my bad writing and spelling so no more this time kiss the children for me and big one for you

From your affectionate husband

Ezra Cross

Strange, Grace considered how communication had changed in the relatively brief span of time from the Civil War to the present, yet how flawed the articulation of ideas and emotions between men and women or, for that matter, between human beings remained. Whether we are carving out symbols in stone, writing elegantly with a quill pen, or texting on a cell phone, we are still so inarticulate, so misunderstood, and so dense in our clumsy attempts to really understand the heart of another living being, she decided.

Had she really been impossible to live with after the death of her mother, and then her aunt compounding the layered grief? Paralysis of a kind had taken hold for a while, but he never gave her a chance to move out of her protective shell.

What must Susannah have thought when she read the intimate details about her husband's bowels and then the lines relating him riding out rather joyfully over the countryside on Christmas day? We are such an oddity as a species, Grace thought. Then she placed a sticky note on the letter since she recalled reading dysentery was rampant during the Civil War, only later discovering, in Faust's *This Republic of Suffering,* 995 out of every 1,000 soldiers had experienced the disease or its equivalent effects at some point during the war. Perhaps the leap from illness narrowed the chasm between life and death, allowing for acceptance of losses all around them without descending into madness or succumbing to crippling fears.

What was Ezra thinking? Moving from sickness to "riding out in the countryside" on Christmas day? Ezra almost certainly had no time for transitions in the hurried rush to compose letters in those sporadic moments of idleness in camp. Although she could almost hear the sounds of the encampment, soldiers preparing food, packing or unpacking gear, singing, scraping metal plates, Grace knew only a fragment of the end of the story, compelling her to read backwards and forward in time simultaneously. It was a fault she was well aware of, however: this rush to reach conclusions before all the evidence, before knowing the records, thereby inserting bias into every equation. I am a dreadful historian, she told herself, amidst trying to order anarchy. History and truth had to be buried somewhere in those letters.

*

"Here you go," said Aunt Evelyn. "I'll tell you about your great-great-grandfather. He cut quite a figure. Handsome, wasn't he?" Evelyn brought out the portrait of the man in his Union uniform.

Beginning with an ending, a tale told to her years ago by her Aunt Evelyn over genealogy charts, photo albums, tissue papers, and all those old letters, Grace was shown the early photograph of Ezra Cross when she was a skinny tall girl. Ezra sat straight and proud in his 20 oz. wool uniform with a gold tassel on the hilt of his dress sword. The buckle at his waist was prominent along with the redundancy of red sash below it. The old tintype had been hand-colored with a combination of pigments and gum Arabic applied to the plate. His thick, brown hair was elaborately curled on the sides but smooth and straightened on top. The faintest blue marked his eyes—the photo expertly retouched—at once intelligent and cryptic in appearance; those small and deeply set eyes under his prominent brows were an indication of contradictions in the man, something the 12-year-old girl was wholly unaware of when she first held his photo. The beard on his face was longer than a goatee and neatly trimmed around his mouth, an extended oval, elongated at his hidden chin. The slight prejudice against a man with a "weak" chin was inherited from her mother's lineage, Grace knew. On his left hand, Ezra wore a white glove and on his right hand was a ring with a stone set into it. Only his thin red lips seemed poorly colored—too red to be natural. His posture was erect and stiff, yet there he was, colorized as in life, an outdated technique, the corners of Ezra's portrait rounded because the technology of the day produced negatives side-by-side on a plate. Part of the image was cropped off when enlarged, resulting in the loss of Ezra Cross' feet—explained in detail by Evelyn, who had an interest in old photographs of the era, although unfathomable to the 12-year-old who wondered why someone would be so careless as to cut off her great-great-grandfather's feet.

Even then, something was missing from the man. A photograph gave away no gestures, the body in repose with open eyes unrevealing, closed mouth silent. If she could have turned the photo ahead a frame or two to see Ezra break into a boyish grin or catch the twitching of his left eye, an involuntary muscle spasm as facial tic—anything might have led in some direction, but all she had was the stillness of an image until all those years later, when she began reading his letters as an adult.

Why had they painted his eyes such a piercing blue, the child asked her aunt so long ago. Grace scarcely knew the little girl who questioned her aunt about some distant relative.

"Because he had beautiful blue eyes, and he was very smart," Evelyn must have told her niece with a tone indicating indignation. Evelyn's pride in her great-grandfather was always in evidence. It was as if the glories of her ancestor's past raised her stature in the present.

"How do you know for sure?" Grace would have persisted even as her aunt expressed some measure of exasperation.

"Don't be silly, child."

"What happened to him?"

"He must have been killed on the way home," Evelyn said, without providing an answer to the little girl's first question about eye color. For weeks, Grace thought about the soldier who never came home, and then this ancestor, this soldier was lost to her in the making of her own life with all its chaotic whirls.

Strangely, she found Ezra Cross again when Evelyn passed away, leaving her the soldier's letters, his photograph, a bit of an inheritance, and another connection to her past. It was after reading Ezra's letters she thought again of the photograph she had seen all those years ago, and it reminded her of a quotation from one of Orhan Pamuk's novels: "My father always said we should pay close attention to the gestures that make us who we are." Where were the gestures of Ezra Cross? Could they be found in his writing? What did his letters reveal? She tried to imagine.

The last time Grace visited Evelyn before her aunt's death, she had walked around her grandmother's property where her aunt spent her last days, crossed the road and wandered under wild crab apple trees where she had played as a child. There, instead of apple trees were anthills, mounds of extraordinary width and height like something out of a photograph from an African landscape she had seen in *National Geographic* magazine. She imagined ants marching out, these alien creatures and creators of this now incompatible landscape, memories of her childhood altered by Salvador Dali-inspired visions.

Evelyn kept the box with Ezra Cross' letters beneath the bed on which she had breathed her last. Grace found her aunt lying peacefully with her arms folded across her chest as if arranged that way, dying in her sleep in the pose that seemed easiest. But the room was cluttered and not artful, used tissues everywhere, as Grace thought about her aunt struggling for last breaths at the end with her pink nightgown buttoned to the neck. Evelyn appeared to have planned on being the one to confront death directly. After a few minutes, while she waited for an ambulance to arrive, Grace sat on a chair in the kitchen and wept for Evelyn. The sheriff who had broken the window to let her in had turned away from her grief while he sipped the cup of coffee she had given him. Death was routine in his business, he said but still he was sorry for her and the family.

"It's too bad she was alone," he said after he thanked her for the coffee.

"She liked it that way. Very independent woman," was Grace's reply, but she did feel the unease of rising guilt. Should she have checked on her aunt earlier? Evelyn had told her niece she had a cold but said it was nothing. Still, Grace heard the thickness in her voice, the gravelly nature of her cough.

Sitting in the present dark later, Grace recalled again those terrible anthills, the great-great-grandfather and great-great-grand-mother she had never known, all in a strange montage of images with the misshapen face of a young soldier home from Iraq somehow transposed over surfaces of these images fell into and out of her visions. Somewhere in the amalgamation of time and loss was a theme, a record of where and how she should turn next, indicating detours to paved roads where she had been traveling, one way now blocked.

FOUR

———

You must be careful how you run

Professor Coleman's office door was closed, but Grace had an appointment, so she knocked tentatively at first and then loudly before turning the antique brass knob, responding to his abrupt invitation. Everything in the building spoke of another age of distinction; even the wood, the architecture had acquired the smell of old papers and historical artifact, of a time and place not forgotten but patiently waiting to re-emerge. Professor Coleman initially appeared irritated at being disturbed, but it was a ruse he had practiced to allow himself time to assess situations.

"Do you have any idea how many of these Civil War letters have been found, archived, and written about exhaustively?" asked Coleman as he leaned back in his dark wood and leather chair, his gesture at once more dismissive than his words, thought Grace. Generally, his students were intimated by Coleman, a man of 53, who had a quiet but sarcastic bite to his words, a professor who offered no sympathy to the plight of every graduate student: overworked and unpaid. Jeffrey Coleman was at work on his own text about the military career of Ulysses S. Grant and made it apparent he believed his teaching duties to be an interruption of his important historical writing. Teaching was his paid career, but his passion was in researching and interpreting history.

Grace considered she had made the mistake of choosing his favorite era to write about, knowing it would draw his critical eye but hoping, at least, he would begin with an interest in her topic. She had done her homework but didn't know if it would be enough.

"I understand there are over nine thousand archived letters in Vermont alone," said Grace. "But there are countless books on nearly every subject, but the fact doesn't mean there is nothing new to write about this particular topic. A fresh perspective could add to the discussion."

"The perspective being yours?" he asked with evident sarcasm but allowing his chair to lean forward again.

"The perspective of the waiting wives of those soldiers," said Grace, anticipating his response. She knew this tactic would resonate with Coleman since the concept behind his text was exhaustively written about, as well. If she had been 20 instead of 42, she stopped at her age, suddenly surprised she thought of it. She never saw herself as her chronological age, an age when, according to her students, you were already old. Her mother's gift to her had been a youthful appearance and hair belying her age. Grace might have vacillated, falling off in deference to the authority figure as she had when she was younger, but time and the events of life had altered her, given her confidence if for no other reason than sometimes it seemed as if there were nothing more to lose.

She took in his office, then her eyes fixed on the man and her mind on the judgment he would make about her proposal. The room, no bigger than a large closet, smelled of oiled and soiled wood, shelves crammed with files not yet stored, as well as bulging bookcases threatening to engulf the living and the inert. It was, as Coleman told her, "My ordered chaos." Somehow, it felt like respectable, earned chaos to Grace as she compared it to her own house of disorder.

"Let me phrase this in another way: If you insist on writing about this topic, I do not believe I will be able to support your seminar paper. I have no idea where you are going to come up with the wives' perspective when you are talking about the soldiers' letters." Coleman closed his jaws firmly. It was finished, he thought. He resisted the instinct to be attracted to her not because he heard she was recently divorced, and he had tired of girls, having had two affairs with students half his age end badly but because he had made a resolution to keep a psychological barrier between himself and his comely doctoral students—no more Freudian transference love going on in his classrooms.

You make your stand here or you fail, thought Grace, shifting her weight from her right leg to her left, aware she should not have worn the new, black heels. Why was she wearing heels? "We clearly know about the letters the men wrote home during the Civil War," said Grace, "but we know very little about the women left behind. Few of their letters to their soldier husbands, sons, and fathers survived. There is important history in her voice, as well, and it is a story we have not delved into with any scholarship. While we do not have their letters, it can be discerned what they were writing to their husbands from the responses. Their perspective has the potential to offer us a fuller understanding of the time." She secretly congratulated herself on this stroke as it had occurred to her to articulate it in this way only at the instant she was standing in the office of male-dominated history texts.

Coleman nearly smiled as if he had trapped her. "How would this work? How do you propose to study the woman's voice if her letters no longer exist? There are few primary documents from the woman's perspective. I'm not sure how far you can speculate from inference." He was at least leaning toward again, expressing interest. "You have a specific woman in mind, I understand? You have to know I don't like the idea of historical writing from a familial perspective; there is too much inherent bias. These letters belonged to some relative of yours, I take it?"

"My great-great-grandfather," Grace asserted. "But I intend to concentrate on the echoes of her voice discerned through the letters of her husband, the soldier/farmer. Somewhere in the lines he writes home, there exists an answer to what his wife had written. There is an exchange, almost a conversation in those missives. Her voice lies in deciphering his words."

Coleman tilted his head ever so slightly.

Grace took a deep breath. "The tone and content of each letter, as well as the specific diction, does more than merely hint at the words of the unseen woman. They are part of a dialogue, responses to her actual words—an intimate conversation between husband and wife, and in all honesty," she was speaking rapidly before he stopped her. "I feel no sense of kinship to this man or woman. The curiosity is historical not familial or genealogical. I'm not sure what I'll find, but there is the possibility of discovery. It's a puzzle I'd like to try to solve."

As she spoke, Grace noted the *New York Times* crossword half completed on Coleman's desk. It was a habit of hers to survey the room she was in, often appearing distracted, but Coleman was of the same species and assumed everyone entered a room like a detective, usually disappointed before the conversation had ended. He allowed the corners of his mouth to curve intentionally, catching her eyes surveying the room. She could tell he was altering his original stance.

Coleman studied her for a moment longer than he was comfortable with, then asked, "You've considered the monetary investment as well as the time allotted for this endeavor? A graduate course does not come cheaply, should your efforts fail."

"I have. I tried to forget about the letters, rewrapped them, and stored these missives in my safe deposit box, but then woke up remembering lines from Ezra indicating Susannah must have written; they are too compelling not to examine."

Coleman began moving files around his desk, as if clearing off space for him to think about the topic from another point of view. "Compelling is one thing. Primary documentation another. Although admittedly, there is a somewhat intriguing concept outlined here. I just don't think there will be enough substantive evidence to support your argument whatever it turns out to be. This is, after all, not a work of fiction. You are aware many students use their first-year paper to further develop ideas for their dissertations. We've talked about your decision to get your doctorate in history, coming from an already well-established career as a high school English teacher. This is a very different, a much more challenging, enterprise. I'm still not sure you're committed to the choice."

"I am."

"It's more than a little unusual to begin a doctoral program—" He stopped himself from saying, "at your age" although the letters were forming on his teeth and tongue.

"I have always been and will always be fascinated by history," she responded. "I nearly majored in history as an undergraduate." Grace knew she was losing the little ground she might have gained in the brief moment of Coleman's hesitation. She reacted almost instinctively, pulling out a copy of one of Ezra's letters and began reading.

Kelley's Creek
December 15, 1964

How sad I feel about Let but all tears that mourners can shed will not reanimate that lifeless body of his. So farewell Lester. Where was Let buried—you did not say in your letter. I grieve to hear of the deaths of your two brothers, my dear Susa, on different battlefields and within a few days of each other. Farewell Let and Edgar. You must bid them farewell and not mourn so long."

Grace looked up. "There is a way to discover what the young wife wrote about," she said with determination. "We know she wrote to her husband about the deaths of her two brothers, Let and Edgar. This is not speculation but a logical deduction. We've discussed potential outcomes and causal or likelihood-based inference in historical writing. This seminar paper centers on these concepts as agents of discovery."

Coleman nodded ever so slightly, but it was his tone carrying the weight of approval. "Counter-factual history—You've read Niall Ferguson, no doubt?"

Scribbling the name in her open notebook, balancing both in one hand while writing with the other, Grace responded, "I will."

"Although, I don't know if Ferguson is necessary here, but you should still read him." A barely audible sigh from Coleman told Grace she had won this opening round.

She had refrained from getting into a debate about the verisimilitude of history versus fictive speculation. It would be better to avoid telling him, *No one ever asks a historian why it ends so tragically.* There are no bitter accusations about why the text is not uplifting with a happy ending in history. We already know they don't end happily, she thought but said nothing of this to Coleman. Better to preserve clarity with a straight line of reasoning.

"Make no mistake, I'm still not entirely comfortable approving this concept—we're not even discussing a thesis yet, but—" Coleman pursed his lips beneath the graying mustache, brushed the back of his hair with his hand and looked not at his student but at the papers on his desk, avoiding her eyes.

"I will write a thesis statement, clearly demonstrating the argument." Here was the opportunity Grace was patiently waiting for, the conjunction "but" allowed the alternative.

"Let me go this far. I will consider reading your thesis and an informal abstract of the paper, as well as your annotated bibliography." Coleman cleared his throat. "I have to caution you, however. If your thesis and abstract are not historically sound, the project is over as far as this program is concerned. You're the one who has to decide how much time you're willing to invest in a project that may be terminated without you receiving credit." Already, Coleman was thinking ahead to the arguments he anticipated about a dissertation topic a year or two down the road. "I would also expect you will read the necessary texts to provide context beyond your ancestor's letters. At the very least, you should start with Shelby Foote's *Civil War* series, James McPherson's work, Stephen Ambrose, of course, and Allan Nevins' *War for the Union* texts. Your soldier ancestor fought on the side of the Union; I take it."

"Yes," said Grace, thinking how impossible all of this would be but deciding not to appear intimidated in the least by the volumes he required simply as background, as she jotted down authors and titles. She also could not help noticing all the male historians he mentioned, but wisely decided not to make that particular point with him.

"Foote may be your best bet for finding a sense of narrative you seem to be looking for," Coleman said as he began to get intrigued about a different approach to his favorite period in American history. "He is a storyteller as well as an able historian."

"Yes. I loved Foote's commentary on Ken Burns' film on the Civil War."

"Yes, Shelby knew how to narrate," Coleman said, openly smiling for the first time since she had come into his office. "Thank Burns for making the Civil War accessible to the masses, in the least. But remember, this is serious scholarship you're undertaking and not a film class."

"Thank you," said Grace, wondering if Coleman was insulting Burns or her, extending her hand, waiting for his cool, dry one in the compact. Coleman suddenly appeared rather cheerful in spite of his desire not to let her know he was pleased in any way with her. He was not done, she realized, when he did not meet her gesture and continued with his list of texts she should read. "When you have some understanding of the context, then you will want to read specific works dealing with the soldiers' letters."

"Do you have ones you recommend?" asked Grace as she thought of knocking all Coleman's books off his desk, in a sudden destructive impulse she managed to repress. He wouldn't be satisfied until she had read every book on the subject, she considered.

"That is up to you to decide which ones are most insightful, but I will mention Emil and Ruth Rosenblatts' *Hard Marching Every Day*. The entire work consists of Private Wilbur Fisk's letters home, but the Rosenblatts' introduction and Reid Mitchell's foreword have relevance to your topic, naturally."

Considering the fact she had just been assigned several thousand pages of reading, Grace prided herself on her calm exterior and nodded in agreement as Coleman finally stood, clasping her foolishly outstretched empty hand. Then he took her hand and held it rather than shook it. The awkward hold embarrassed both of them. She left his office feeling ridiculously confident but simultaneously overwhelmed with the possibilities stretching out before her, the words of Susannah submerged in Ezra's letters, the mysteries deeply embedded.

Without thinking, Grace left the door to Coleman's office open; a closed door allowed him to determine whether or not he would answer and for whom.

Exasperated again, the professor walked over to shut the heavy door just in time to avoid another student sans appointment. He deliberately did not look down the hall at Grace exiting even though he was curious about her in a way that slightly troubled him.

In her son's car she had borrowed while her own was in repair, Grace suppressed a little victory yell and then began to wonder where she would go from there. These victories seemed a little hollow when there was no one to share them with, she thought, remembering Bill coming in the door and picking her up, celebrating because he had been promoted years ago. He would never pick her up in celebration again. Nor would she share any good fortune of hers with him ever again.

What had happened in the interval from the time he could not wait to tell her something and the time he began slipping out to work late "at the office?" There must have been signals she had failed to notice. Although part of her knew the answer, she was not willing to shoulder all the blame. Was she so burdened grieving over the loss of her mother and dying brother she did not discern her husband turning away from her? Self-delusion was easier than accusing him at first.

Only later did she discover it had been Beth all along, even before her mourning for her mother and brother. Strangely, she gave little thought to this younger woman, knowing instinctively the break had been between Bill and her. If Beth had not walked up to Bill and leaned a little too closely against him, complimented and flattered him, some other woman would have, or Bill would have moved closer to another woman. Bill's decision. At times, she wondered how much she helped him leave, not encouraged because it was never a conscious movement.

For some reason, it was too hard to see the moment, the incident when she realized she no longer loved him. By then it was also obvious he had some time ago fallen out of love with her, as well. It all came far too slowly to precisely define. There was the night he feigned to be too tired to make love, and the evening she walked down to the lake alone while he sat in the cabin and drank a bottle of Bordeaux alone. At some point, she kept expecting him to join her but he never did. Perhaps, he expected her to return to him.

Such speculation only left her feeling sad and confused, however; she pushed the thought away with a deluge of historical papers. By the time she walked in her front door, took off her coat, and circled the outer edge of the floor covered in letters, she had decided upon a tactic. Sometimes, movement felt like hope.

FIVE

———

I have a few leisure moments to myself

Grace decided to catalogue evocative comments from Ezra indicating a response from his wife, positive comments in one column and the negative ones were separated into the other column. The simplicity of her methodology intrigued her: quantitatively measuring qualitative responses. She could further set up sub-categories of topics of dialogue between them. Setting up the columns and drawing the line down the middle seemed tremendously productive to her. It was almost mathematical in a way, she mused. It freed her from reading the letters in order; the methodology was inherently chaotic, a practice she felt more comfortable with as she chose a letter the way Morrison's Macon Dead chose his children's names in her novel *Song of Solomon,* she thought, knowing she was still operating more like an English teacher than a historian.

The first line caught her eye, Susa having fallen and injured herself. This response would begin in the negative column, it seemed. *Camp Sullivan*

Near Halltown VA

March 19th/ 64

Dear Wife

Yours of the 16th I received last evening and I was glad to hear from you but I was sorry that you fell and hurt yourself You must be careful how you run in the future.

I hope you are not seriously hurt but I am not disappointed in the leaste in hearing of Maryettes babe--perhaps you do not believe in dreams but I must say I do for the verry night ettes babe dide I drempt that I and Sergt Hamlin were on horseback and we came to a place where there was a funeral prosession and there was a deep and wide ditch dug and the dirt was fresh and the ditch was in our way but we could not go around it for we had to go ahead so there was only one way for us and that was to jump our horses acrost the ditchy but the men in the prosession said we could not but told Hamlin we could so we started and our horses landed safe on the other side with us on their backs we rode on until we came to a house when we dismounted and went in and to my surprise, I found you and Maryette holding her babe it is a rather singular dreame I told Gillick and Cale that morning after I got up that some of my friends was going to bee sick or die and so it has proved but may we have grace to say the Lorde gave and the Lorde taketh away and blessed be the name of the Lorde. I am as well as usial and I hope this will find you my dear one and friends all well We are under Colonel Averys. Some expect to go to Martinsburg. I wrote you a letter yesterday. I went out this morning and this will not go out until Monday but you will see by this that I have received all your letters to this date. So no more this time. give my kind regards to all enquiring friends My love to you and the children.

From you affectionate Husband

Ezra Cross

Settled into her tiny library in the cottage again, Grace made notes corresponding to the arrows she placed on the letter of March 19th, 1864. How did Susannah take her husband's comments about Maryette's baby? They must have seemed callous to her, but Grace knew the life of any baby at the time was so very tenuous it must have been commonplace to lose one and equally common for a man to appear unaffected. Yet, still, how could he write, "I hope this will find you and my friends all well," when he knew of the death of the baby? Susa—Grace was already thinking of her by her husband's pet name for her—must have thought of his carelessness or thoughtlessness and wondered how he might have been changed by the death and destruction brought about by war to the extent it all made him seem almost immune to the death of a dear child.

Susannah had written of the death of her friend's baby, and Ez had responded by writing to his wife, "I am not disappointed in the least in hearing of Maryettes babe" because he was pleased with the accuracy of his premonition? Was this arrogance or simply indifference? Arrogance a trait arising out of the primitive superstition predating his Christian views? Or was he merely a self-centered man indifferent to the suffering of others? The last made no sense from his other letters.

Grace imagined Susa throwing the letter to the floor and crying before later picking it back up and neatly folding it away.

Noting the co-mingling of superstition and religious viewpoints at the time, Grace considered the self-congratulatory tone of his dream sequence should have offended Susa, but perhaps it puzzled his wife or hurt her further. Was Susa impressed with her husband's abilities as a soothsayer or angry at the way in which he seemed to dismiss Maryette's tragedy in order to paint it in terms reflecting his skills and prowess as horseback rider and fortuneteller? Was he even reading what his wife wrote? Grace recognized a moment of panic her approach might not be possible. There appeared to be simply too many possible interpretations to gauge Susa's actual responses with any authenticity, but then Grace reasoned other historians hit the same walls. The trick was finding a way around if not over them.

"Ezra," she said out loud. "How could you have been so thick?"

Realizing she was criticizing the actions of her great-great-grandfather rather than analyzing, Grace corrected her course. She surmised it was likely Ezra was interrupted many times during the period of writing a single letter, perhaps forced to concentrate on some other business of war or camp requirements for hours at a time before returning to a letter, so the discontinuity and occasional strangeness of his remarks might have been the result of him having forgotten what he had written earlier or even what she had written. He was writing not for posterity but to unburden his heart and let his wife know what to do. There were multiple examples of this time break found in his letters. It was a wonder any of those soldiers' letters had found their way home.

Susa wrote to tell him she had fallen, and he admonished her, "You must be careful how you run in the future," and at the end of the letter, Ez seems to have forgotten his wife had written to him of falling and hurting herself at all, for he wrote, "I hope this will find you my dear one and friends all well." Grace made a note she had begun referring to Ez rather than Ezra because he was already becoming familiar to her, as well. Susannah and Ezra had ceased to be historical anecdotes and had become human beings, as if they were in the room with her when she was deciphering the letters.

At this last conjecture, Grace pulled Susa and Ezra into the tumult of her contemporary setting. Ez's inability to be comforting to his wife in the time of the loss of her brothers reminded her of her own losses. She had expected some comfort and consolation from Bill when her mother died followed so closely by the deadly illness of her brother, but there was none. Why had he been incapable of helping her get through these terrible losses? He seemed to imply it was her fault if he was remote or distant, or was she just reading into every nuance? Her students had been far more generous in their sympathy, quietly doing their work after she took the phone call in the middle of class, the office secretary speaking rapidly. Grace turned to look at them, and they sensed it before she said anything. They could not have been better behaved.

Only months later, after Bill had moved out and left her a message on her answering machine did he confess to loving another woman. He actually asked for a divorce in measured phrases and foreign tones over the phone on a message machine. Even if her mother had not died and Grace had not been in mourning, she instinctively knew Bill would have entered into his affair. He was feeling the weight of mortality—a certainty she could not stop—and the younger woman who could bear him a child again would forestall that quickening feeling, at least temporarily. Knowing this, however, did not make Grace feel any better. She had loved Bill even less for his fears. No longer. Although his betrayal stung, she no longer wanted to be in his presence.

*

"My dear Grace," said Jenna who appeared as the daughter woke. "You know this has been too hard for Bill. He doesn't want to think about death all the time. You need to let this go a little, darling."

"Mother, I love you, but you always took his side, didn't you? I'm wondering why right now."

"You're so foolish. I took his side because it is the side needing defending, and you know I gave you the perspective you were seeking."

"I'm not so sure. I think I would rather have had you always take my side in these convoluted arguments in life and death."

"Of course, I'm always on your side. I just thought if you could see it from Bill's needy perspective, you might be happier. He wants to believe he's too young to die or to think about death. I just wanted you to be happy."

"Oh, Mom. What is happiness anyway?"

*

After having felt depressed for so long, Grace found the surfacing of anger to be oddly restorative even though it was also humiliating—easier to hate or immensely dislike her ex-husband than simply miss him. In one of the oldest acts of purging, she had burned her youthful love letters from Bill. For days afterward, she was torn with regret. As a historian, she knew this was blasphemy, but, as a woman in the midst of divorce, she felt it necessary for survival. The contemplation of the action reminded her Susa had never burned nor carelessly treated Ez's letters but preserved them lovingly, individually wrapping them in small bundles in blue ribbon until Evelyn unwrapped them all those years later. As was typical of her response to pain, Grace redirected her attention to what was emotionally manageable at the moment.

Returning to Ezra's letter about premonition and dreams, Grace wrote down her question: what was the prevailing attitude toward such dreams? She needed to research the topic further. How curious it was Ezra wrote of his dream prophesies with all of their paranormal implications in the same context as he wrote of what was "proven" experientially, as if demanded by scientific methodology. Ezra Cross was a man of contrasts and paradoxes. The historian would be looking for patterns not idiosyncrasies of the individual, she considered. Or were the anomalies as significant as the typical characteristic in identifying paradigm?

She needed to write down exactly what she knew in terms of factual information that had been historically documented. Grace jotted down a few notations: 1st Veteran NY Cavalry, also known as the NY

Volunteers. Formed in Geneva, NY in 1863. He was mustered out for the last time in July 1865. He never made it home. The last sentence set off fireworks.

Col. Taylor recruited the regiment. Ez joined in Binghamton, Company F, and left New York State on October 10, 1863, but that was already his third enlistment. The first had been in 1861, at the beginning. He wrote he had been made a lieutenant in August 1861, after the Battle of Bull Run. Everything must have changed after Bull Run, the number of deserters written about by Ezra in a letter to Susa. The extent of the desertions during the Civil War was mind-boggling, thought Grace, as she made a few notes about further research she needed to do on the topic. The list of topics to be researched was longer than she had, at first, anticipated, but perhaps she could combine some of these topics as they overlapped.

She remembered a line she read somewhere, then recalled it was in one of Orhan Pamuk's novels; yes, *Silent House*, and she pulled the book from her top shelf, thumbing to the chapter she recalled, finding the quotation: "There must be more to history… than just copying things down and linking a string of events together to make a story…I've no doubt the true appeal of history is the pleasure of the story, the power to divert us."

It had occurred to her before: ideas of both the importance of narratives and their "power to divert," an appeal which echoed. All of her searching was also diversion from her losses, her pain.

Picking up another letter, Grace thought here was Ezra after the battles of Bull Run, listing the men in his company who had deserted. Of course, there were desertions; there were bound to be in every war, but the sheer volume of those numbers during the Civil War belied the accepted notions by nearly everyone who was not a historian of the period. Ezra made a note of the father and son who had deserted his company. What became of this father-son tag team? Ezra knew no more of their fate than she did all those years later. Did they return to the war later or head home? Grace considered whether they were charged with desertion, executed, or eventually mustered out. Where was truth in the retelling if one had to invent? As soon as she began speculating on the fates of those missing, she was in fictional territory, yet the historical record left too many unanswered questions.

Following those names across paper, she could discover the father and son had paid no physical price for leaving the horrors of battle as did so many of those who deserted, walking away from the brutality of close combat during the Civil War. Was it still possible to find whether they had been captured and executed? The effect of deserters on the rest of the men must have been demoralizing. From her readings, she knew there were more executions of those who disserted during the Civil War than during any other American war, but there were far more who disserted who paid no physical price, too. Of course, deciding to walk home from the beaches of Normandy was a very different prospect than walking home to Pennsylvania from Maryland. She could almost see deserting father and son on the move, their rifles discarded, their uniforms exchanged for civilian clothes as they hid behind trees then leaped across streams, all the while thinking about escape and home. Or, perhaps, they headed west where no one would know them, starting again.

Distracted from one line of research, Grace spotted writing at the top corner of a letter, so she picked it up. On the letter dated November 2nd, 1861, Ezra had written, "[Hear] you will find a kiss."

It was the only postscript of its kind in all of his letters to Susa. Circling the room, she searched the other letters to make sure no other such postscript existed. There were none. Its singularity gave it prominence, perhaps unduly so. As the war wore on; there should have been other such demonstrations of affection in his letters. Susa would have been looking for another of its kind, searching in vain for the sweetness she had lost so near the beginning of the war. Where were the other letters blowing kisses to her? Hunting for a line referencing a kiss to Ezra's wife, she found no other. Its absence was telling.

Grace carried the missing soldier and his young wife with her when she wandered around her little cottage, looking for items to put away. It was somehow easier to think of Ezra Cross and Susa than her still living soldier Tim whom she knew was helplessly lying in a bed, feeling forgotten by nearly everyone except his parents. She realized the extent to which she tried not to think about Tim's injuries or his kindness when she visited, or the sternness with which his parents' gestures and stares held her at a distance. No, she held herself at a distance, she knew, but could not apologize for at this time. The young man granted no mercy in his stare, his helpless stuttering, his nearly limbless body reminding everyone who dared to look they had no reason to ever even once complain. Somehow, it was easier to care about a distant, long-dead soldier and his wife than one living young man unable to feed himself without assistance 30 minutes away.

After arguing with herself about the importance of her research, she impulsively decided to go to the grocery store rather than to the VA Hospital. She must do something, and moving in a direction away from kindness seemed barely acceptable. Storing supplies was necessary, but even while shopping, selecting plums, she understood her avoidance was akin to cowardice.

As she headed out the door, her sweater pulled away from her, snagged on a nail which had been working its way out of the wood for a very long time but had finally reached the right distance to a passing figure. A long loop hung from her favorite blue sweater, and she fingered it for a moment, then walked back inside, rummaged through a drawer until she found a hammer. She hit the nail squarely on the first try, driving it deep back into the wood, then found a paper clip to use as a weaving tool, pulling the yarn back through the sweater. Somehow, solving this small problem changed everything.

Whatever the issue, she would learn to master it or at least muse over the troubling spot until resolution. Without further consideration, she left the house and headed toward the hospital rather than the store again as she had originally intended, propelled by the fact she had never made repairs to her house or, consciously, to herself. There was a necessity beyond house repairs. His name was Tim.

SIX

I would not write to you again
until I got an answer

When she arrived at the hospital, Tim was sleeping as he often was, and she hesitated to go in, uncertain if his dreams carried less pain than his wakefulness. She lingered in the doorway. Before she could turn to leave, however, he called to her.

"IIII kkkknow you're there," he said opening his eyes slowly. "YYYou wwweren't ggggoing to gggo, wwwere you?"

"I didn't want to wake you. I thought you might be dreaming, and you were smiling."

"I wwwas?"

"Yes. Your face looked so peaceful, and your mouth was turned up ever so slightly." Grace suddenly felt embarrassed she was watching him too closely and had betrayed this observation. Unnerved, she decided to say nothing more about it but walked into the room with a book under her arm.

"IFFFF IIII didn't know you were mmmmarried, I'ddd say you were ffflirting." "I'm too old for you, and you know it," was all Grace would allow to stumble out, fearing she was about to begin stuttering herself and afraid of how Tim might believe she was mocking him.

"IIIII'mmmm older than I lllllook. MMMaybe you're ttttoo young for me." Tim's eyes were wide open and the dreaminess of sleep had disappeared. Even in his constant pain, he was funny and clever.

"I believe you are, as in wisdom rather than years," Grace said, recognizing his meaning could be taken two ways. She offered him a Styrofoam cup of water with the bent straw to his lips.

"Hhhow'd yyou know IIII wwwanted a dddrink?"

"I'm always thirsty when I wake," said Grace.

"SSSSShe lllleft me, mmmmy girl."

"I'm sorry, Tim."

"Sssssshould I wwwwrite to her? I mmmmmmean, would you help me wwwwrite to her?"

"If you want to, of course, but do you really think it is a good idea?"

"NNNNo. It's a sssstupid idea. III jjjust wwwanted to tell you something."

"What did you want to tell me?"

"III ccccannn lllllet her gggo."

"Would you like me to read to you?"

"Yessss, sssomething sssexy." Grace must have looked surprised because he immediately corrected himself. "JJJust kkkidding. Anyththing wwwill do. IIII gotta ttttry, yyyyou know. II alwaysss sssstuttered befffore the wwwwarr, bbbut never this bbbbadd."

While Grace read to him, she felt his eyes on her expressing gratitude, and she began looking at him in a way she had not noticed before. She was thinking of him not merely as a wounded man but as a man capable of giving and receiving love, as person capable of learning and listening, of longing.

He bravely listened while she read, but she could see the increasing heaviness of his eyelids closing against his will. Then he was asleep, and she knew he would be disappointed not to find her there when he woke again. She imagined the drugs he received intravenously kept him in a near constantly groggy state, but there was no other humane way to treat him. Without the dosages of multiple drugs, he would have been in constant agonizing pain.

It was later than she planned when she finally left the hospital and forced herself to go to the grocery store. Tim was no longer simply a patient to her, she realized. She had trouble getting him out of her head even when she tried to think about other things now. But she still had to attend to her own life, and the one advantage of shopping late was the store was nearly empty; she went through the checkout line quickly. For no reason she could discern, she was feeling a little better. No, she knew. It was Tim, but why he made her feel differently made no sense to her. Tim was the reason. He was reason enough.

Driving home, she had an idea for the paper, so she hurried inside to write it down, a grocery bag cradled in each arm, her pace too quick, the step up to the porch too sudden, and her right foot fell away behind her, all the weight descending upon a wooden plank her chin met. The shock of it charged through her like electricity, numbing at first before the howl of pain tickled somewhere in her head and took forever to reach her lips. Cursing, she decided was a good sign; she was not dead or unconscious. Why the blow didn't knock her out was a mystery. The groceries spilled across the porch, a glass jar of spaghetti sauce broken, looking like blood in the dim light, but her blood was contained in her body still; the bone in her chin split and dislodged, a chip loosely floating in the rush of fluids beneath the unbroken but badly bruised skin. She thought about crying, but the absence of observers altered her response. The sight of Tim's swollen head came to her again. He was blown up in a war, and she had fallen on her step for no reason, helping no one, sacrificing nothing.

Within a few more seconds after she caught her breath, she stood and gathered the rolling head of lettuce, the can of beans, and the plastic jar of mayonnaise. Whew, she thought, at least I bought a few plastic bottles! And gathering up the mess, she realized she had forgotten her brilliant insight, the one spark from the Muses graciously given to her in the car on the way home. Her chin began swelling almost immediately, the purple crown at the base of her face suggested her countenance had been turned upside down. Closing the door, she set everything down in the galley kitchen and closed her eyes. Tim's swollen face greeted her again. Then she reached for the ice cube tray, knowing the swelling would only be worse unless she somehow treated it immediately.

For hours, she gently touched the homemade ice pack to her chin and the lower half of her face, then pulled it away before returning it. On top of the pain, she felt ridiculous—to have injured herself over nothing; she could not even blame a dog or a broken step—just a careless and inattentive action. That was all it took sometimes to change a fate. She reached for Ezra's letters, but it was Susa Grace was thinking about as she scanned the notes. Susa's lost letters to her husband, those lost to everyone except the woman who held her family together.

*

Lester, I imagine you walking in the door and picking up Willi as if he were a rag doll, tossing him over your shoulder as we all yelp with laughter. You were my favorite, you know, tho' I loved Edgar dearly. How is it possible you aren't never coming' home again? My dear brother, how can it be you slung your arm around my shoulder and told me you would make sure I was always watched out for, and nothing would ever happen to me? Such rash promises from one so young and strong, so invincible. I didn't think your early death was possible. The farm should have been yours or Edgar's, and now the county has sold it. I don't expect you'd be angry with me for I had no money to help Ma or Pa pay the taxes. Pa was never much of a farmer, as you recall. Do you remember when you cried 'because I was marrying Ezra? "He's too old for you," you said. "Like a gussied-up toad." Harsh of you, but I forgave you. He is a good man, Let. He tries to make me happy tho' I don't know if he will come home from this terrible war either. I can't even write you a letter anymore, so I'll jus' be talking to you now and then 'cause I can't let you go like this. You and Edgar. I can't get my mind around it. You both gone. Are you together again in Heaven? If not, I hoped you didn't know he got killed, too. It's so terrible lonely to think of you both not in the world anymore. I'm ashamed of how weak and small I feel, like I could be blown off by the next gust of wind, and no one would notice 'cept my babies, and they'd only notice cause they's hungry.

My dear, dear brothers, pray for me. I am only a weak sinner who is deep in sorrow and lonely.

SEVEN

———

A calm and sure retreat

Death *was defiance. Death was an attempt to communicate.* Mrs. Dalloway, as well as her author Virginia Woolf, must have believed in the power of the act to communicate, but such annihilative communication cut off all further discussion. Grace could picture herself as both Mrs. Dalloway and the young man who took his life in that novel. She felt it so strongly she moved into first person narrative to find her story.

Tucking Woolf's novel into her bag, she looked up to check on any changes to her flight time. There were still three and a half hours to go during her layover at Kennedy Airport. Virginia's sentences moved her in a direction from which she was not certain of returning, so she recognized the paradoxical need to get up and walk around while waiting. There were only so many places she could go even in an airport as large as New York's JFK, resulting in her second visit to the gift and magazine shop in the terminal.

Crowded with celebrity gossip magazines hugging the entrance and exit, the store offered diversion, and she picked up a copy of *People* and flipped through it while standing in the doorway. There were pictures of newly married or engaged actors who would likely be newly married again two years from then—no, two months from then—the same ones looking for love in an industry which promised to pair them with the next hot star. Grace knew she was looking for something else, not this culture of celebrity obsession. Was Virginia Woolf already formulating a plan of her own or still moving in abstractions as she wrote those lines about Clarissa nearly twenty years before she stepped into the Ouse to drown? Grace tried to imagine filling her pockets with stones and then attempting to climb over the edge of a rowboat, falling rather than leaping into her lake, banging her head and landing back in the bottom of the boat.

"Are you going to buy that magazine?" A heavy-set woman with bright red hair and wearing a great deal of make-up was pointing at her, and then adjusted a badge of identification. Only then, did Grace realize the copy of *People* was still in her hands.

"No. No," she said more definitively the second time. She moved deeper into the shop to avoid the militant clerk. Stopping at the magazine racks, she picked up a copy of The New Yorker, flipped to the poetry page and read, "After My Brother's Death, I Reflect on the Iliad," a troubling, wonderful poem by Elisa Gonzalez. "Yes," Grace thought, as she, too, imagined being consumed in fire, grief finding levels below levels when another arresting title and cover art compelled her to pick up a book. It was Maira Kalman's *The Principles of Uncertainty*. She bought this one.

Twenty minutes into the quick read, she carelessly bookmarked a page with her boarding pass: "How are we all so brave as to take step after step? Day after day? Bravery is suicide on one end of the spectrum of existence, and bravery is endurance at the other." Who is this woman? Grace wondered about the idiosyncratic Kalman with her hypnotic illustrations and cryptic notes accompanying them. How had she not discovered Kalman before?

Five-hour layovers require patience, companionship, or an ability to amuse oneself nearly endlessly. But what did Grace know of endurance in relative terms? Her soldier friend Tim understood endurance in a way defying logic. She had already begun to think of the maimed young man as her friend even though she was only a volunteer at the V.A. Hospital where he would be living most likely for the rest of his dramatically shortened life. She would never ask him, of course, if he had wished to stop breathing even though he had already shared the intimate details of his break-up with his girlfriend and his abbreviated statements about lack of future. The English teacher and reader in her recalled Faulkner's writings about the idea there is no future, only present imploding with past.

A cockroach near her foot drew her attention. Its lack of ability to calculate risks made it seem brave and daring. She moved her foot to avoid it, and then noticed the insect's strange sideways motion. Someone had already stepped on it, a glancing blow, however, partially crushing its exoskeleton. Was it really possible other life forms had no awareness of their existence? It seemed a cockroach knew very well it was still alive, and Grace was ridiculously rooting for the injured insect to make it to the next shelf overhang in the airport cafe. Was bravery simply this autonomic response in the face of hopelessness? The soldier who raised his sword a century and a half ago to lead his men valiantly into the onslaught—was he brave or simply recognizing the hopelessness of the situation and pressing ahead? Is the deserter really a cowardly villain or a pragmatist? It was possible no one would ever go to war again if everyone actually thought things through to their inevitable conclusions.

The historian in her should have been looking for the soldier's voice, but she found herself searching for his wife's words and thoughts. Through a historical telescope, Grace could see the pores in the skin of a Civil War soldier but nothing to his left or right. There was no peripheral vision, yet somewhere off to the side, the man's wife stood holding a baby boy or girl on her hip, a ladle in her hand, gazing at another lad running past her rustling skirt. This 19th century woman remained less abstract than her husband although she left not a word behind. The history was always related from the letters of her husband, from the generals, the politicians.

For an instant, Grace wondered if it had been a mistake to shift the emphasis from the soldier to his waiting wife. Finding enough evidence of the woman's voice would be more difficult than she originally thought. Sitting at a dirty table at JFK, she took notes on the other side of the bookstore receipt because she had forgotten her journal. This was not amusing—a writer forgetting only the most basic elements of craft. But she only jotted down a few phrases before stopping. Every time she thought something coherent, it seemed a sparrow darted down from a tangle of pipes above and hopped around as if investigating a city park and not a terminal. There was that word again with its utterly hopeless connotations—terminal. There she was on her way to her brother's funeral. At least Jenna did not live long enough to see her only son, the great joy of her life, die slowly, she reminded herself.

In every direction she tried to move either literally or figuratively, there appeared to be a closed door. Just enough room on the boarding pass for the description of a little girl, Hispanic, she thought, with her bangs cut very straight across her forehead. Like the sparrow hopping around, the child is suddenly jumping around beneath her table. Across from Grace, there was a group of adults laughing and talking animatedly, but she knew they belonged to this child. They were a large family. Not all the children could be with one mother and father, an aunt and uncle, too, perhaps, maybe even a cousin. The youngest child was enjoying everyone's indulgence. Although a few of the adults appeared to have forgotten about the little girl. She was giggling at Grace's feet, and she didn't understand the joke. This adventure they are on envelops them, Grace thought, holds them together tightly. She wanted to call out to them, "Don't forget this child!" But just then, one of the women looked over and spotted the girl sitting on the floor under Grace's table. Called to her. The little girl leapt up and bumped her head, nearly knocking the table over before beginning to cry. They all laughed again, but the mother swooped up the child and comforted her, kissing her hair—a joy Grace could not enter, observing from outside their familial bubble.

Suddenly, she wanted to join them, pretend to be an aunt, nuzzle the child, point out the birds sitting on the steel beams overhead, but she was so far outside their world there were still oceans between them despite the distance they had all traveled.

"Last call for passengers to Istanbul." There was the disembodied voice calling for passengers to board a plane for Istanbul, Cuenca in Ecuador—all these exotic, fantastic locales. Just as abruptly, Grace wanted to go to Istanbul. If she got up and headed toward the gate, would anyone wonder why she was leaving to go to Turkey? She checked her ticket again. It read DTW—Detroit Metro Wayne County Airport. No mistaking its end point.

Two young men seated themselves at the table beside her, pulling out a deck of cards. They immediately engaged in an intense game, slapping cards down so hard the pedestal table nearly tipped over; one yelling out victory or defeat with each hand. It seemed they came to the airport only to play cards. This was their destination. The moment was all—who knows where they were headed? The trick of it was to make connections. Ah, Grace nearly said out loud, only she was enjoying the pun. The novelist engaged in discourse with the historian, only they were the same person in this case; the historian's task was to uncover the connections beneath the surface of the dust of ages, lay them out in a timeline rejected as false construct. She was making connections that did not exist, imagining she could pull filaments together as she walked.

And then she was back in this foreign country: isolation in the midst of all of these people more pronounced. Here a Vietnamese family—behind her teens from South Korea—to the left, a French couple or perhaps from Quebec. Their syllables roll off tongues, falling and disappearing near the end of words. The man in front of her was speaking Arabic on his cell phone.

There were a few empty seats in a waiting area. Sitting down next to her was a man speaking English. "Yes. Yes. You need to take the beetles out of the freezer." He got up, gestured to his disembodied assistant, this entomologist who might as well have been speaking another language for she had lost his conversation embedded with scientific lingo. She caught the word "diapause" but would have to look it up later for its precise meaning. Then she tried to imagine life as an entomologist. It sounded exciting from a distance but probably was not nearly so glamorous in the lab, identifying little beetle parts, as it appeared in an airport terminal. Already, the entomologist had moved on, unable to have his conversation without physical maneuvers. Grace watched him gesture until the crowd swallowed him.

She wanted to follow and ask him questions about his study. Why were the beetles in the freezer? She was thinking about Kafka and "The Metamorphosis," the man-beetle lying there on his back, identifying his beetle parts—the stuff of our nightmares and psyches growing weaker and weaker until we all, each and every one of us, disappear whether into the earth or as an insect poked about by a cleaning lady or some child at an airport.

"Hello, Sophia. I bought a blanket for you to cuddle with. You can never have too many blankets, sweetie." The grandparents of a little girl are talking loudly on their shared cell phone, laughing then cooing to this unseen child who felt present simply by the familiar way in which they addressed her. Grace would have liked to see Sophia, imagining her to have intelligent eyes, sparkling with excitement when her grandparents called. She wanted them to reach her safely but felt this growing sense of foreboding. It was not lost on her that her familiarity with death had made it seem imminent all around her.

The congested airport was like an electrical conductor with impulses darting about, yet with each group or individual articulating in an insulated cell. Still, the world seemed smaller, increasingly so; it must have felt enormous when Susannah was waiting for the end of the Civil War, while she was waiting for her husband and her brothers to come home. It must have been discerned as if they dropped off into the abyss when they boarded those trains. Susa was never to see any of them again. And here Grace was, flying to see her brother but would never see him again. He was a wild man, his blond hair standing straight up when he water-skied with the towrope between his teeth, she recalled. She still could not believe he was dead. His sons bear an uncanny likeness but are more somber; sobriety hard earned, she thought.

"I'm sorry about Richard." Bill's voice had sounded so artificial over the phone. She had no immediate response for the moment, so he continued, aware of the awkwardness of silence. "I've got an important account to close, but if you think I should go to the funeral, I mean, if you really think I must be there, I suppose I could still make arrangements at this late hour. You know, I always liked your brother."

"No, it's not necessary. Thank you for calling." She could hear Bill's exasperated sigh on the other end of their stilted, awful conversation.

"Well, then, tell them. Tell them I extended my sympathies. To you, too, of course. I know you were close to him." He sighed loudly. "I'm sorry, Grace, about your brother." What more was there to say, he wondered. "Have a good flight." Even to Bill, his comment sounded ridiculous. He hung up. Ah, the extent of the conversation between a man and woman who had known each other intimately for 22 years. And she remembered how famously Richard and Bill got along, as if they had been buddies growing up. Oh, they were for a while. She didn't want to spoil even the memory and tell Richard how Bill had left her. She was so glad she hadn't burdened him with her problems. That was another life—when they were children in another lifetime.

A boy bumped her chair, knocking her bag over. He looked up at her. She wondered if he would say anything, but he stood frozen. His parents' eyes were directed her way to see if they needed to react. He was too adorable even in his recklessness—sighs of relief could be detected. She was already imagining his life somewhere far off, flown to this airport by what imperative? Why had his family arrived at JFK and, obviously, intended to travel on since they awaited another plane? This connection only lasted an instant before they all moved back into their own spheres.

In a couple of hours, she would be flying in the direction of her brother's home, at least where his home once was, leaving this infusion of the world's energy perpetually bottled. How was it anyone of us is so brave as to allow ourselves the indulgence of annihilating memories? She reverted to childhood fears, making her think of her son when he was a young child. Jason used to crawl up on their bed in the morning and ask questions until Bill would finally say, "That's enough. He's too big to still be getting into our bed." Sadly, she could still imagine sharing a bed with Bill, but she no longer wanted to do so. She watched people's reflections in a huge window as it grew darker outside. Everyone leaving.

On the wall was a billboard picturing Gwyneth Paltrow dressed in white, holding two Labrador retrievers, also white. There was softness to the photograph—airbrushed. In large black letters, the advertisement read, "I live for moments like this." It was a perfume commercial, but for some reason, she felt immensely irritated with Gwyneth even though she generally liked her work as an actress. Gwyneth lived for photo shoots, for attending concerts where her then husband performed, for walking down the red carpet in Hollywood, for holding someone else's perfectly matched puppies? The disparity between the fantasy and reality in which the rest of human beings inhabited stayed with her. What would it be like to wake up to find herself an unearthly beauty surrounded by opulence and every whim catered to, the perfect white pup, the designers fighting to highlight her good bone structure? Perhaps Gwyneth didn't see it that way at all.

She decided to take the next moving walkway to her fate, she meant, her gate—what a Freudian slip! There was the STAND side of the walkway and the WALK side. She had this wild urge, this incredible urge to be defiant and STAND on the WALK side or WALK on the STAND side, but, of course, she did not.

At the end of the movable walkway, there was a bar. Airport bars have this ridiculous élan to them with their wooden veneers appearing to have been there long before the airport was built, she thought. It was as if they were expecting Humphrey Bogart and 19-year-old Lauren Bacall to take a seat in the back. Grace could see them leaning toward one another, oblivious to the rest of the world, yet knowing the world was compelled to watch their every move.

Her brother should not have died. There was no possible way for her to accept this new and devastating information. The rational mind was divorced from emotional context. There was so much anger seething around, just under the busy veneer of life, but she considered the idea it might be anger that saved her temporarily. Death seemed as if it had become her most constant companion.

She looked up to see a young man coming toward her in a motorized wheelchair. He was dressed with a suit jacket and his shirt unbuttoned at the throat. He stopped and looked up, saw her, she thought, since he hesitated. She almost expected him to speak to her. He cocked his head as if trying to focus on what to say, but then he motored on his way again with surprising speed and determination. What was this fleeting contact? Or was it all only imagined? She stopped at another bar further on for an iced tea.

The time between planes was like purgatory in which we are meant to reflect on our mistakes or losses. Mistake number 1: she should never have married Bill. No, not right. She would not have had Jason who could never be a mistake. So, she did not move past the first number in her catalog of life's errors. The bartender forgot the lemon. He was not sympathetic, offering no comment or nod the way they do in the movies, just grabbed a lemon from under the counter and plunked it in her glass. His indifference was somehow reassuring. She did not want any more perilous or imagined connections right then. Better to be moving through this indifferent universe.

She pulled out and opened Kalman's book again, even though she had finished reading it earlier, lost in Kalman's variously wonderful and grotesque drawings. She stopped on a page with the illustration of a very wide nun on a bright yellow background. For some reason, the image made her smile. How did Kalman know she needed this book, her pictures, her sad and thought-provoking lines to make her feel again?

When she looked up, she noticed a young man and woman. They were obviously in a new relationship. He reached across the bar table and played with her fingers; she tilted her head down without taking her eyes off him. Did Grace ever look at Bill that way? Of course, she did. That almost—no, made it worse. She was once so in love. They were crazy for each other, and then things changed, ever so gradually. So slowly she could not remember a precise moment when she knew they were done.

"Sending out an SOS. Sending out an SOS." Sting came on the speaker; the bartender had turned on the music, and she found herself involuntarily humming, "message in a bahhhtle." Anonymity discovered in the airport allowed for singing in a public, disconsolate place in which all of humanity appeared to be coming and going, arriving and departing. No one looked at her as she sang softly. Strangely, it was in this chaotic environment of the airport she finally found her calm and sure retreat. On the long path to her gate, she stopped again, examining little white pills in her purse before flushing them down a toilet.

*

I heard his step on the stair last night, waking to it, but he was not there, and I turned to look behind me, knowing Willi was asleep, and he was not there. George is silent in his bed, Jennie, too, I know after getting up to check on them, George's forehead damp from struggling in a dream. If I fall asleep again, the ghost will haunt me, but I dare not lay awake any longer. A shadow has fallen upon me. I'm too young to feel so old, but there is no hope.

This ghost, this spirit wears the clothes of my Ez, but I do not recognize him or his eyes, long past knowing, past understanding, fixed upon something I cannot give. I sit up in the bed, hear my measured breathing, recovering from what I do not dare to imagine.

I do not believe this war will ever end until every man, even my Ez, has given his life. Why did he enlist before he had to? What is this call men hear whispers below the hearing of wives and mothers? My brothers gone? I still do not believe they will not return, scoop up George, toss Willi in the air—they would have tossed him if they'd had a chance to—laugh as they enter the kitchen, tasting my pie, teasing me, saying it has no sugar, kicking mud off their boots, and always pretending to apologize for their mess.

In my dream, I run up to them, hug them fiercely, and ask them why it is my husband feels like a stranger or a ghost. But my tall brothers do not answer me. Only then do I notice how thin they are, how worn their clothes. Now they are ghosts.

I must be wicked to sometimes imagine Ez already dead, so I pray, but the harder I pray, the more difficult prayer becomes. And my children sleep unknowing, their mother considering all things, even the most unnatural, not the fear of poverty which I have grown to know and dislike as a mean cousin but the fear of my husband not returning or, far worse, returning a stranger who climbs in my bed. Do I still love him? Am I angry with him for fighting a just war? Such selfish, wicked thoughts come around again when I close my eyes, so I keep them open until they burn and the sun enters with its harsh face beneath the curtain, making its presence known.

The baby cries, the children are up as if the sun tapped them on their little heads. That's something Ez would say. I wonder if I'm getting more poetic like him or is he just giving me the words because I remember. I don't sleep anymore. I wonder what death would be like. I don't mean the death of a solider—all glory and honor, just the plain death of the nameless, waiting woman whose work is never finished?

EIGHT

——

I have faced death several times

Arriving at the funeral home, Grace felt herself falling away again. The moment belonged to her brother who was not hers at all. No one belonged to anyone, she thought. Here, his life was set out on large posterboards with photos of him dancing at his wedding, his multiple graduations, him holding up a largemouth bass with great pride, him reading to his young son, him with his arm held in the air by a referee after winning a wrestling match, Richard looking into Ellen's eyes with love, the still young man walking away and turning his head one last time. At least, that is what it felt like to Grace. Those photographs of her brother, making him tangibly present in his absence. This was too soon to be seeing her brother in a casket. She supposed it was not only about self-protection but the loss of words when grief overwhelmed everything around it. Sobbing and stifled sobs enveloping them all.

At Evans Funeral Home, Grace held the arm of her great aunt, watching her nephews standing in front of her as young men, protective of their mother and her sudden fragility. No, that wasn't right, Grace thought. Her sister-in-law was stronger than ever but horribly saddened. Sam, the younger of the two boys, looked like his father, and then Grace was thinking not of Sam but Richard as a boy. The casket was closed. For that much she was grateful, but then she kept expecting to see him once more, not in death but coming through the door.

*

Richard began formulating what could be considered a decision to allow his 7-year-old friend Johnny to cut the wrapped fishing line. Still working furiously, knotting the 80-lb. test line he had pilfered from his father's tackle box, Richard assured his buddy, with his sister's acquiescence, the stratagem was sound. The nearly invisible line extended from the sapling to the stump of a tree felled by insects and rot to the forest floor made soft by moss and pine needles. Grace, eleven months older than Richard, must have said something about the fact it was "not a good idea" and "somebody might get hurt," but she was primarily a spectator on the scene. The mastermind, all furious limbs and actions in pulling, stretching, and holding, shouted, "Ready?" before slicing through the lines with the pen knife his grandfather had given him for his birthday, and Johnny was riding a wild stallion. He should have just fallen off or the tree limb broken, but the plan worked, and amazingly Johnny was catapulted into another part of the forest as Grace and Richard stood looking at the white piece of sky their smaller friend had passed through and then turned to one another in terrible but extraordinary wonder.

Only many years later, it occurred to Grace—who by then had her own son—her life might have changed forever in the whoosh of air and whipping line, the moment Johnny fell twenty feet to the forest floor on his back with the "wind knocked out of him." The moment in which Johnny was still alive although he couldn't talk, or cry, or laugh because he wasn't sure what had happened or even if he was alive as he fortuitously landed on a patch of earth softened by recent rain and a nesting doe. Grace reached the little boy first even though Richard was quicker because Richard preferred, just this once, his sister precede him. Johnny lay with a small branch across his face, and his arms and legs splayed.

"Oh, no. Are ya okay? Johnny, are ya all right?"

"Is he alive?" Richard asked tentatively, approaching as if he would be bitten.

"Stay here. I've gotta get help," said Grace, standing up and running through the brush fast enough to earn a first-prize ribbon in the upcoming junior high school track meet, opening welts from the thorns and branches reaching out.

"I'm sorry, Ahhhhhhhhh," said Richard, by now weeping in a heap next to the little guy. But Johnny's eyes were wide open, clear, and comprehending when Mrs. Keats pulled the sister away from her friend, felt for the little boy's pulse, and listened to
his heartbeat.

Johnny then did the most unexpected thing. He sat up, brushed himself off, and said, WOW! That was great." It was typical Johnny.

*

As she thought of that particular experience, Grace nearly laughed before being brought back to the moment in the funeral home. Richard would have laughed, too, she thought. Sam leaned back and whispered to her: "I was just thinking about this move dad was trying to show me a few years back, this move called the grapevine; it's a finishing move in wrestling. You see, you wrap your arms and legs around your opponent's and pull up and out at the same time. When Dad pulled the move on me, I was done. You're going to think I'm exaggerating when I tell you, he was the best 145 lb. wrestler ever. Okay, so I never saw some state champion from Iowa or wherever, but I've watched the videos—and you can see him pacing the sidelines furiously during the opening matches."

Grace reached over and hugged her nephew tightly. She could feel before she heard the sobs breaking down in his chest, the jerky motion of his strong, convulsing body, and she was helpless. She held him tighter then finally let him go. His mother leaned forward and wrapped her son up again.

But Sam, like his brother Ben, reined it in quickly and stood up before the large group in the room to speak a few words, remembering his father. Grace had moved to help Ellen who rested her head on Grace's shoulder when Ben finished speaking. "I can't do this," Ellen whispered to her.

"Yes. Yes, you can because they need you to," said Grace as she nodded toward her nephews who looked very handsome and smart and terribly sad and young in their suits. "Richard would be proud of them and very proud of you, too. You are so much stronger than you realize."

"No, that's you, not me" said Ellen, but she pulled herself straight again.

Ellen held her head up, wiped her eyes, and looked at her sons. She squeezed Grace's hand too tightly. Grace realized the only way she was able to get through this death was her sister-in-law needed her to be strong. She wanted to see her brother again, but not as he was at the end, his body dissipated during his long, slow illness, the unforeseen cancer because cancer is never bargained for.

Grace closed her eyes and remembered how Richard had looked, a sort of scruffy Robert Redford, good enough looking to have been a movie star himself. She allowed a moment to collect herself and look around at the roomful of people who loved her brother as she had and saw the sadness, loss so profound you could touch it, and in the collective sorrow, there was not so much comfort but small relief. The feeling of loneliness dissipated.

After the funeral service was over, Grace offered to collect the white boards with the photos, her brother's wrestling trophies, the scrapbooks and other personal items for Ellen and told her she'd meet them back at their house. Ellen nodded in gratitude.

When everyone had left, Grace was alone in the room, and she expected to sense her brother with her. Richard was always a quiet man, but there is no mistaking his silence as the pale shade of death. Perhaps she would be able to share a communication, sense his passing, but she only felt the profound emptiness of the funeral parlor. At first, she was surprised at how well she did: methodically collecting those remnants of her brother's life was not a summary or a true reflection. It never was for anyone. All the motions did was point to all that was missing.

When she picked up his favorite fishing cap, she broke down. It was only a green cap, but it had held her brother's head, and now it was all she could ever again hold of him. The rush of emotion was so sudden and violent she had to grope for a chair and wait until sobs subsided, her shoulders sore from effort. Her eyes were burning, and she was relieved for all of the physical discomforts of grief distracting from mental anguish.

Packing the last box and setting everything in the back of her car, she went in to splash cold water on her face and looked up at her puffy lids and swollen skin around her eyes. Logically, she knew the cause, but she could not shake the feeling it was more; emptiness at the center of her was a well deeper even than the widening space left by the death of her brother. And she felt guilty. This sensation of devastation was not for Richard alone. She understood why Bill had left her. The sorrow—her connections ripped away until there was only a raw edge, a frayed lining of the inside turned outward—her body a vessel of loss had been too much for her husband to bear witness to.

She understood; perhaps even forgave him a little, at least in the moment while the water cooled her face and washed away visible residue of suffering.

NINE

I certenly think you are to blame

The galley style kitchen had always seemed too small for Grace until Bill left, but as she made supper for herself and her son, the ease with which she moved from the old Sears stove left in the cottage to the ceramic yellow sink, stained with colors long ago embedded in the surface, was oddly comforting. The mismatched appliances and camp furnishings spoke of a more casual life, a life following its own internal clock from another era. She had already realized it was the style she preferred. Her parents' camp had come to her through Jenna's will, but she had never thought of living there alone. It had always been a place of family. Now the shape and dimensions appeared to change as she moved through rooms which shrank to fit the size of a woman who was now most often alone.

Her son's occasional presence was powerful, and she had to avoid the temptation of wanting him too much, impinging on his life to fit the new needs of her own. So, what do you think?" Grace asked her 19-year-old son, Jason, who by now was certain whatever he said would not be the right answer, but he knew he always had the upper hand with his mother, even if she still had some power to restrict his movements. He forged ahead like one of the Civil War privates under ridiculous orders.

"That's your specialty, not mine," Jason said, suddenly inspired, as he tasted the sauce on the stove with her stirring spoon.

"It's not ready yet," said Grace, moving him slightly with her hip. "I'm not looking for an academic critique, just an opinion."

Shrugging, Jason was about to offer his opinion in spite of his better judgment. "Thought you were focusing on the woman, on the soldier's wife? It sounds like you're getting too caught up with the soldier and why he disappeared. Does it really matter why he never returned home? I mean, it's not as if you could discover the answer to a mystery over a hundred years ago."

"Nearly a hundred and fifty, and yes, you're right! I keep getting lost in the unsolvable mystery of it."

"Maybe because you really want to write a novel rather than a history dissertation," Jason said, unafraid of his mother's reaction to his honesty. He knew he could say anything to her, particularly at this point in her life. The fact his father left them made him angry but not devastated as his mother seemed to be. He, too, had loved his grandmother, but the relationship was different, and his grandmother was of an age when people died quite naturally, he thought. Part of him wanted to comfort her and the rest of him wanted to flee. She needed him too much. It was a burden to be an only child.

In the moment, she reimagined an entire scene from their past when he was still a little boy. It was not a memory but, rather, a reoccurrence of past imploding present.

*

Canoeing up the river, which fed the small lake she lived on, the morning with her son at the helm, wearing his lifejacket, the boy paddling as they navigated over a membrane of water between rocks and fallen branches. She had wanted to take him on this adventurous trip for some time, but it was never the right moment until she looked at his growing frame, his long legs loping across the yard to grab a football out of the air, and suddenly and urgently knew the moment had nearly been lost. So, she said, "Hop in; we're going for a canoe ride while it's still summer." Jason surprised her by responding, "Okay" and helped her lift the canoe and carry it down to the water. They worked hard at first, not talking, just paddling in smooth, rhythmic strokes seemed to connect them by both blood and movement over water.

"I have wanted to go up this river with you for a long time," she told the back of her son as she tried to talk steadily, not revealing the fatigue in her shoulders and the suddenness of aging.

"Why didn't you just ask me before?" he said simply and directly as he always talked to his mother. "Look, did you see the turtle?" he asked, a child again.

"A snapper."

They stopped paddling and let the canoe skim slowly over the brown swirls of water where the large snapping turtle slipped into the mud, turning the water smoky. Jason turned his head and smiled at his mother. It was only a turtle but a big one. Perhaps they would see a trout or other fish. They continued up the river silently paddling, sometimes quickly then slowing to take in a sound, a rustling in the thick brush may have been a large bird or a small animal, a muskrat up along the banks.

Pulling the canoe over, they stopped and got out where the water was too shallow for their weight. They both had bare feet, so hopping in and out of the quick-moving water was a relief from the heat of the late summer afternoon. Grace wondered at her son and his absolute quietness. It was difficult for her, but she tried not to break the silence. As the canoe wound around a large, rotting stump, they came across a blue heron standing on one leg in the water. It turned its head to stare at their strange figures then slowly lifted its giant wings and flew right over their heads like some shadow of an ancient pterodactyl.

"Oooh." He let out a gasp. They had arrived at the stretch in the river where the brush along the banks was so dense nothing could be seen of houses, fields, roads, and civilization. One branch leaned so low across the water Jason had to duck and warn his mother. She just barely missed being hit in the face with the whipping limb. Then all thought of work and school and the trappings of civilization were lost for a time. There was only the exertion of muscles in her back and arms, pulling the canoe up the river.

Grace was not even thinking about turning back before dusk when they heard a thundering sound coming from something up ahead. The canoe arrived at the point in the creek where a herd of heifers stood— some in the water, some at the banks—come down to drink, then out of curiosity, were actually running in the stream toward the canoe. Grace yelled at them with Jason joining in, waving his paddle wildly to scare them off, sure the noise would frighten the animals, but the heifers kept gaining on the canoe in the shallows.

Sticks and rocks jutted up, providing unwanted drag. Suddenly, Grace thought of her foolishness and selfishness in wanting to share an adventure with her son, as the heifers seemed aggressive and very large up close, unafraid of the humans. They were running toward Grace and Jason, snorting like wild pigs, and sending water flying in tiny jets all around mother and son. It was a terrible moment of guilt, as Grace felt the danger of her son too far out in front of her for her to take the first blow, the lead heifer charging with his head down, nearly upon them.

Jason hopped out of the canoe and pushed with all his weight against the current as his mother paddled backward with everything she had in her aching muscles. Just as quickly as the danger presented itself, it passed, and the canoe suddenly hit deeper, swifter moving water carrying them out of reach. The heifers still snorting, one pawing the bed of the river as a bull, standing in the middle of the stream and looking after them; the quarry had gotten away. Afterward, Jason and his mother laughed as the river widened downstream: pure relief and wonder at their fear over a group of young cows.

"They were only cows," Jason said at last.

"Yes. There was no real danger," she said. They laughed then were quiet the rest of the trip back to her mother's cottage.

And a moment later, Grace turned to meet her son's grown-up face and brushed his curly head gently, leaving her studies to carefully observe her son, who had long disliked her habit of touching his head when she wanted to show affection. On one level, Jason knew his mother was hurting from the impending divorce, but it was not a subject he wanted to broach or think about any more than was necessary. He indulged her in a quick, one-handed hug, awkwardly, before bounding upstairs to shower in preparation for going out for the evening.

"You're staying for dinner, right?" she called after him, trying not to sound too desperate. "Jason?"

"Yes, but I've got to leave in about twenty-five minutes," he yelled down the narrow, steep cabin's stairway before slamming the bathroom door.

"Thirty," responded Grace. She knew not to push too hard, so she pulled out the plates to accommodate her son's schedule although she was hoping he would stay and visit for a while longer. Jason was not leaving her as Bill had done, she reminded herself.

He was just being a young man getting on with his life, she had to admit. How had he gone from the nine-year-old who didn't want to hook the worm because, "I feel bad for it," to the self-assured young man who breezed through life with such seeming abandon so quickly?

But thinking of Jason's childhood sweetness reminded Grace of other losses. It was in those moments she recalled how young she had been when she discovered she was pregnant with her son. Bill seemed to want to get married, but now she found herself questioning every move he had ever made toward her, as well as his decisions. If she had not been pregnant, would they have married? The idea Jason might not have been born was far worse pain than any she had yet had, so she stopped speculating on her own ancient history.

She began to think of her research as a diversion, which she could focus on in the absence of someone else's life, with the energy and dedication normally reserved for one's own life. She and her son ate so quickly their conversation was minimal. She resisted the urge to admonish Jason not to hurry through dinner. Returning to her books and her library after eating involved an urgency she did not analyze. She would be alone again but not alone because Ezra and Susa were waiting for her.

What was known, passed down through families—but not ever substantiated through documentation—was the fact Ezra never returned home. What was known was he survived the battles, diseases, accidents, and three minor wounds incurred during the bloody Civil War only to die or disappear before reaching his wife and children. What had happened? The oral history, remarkably unreliable, only suggested to Grace the idea Ezra had been killed or accidentally died or something else? Grace was not even sure if Ezra's body was brought home. If a body was brought home, was there any certainty it had been his? She speculated on how Susannah reacted to this most ironic of ends to their union. Did the waiting woman struggle with this mystery for years? She had, after all, kept his letters, carefully bundled them, tied them with ribbons, and passed them to her own children as keepers of their history.

Grace stared at the copied letters strewn about the floor, covering nearly every square inch of it, so she had to step tentatively, in order not to disturb the woven rug of words.

"When can we use this room again?" asked Jason, as he inched his way closer to the doorway in an exaggerated movement, ready to make his exit. His mother's nose twitched at his strong aftershave and recognized her son was on his way to meet a girl or girls.

"You know it will be awhile," she said, looking up and laughing at the sight of her 6' 5" son pasting his lean frame against the wall of the study in order to get to the door. "I am sorry about all the papers on the floor. What time are you going to be home?"

"C'mon, Mom. I'm nearly twenty; I'm in college!"

"I know. I know," protested Grace, feeling helpless.

"It'll be late. Don't wait up. I'll be fine. You really don't need to worry about me." He leaned over and put up a large hand to wave and then was out the door. The motion and concussion produced by the door slamming caused the broken ceiling fixture to shift slightly, dangerously close to falling apart.

I need to have that light fixed, thought Grace, but the idea it might fall on their heads always seemed the least of her worries about things coming apart. Bill wouldn't have fixed the light either. He would have waited for it to fall down before calling in someone to replace it. When she thought of this, she suddenly decided the light must be removed. She would have to call an electrician in the morning. There were so many calls she would need to make or, then again, maybe not.

"Jason?" She got up and called out the door, hoping to catch him, wanting to ask him about the idea of volunteering at the VA with her because she thought it would be good for him, too, but the timing was never right, or he was resistant on some other plane, able to avoid those conversations he would rather not have with his mother. He was already gone, of course. Grace would wait up for her son, however. She always waited, alert. It would be impossible to sleep until she heard the whooshing sound created by the door opening and closing in the middle of the night, Jason dropping his huge sneakers next to the antique stand her mother had given her and his footsteps on the stairs creaking in certain spots, giving away his practiced stealth. Then she would let herself release all the active stories she kept on file in her head and allow her subconscious to take over, discovering fragmentation in dreams.

In spite of their imminent divorce and the sense of failure her broken marriage left with her, Grace tried to wake up hopeful most mornings even as she ended her evenings in near despair. She loved the early hours before Jason stirred when she knew her son was safe in the cabin; she could read or write in the quiet before the world's schedule took precedence. Taking leave from her high school teaching job allowed her a new freedom, but it was an unnatural act causing angst. What would happen if she actually finished her doctorate and applied for a job? Would she leave this place? Would she be willing to take a job in another state and start over as if she were a young woman instead of a middle-aged one? The idea was both liberating and terrifying.

*

Because Jason had come home at an earlier than usual hour the night before, Ez, not her son, was foremost in her mind when Grace went to the kitchen to heat water. Her mother Jenna had given her a beautiful copper teakettle, the one sitting on the stove unused. It was simply too lovely to ruin with the hard water from the well, iron producing heavy deposits on anything it touched, so Grace used the microwave to heat her tea, something she knew was terrible for producing the best taste.

Leaving the teabag suspended, darkening hot liquid, Grace returned to the library with the feeling of a detective. Just letting the tea steep reminded her Jenna had liked weak tea, always telling her daughter to take the bag out quickly. Neither of them was an aficionado of fine teas.

While smiling about this little detail of routine, Grace suddenly found herself with Tim Fitzgerald. It was as if he were sitting in the next room looking at her, wondering why she had forgotten him. "I'm sorry, Tim," she said out loud. The pressure of volunteering in such a depressing place was overwhelming at times, she told herself, trying to excuse her missed visits. But she really wasn't avoiding him, admitting Tim had become someone she looked forward to seeing. This fact alone did not give her solace because she was not sure what that meant anymore. Was she becoming more generous, more tolerant, or merely needier? A story or stories awaited discovery. She left Tim in her thoughts and was back in her study with piles of letters.

There were many kinds of tyrannies, Grace considered before she set about creating a chart of particular key phrases, indicating Ezra had heard from his wife by letter, with lines for the date of the missive and exact quotations in context. Grace would type these columns and notations on her computer in the afternoon. A second chart indicated key evocative words Ezra had used to indicate his feelings about Susa in one column and about other matters or people in a second column. Cataloging made Grace feel centered again, almost the academic historian she was attempting to become. This was a conscious decision—to evolve—to remake her life by following other lives. As she drew the lines of her chart, she imagined herself to be a meticulous mathematician, in addition to the historian. A third column was added for direct references to Susa's words to her husband that could be deciphered from Ez's letters in response. Inference.

As Grace undertook the task, she was certain it would reveal secrets, but the doubt crept in almost immediately as she began her task. If all she could enumerate were conjectures, Coleman would likely make her toss the whole project. She was the student now, not the teacher, and the change in roles was both exhilarating and daunting, even a little frightening, taking her marching orders from someone else. The letters waited patiently as if she only needed to walk up and begin the conversation. She thought of them as distant relatives who masked their voices.

TEN

—

You probably will not see me again

Some mornings, Grace anticipated the words of her ancestor, almost as if the man she had never known was in the library with her. As she read his words, Ezra woke again.

Camp Stoneman

Saturday evening Jan 19ᵗʰ/64

Dear Wife

I have said that I would not write to you again until I got an answer to some I have written to you but I have changed my mind a little and concluded to write you a few lines to let you no that I am yet in the land of the living This is the fourth one whether you have written or not I am unable to say but if you have your letters havent reached me they proberbly have gon to the front but if you are able to write and have not done it I certenly think you are to blame I have not herde from you since yourse of the 27ᵗʰ of Dec 1863 and that is a good while I reccon but I have written four letters with the penn you sent me in that letter The letter I wrote you about my friend Gillick coming with his wife to see you when he got home his wife was verry ill with the petred sore throate consequently he did not go up to the forkes as he intended and besides the letter I sent with him to mail in Binghamton I have written two besides this one and one of them had a fifty dollar green back in it likewise I sent my commishion at the same time. I hope you have got the fifty before also I wrote Mr. Lowell about that 3.00 bounty from the county. Write me soon as you get this and direct your letter.

Ezra Cross

No more this time from your affectionate husband

*

Grace noted the tone of the Camp Stoneman letter seemed rather accusatory, particularly in his lines, "if you are able to write and have not don it I certenly think you are to blame." Would Susa have either felt guilt for not writing more or annoyance she was blamed for the mail system? It was possible Ezra was joking with her. No, the wording was too matter-of-fact with too many details of exactly how many letters the lieutenant had written before a response was received. He could have been using sarcasm, but the idea didn't fit the age or circumstances.

Reading between the lines for tone was going to be more difficult than she had previously imagined, Grace almost immediately doubted her entire system of cataloging. Did Susannah write as frequently as her husband, or did she find the practice nearly impossible with her chores and caring for three small children—one still an infant? Who was her support at home? From their correspondence, it appeared Susa had no help at home. Perhaps the mother of three found herself stronger rather than weaker after the absence of her husband.

*

Maryette's baby died and I wasn't there to help her. She cried all night, wrapped the dear little thing up in his blanket and held him. I

90

don't know how long she would have sat there if Emma hadn't stopped to see her and taken the dead child away. I stayed with Maryette all day and will stay tomorrow. Willi is being such a good baby, quiet, instead of crying, and the children aren't running around as usual tho' they're too little to understand what's happenin'. George is my little man, fetching what I tell him for Maryette.

I asked Maryette if it troubled her to have my baby and the boy and girl there with us and she said, "They're a godsend. I do believe she meant every word, or I wouldn't have stayed on with her like this. I'd like to be with her longer, but we're running out of food tho' Emma promised to talk to some ladies from the church to get some provisions for us. If her Jimmy could be with her 'stead of at the war, her heart might find some peace. I cannot bear to see her suffering in this way and wonder how it was my son was born so easy, all of them coming after a few hours of labor. I wonder what Ez would do if I had died bearing his son? Would he grieve over me or be glad I left him a son as his mother wanted?

Sometimes I wish I was the one who was off to the war. Washing Maryette's underclothes takes my mind off my guilt for now. Always this guilt over living, over thinking, over wishing for something else. But I can't start wishing for him to come home because it's just when I'd hear the bad news. And if I keep thinking like this, it'll be my own fault if something happens to my Ez. I can only concentrate on Maryette a short time more because I've got to figure out what to do about where we'll live.

Counting the number of Ezra's accusations about Susannah not writing as often as her husband had, the historian was surprised to discover a theme of unequal devotion woven throughout the letters. It appeared to indicate a strain in their marriage. Ezra had accused his wife thirty-three times of not writing often enough. Susa's guilt was quantified, according to her husband who had left her alone without means. Grace got up after counting and cataloging these responses of accusation, troubled by the bitterness she had found. Although not in the least hungry, Grace thought the idea food might interrupt this awful meditation on blame leading her back to her own circumstances about whom had been more to blame? Bill for his infidelity and indifference or her for her obsession with grieving, a condition she had no choice in avoiding.

Another letter, dated much later, evidenced Ezra's betrayal to his wife. In writing to his parents of his wife's lack of writing to him, he was accusing her to those most likely to find fault. She had already read enough of the letters to know a strain existed between Susannah and Ezra's mother. Grace read again the letter dated *November 1, 1864.*

Kellys Creek, Western Va

Nov. 1st/64

Dear Father and Mother

As I have a few leisure momentes to myself I will improve them in writing you a few lines by way of a joke not not a joke either for I assure you I was never more serious in my life. I have written to Su several times within the past three weeks and have not as yet received an answer. I received a letter fro her dated Oct. 13th since that I have not herd from her and know I wish to no whether she gets my letters if she has whether she has answered them. If she doe not get my letters their must be a pair of ...I sent five dollars in letter direct to George I also sent by A.C. Andrews of Binghamton a letter directed to Mary Cross with one hundred and five dollars in it. He/Andrews said he would mail it at Binghamton as he was goin directly home. I thought it would be the safest way to send it. He left here the 29th of Oct. I was afraid if I sent it by mail from hear that it might get into the gents before it would to the Forks--and you no that I or my family could not afford to lose it for to tell the truth I have faced death several different times this last summer to get it. Yet I will not brag about it. Neither do I regret of having been thus exposed to death but through the goodness and Mercies of a Just God I yet enjoy life and health for which I feel thankful to him who doeth all things well--our mail has not been verry regular since we came into the Kanawha Valley or for that matter since we left Harpers Ferry last spring--one time this last summer when we were kitting up and down the Shenandoah Valley so much I did not get a letter in a little over two months I had about given up hearing from home again when lo and behold as the mail was called off I hear my name called verry mutch to my surprise however but sure as fate there was a letter for me not onley one but eight they soon surred me of the blues I asshure you for I had them right smart I reccon speaking after the manner of a V. gentleman--the country is verry rough and mountainous but abounds with coal. There is no news of any importance with us but stirring news from Sheridan.

I must close. Write soon.

From yours truly

Ezra Cross

Pulling open the refrigerator door, she found a package of ham dated two weeks earlier. The gooey consistency of the slice's surface and its faint order made her more than suspicious. It would be bitter if she died from tainted ham because she had been too preoccupied with history—her own as well as Ezra's and Susa's. Tossing the package into the garbage, she searched for a can of soup and thought about how Susa and her children would have been hungry much of the time. All of those simple extravagances of life had become routine in so many households in this country, she considered. Even deprivation is subjective. Foregoing eating, she returned to the letters.

Why was Ezra accusing his wife? He had to know writing to his

93

parents and accusing Susa of not writing was a betrayal, didn't he? Was he simply lonely, naturally jealous, or rightly so? It put him in a bad light with Grace when she had so wanted to find him heroic and a gentleman.

In thinking about Ezra's parents, Grace had an image of her own mother the night she took Jenna to the hospital nearly a month before passing away. She recalled standing in the emergency room beside her mother's bed, holding a bloody towel. Jenna didn't cry as her daughter expected. The fall seemed harmless enough. How does one nearly amputate an ear by falling against a bedstead out of bed? Jenna seemed more like a child than a parent as Grace soothed her with words she scarcely remembered.

"What have you been writing lately?" said Jenna, trying to divert attention away from her recent and sudden episodes of clumsiness as she called them.

"Nothing, Mom. Can't write anything creative lately." The dried blood on her mother's pajama top made this once imposing woman appear so frail.

"Why not? You always used to write." Blood had stopped soaking the towel, and Grace wondered how her mother would react to the stitches that would certainly have to be used to reattach part of her ear.

"I don't know. It feels like a dried-up river bed with the stones all bleached white and exposed."

"Sounds like poetry to me, dear. Every writer has those times, I expect," said Jenna. "Oh, no. I'm still feeling a little dizzy."

Grace pressed the nurse's button. "The doctor will be right along. You will be fine. I'm sorry, Mom."

"What are you sorry for? You didn't knock me over in the middle of the night. I'm just sorry I had to get you up and call. But I couldn't stop the bleeding, and honestly, I got a scared. Feeling foolish now."

"You're not foolish, and you did the right thing to call."

"My dearest Grace, you have written a lot. Don't get discouraged. You're too young to be so despondent."

"Not really. I mean, I haven't written much. You've got a nasty cut, but the doctor will stitch it up. My writing is not what's important at the moment, but for the sake of conversation while we wait for this ER doc, Joyce Carol Oates has written something like 119 novels. I can't even get all the way through one."

"Joyce Carol Oates? What did she write? I've never read her."

"Oh, Mom, trust me, Carol Oates is very well known. Her novel *them* won the National Book Award. And not long ago, she wrote *A Widow's Story*." Grace suddenly felt silly reciting these facts to her mother who would not have known anything about the esteemed writer.

"If you really wanted to, you could do it. You could write as many novels as Joyce Carol." Jenna closed her eyes, and Grace remembered her mother that way, always giving encouragement even in the face of disaster.

"It's not just a matter of will, Mom."

"Well, what else is it? Don't tell me you're not talented because I still recall the little books you wrote as a child. Have every single one in a box somewhere. Do you remember the one about the turtle?"

"Oh, please, Mom." It was all Grace could get out before Dr. Hayes came into the room, looking skillful and unconcerned. He was reassuring even. Yet, it was not long after the evening in the hospital Jenna died. Although it had not been sudden, and Grace felt prepared, the reality of her mother's death from a series of strokes hit her harder than she anticipated. Never had she seemed to need her mother so acutely as after the news of Jenna's death.

Heating the corn chowder, she had made from scratch, Grace wondered why she was thinking of the incident with her mother. Was the impetus what she read about Ezra writing to his parents?

And what was Susa doing or thinking when her in-laws accused her of not writing to their son? Did Susa write when her children were sleeping, exhausted herself, the letter stamped and taken into town to be mailed in good faith, like a belief in a higher power, only to be betrayed by a system delivering her letter days too late, arriving in camp after it had been disassembled, the lost letter picked up by a passing soldier from another regiment? Had the passing soldier opened it with a bloodied finger, read it slowly, wondering what Susa looked like, dreamed of her with red hair, picturing it a much deeper shade of red than it was, wanting her? Had Susa's letter been in this stranger's breast pocket, blood spattered, and then later trampled by horse hooves, broken into scraps, and finally entombed in a shallow grave?

ELEVEN

I was angry with God

All night, Grace kept her Ezra's words while she turned in her bed. They would greet her again in the morning before the sun had fully risen over the hills.

Dearest Edgar,

I'm writing this letter in my head 'cause I'm told you was killed in battle the same day as Let. Were you side by side? Could you see him? Did you know he was gone, too? I couldn't pray when I first heard 'cause I was angry with God. I know that is blasphemy, and my soul is in jeopardy, but I'm still fiercely angry, so angry I almost don't care if my soul goes to hell, so long as yours does not. I know you would not be happy with me about that, and you'd tell me the story about Job who had more trials than me or even you who's now dead, but I'm not as strong as Job, and Job didn't have to nurse his babies, so I can't cry till my milk's dried up. And I'm not God's favorite. Sometimes when George's hollerin' and the girl's crying and there's no food, and I don't know where I'll be living...a selfish thought I can't finish for fear you'd never forgive me.

I've grown more selfish and mean with this war, but you would not believe how cruel Ez's mother was to me. Still, I apologize to you who died fighting for us for this complaint. I want to ask you, 'Was it terrible painful? Did you know it was going to happen? Was there a premonition? I did not sleep at all the night before I herd you was killt. You might think I'm terched, but it was a strong feeling come over me to be nervous for someone I loved.

So, you can imagine when I herd the truth about you. I was certain I would never sleep again; afraid I might imagine another death and have it come true. It was only a little later I learned about Let, and I dared not dream these nights since. I try to stay awake but then doze off and feel myself dreaming. I jump up and shake my head of dreams. Maryette said she dreamt of losing something and searchin' for it frantically, all nervous when she woke before her baby died. She was not doing so well, and I'm afraid for her. Sometimes, and it is hard to admit, but I am afraid for me and our babies, too.

But you probably want to know if I miss you, and I do, and I can't hardly believe you're never coming' home. Father broke down when he herd the news and cried like a little child, and I felt such compassion for him as I've never felt, but when I touched his shoulder, he yanked away, stood up to his full height and said you and Let was worth twenty of me, and I know he was right, but I couldn't exchange my life for yours even though I would of if only I was asked. Well, I would if I didn't have the little ones.

Mother screamed in her bedroom, carrying on something fierce, and I daren't go in to her even though I was feelin' great pity for her broken heart. I don't want you to think my heart isn't broken too because it is. But I know for certain you can hear me now as I'm composing' this letter in my head to you, my beloved brother.

Tell Let, if you can, I'll be talkin' to him soon as I can stand to think of him dead or not in this world of ours anymore. I don't know why I should go on living when both my brothers are gone. The whole of this earth seems crazy with grief and pain and loss.

*

The doubting historian reread Ezra's words: "I should like to hear from those I love nexte to my God." Then she whispered them. She thought, she, too, would like to hear from those she loved next to God—the contact we were looking for, often times with no more success than Ezra Cross, scribbling a note to his wife, a woman he would never see again. From the letters strewn across her floor, Grace could infer Susa's words and anguish.

TWELVE

God knoes that I love my Dear Wife

Fifty feet out from shore, the rock's eye looked out before disappearing again, surfacing and submerging its bulk with each traveling wave, the lake lower than usual in the autumn. Grace dipped her bare feet in the cold water and stifled a surprised shout but did not pull her feet out completely. If you came across the lake quickly, failing to notice the rock's eye, its ragged edges below the surface would gouge the prop, crippling her, Bill had warned her. You had to know the small lake and its hidden landscape, the valleys where the trout slumbered and the jagged edge of below-the-surface mountains where the walleyes hung suspended. The pike could be anywhere, the lone wolf of the water, cruising for fry.

"It's the only fish worth catching," Bill had told her once, "not because they taste better than any other but because they put up a fierce fight." She still thought of him as her husband and realized she probably always would, but at the moment, she was relieved it was done. He had called that morning to tell her she could keep their camp in her name if he could have the sailboat, the one of their two major bank accounts, their house in the village, and his old albums.

"You've got a teacher's pension, don't forget," he said, trying to get her to agree with robbery. She didn't speak for a moment before saying, yes. He was aware she had come into sums from her Aunt Evelyn and her late mother. Grace did not need the cash, he surmised, but he had no idea how frightening it was for Grace to feel the burden of carrying all her bills alone.

Any lawyer would have advised her not to deal without negotiating because she was sure to be getting the poorer end of the bargain, but Grace no longer wanted anything out of their marriage except their son and her little camp on the lake, her solace even when glazed over with ice in the winter. The fall colors of the leaves on the hillside reflected in the mirror image of water were painterly and so elegant it seemed unnatural. She noticed all of this even in sorrow. With her feet moving back and forth, Grace considered the dissolution of her union with the man she had known since she was still a girl.

"You didn't answer your cell phone. Thought I'd leave a message. Gracie, I'm, I'm sorry if you were hurt. It was never my intention." Bill's voice on the phone sounded like he was someone other than who he really was.

"Please don't call me that anymore," she said pointedly. He wouldn't pull her into the maelstrom again, thought Grace, trying not to sound bitchy or weepy—either would be unacceptable.

There was silence for a long moment. "All right. Grace. Let's just be reasonable adults about this. We just want to get through this as painlessly as possible, and I'm sure you do, too."

Grace heard the "we" and realized it no longer applied to her.

"You can have the camp; you know it's the more valuable of our two properties. And it's now insulated. You are not in a position where you couldn't live there in the winter. There are a few things I'll need, of course, my fishing gear, my tools, but you can have the rest. The books are all yours. I've spoken to a realtor, and he thinks I'm being too generous. Even if it's a lot smaller than our house in town, it's worth quite a bit more just because of location."

"I'll keep my mother's house on the lake." She thought of the mallards, osprey pair, geese, and occasional cormorants diving. Grace emphasized the word "mother's."

"I realize it's your property, but the law looks at all of it as joint property, you have to understand."

"The books were my father's. Allow Jason to choose where he wants to live, but I'll agree to joint custody. That's all. Our son needs both of his parents." She had decided to be rational, or perhaps it was irrational, but certainly sounded conciliatory, not to think of Bill as the man she had been married to all those years and his betrayal, his secrets, his liaisons with another, younger woman in the oldest trick in the book—a friend's wife. She couldn't decide if it was better to have the other woman be Bill's friend from work or someone she had known as well as Beth. No, not true, she reminded herself. She did not know Beth at all, she decided. How could a friend have done this? It was so clichéd, she wanted to scream, but he would not know it, so she didn't scream or throw insults. Calm, she thought, stay calm.

The conversation was abrupt but not uncivil. Agreeing to her terms readily, he was surprised at the fact she did not weep or curse over the phone or ask him about the total value of his vintage albums and his old coin collection although he suspected she knew very well. His highly competent wife knew everything. He was prepared to bring up all of his expenses and debts: buying Jason the used car, her newfound inheritance from her mother and aunt, money to which he might legally have some claim. He was even prepared to buy her a car f it would keep her from asking too many questions or asking for alimony, but she didn't. The relief of the burden overwhelmed him almost to the point of gratitude.

"My lawyer will draw up the papers. We don't need two lawyers haggling, and it'd be an extra expense for you."

"Thank you for thinking of me," she said, unable to avoid the sarcasm spilling out like water.

"Look, you don't have to get bitchy here." Before he had completed the sentence, Bill knew he had not intended to go there. He tried to get out of that space quickly. "Uhh. Say hello to Jason for me," he added, as if his kid was a distant relative. Then, he offered the obligatory familiarity before hanging up the phone.

"Bitchy?" she said to no one in particular after the connection went dead. Grace stood numb for a moment after dropping the receiver on her landline phone. She decided at the moment to change her cell phone number, too. It was not possible to go on having feelings for him and impossible to cut herself off from her life story with Bill. She hated him for his awkwardness at the end of their union, his seeming indifference, his carelessness, his infidelity, his selfishness as much as for telling her to "say hello to Jason." He had been a good man for so long. Was there a time limit?

She wanted to yell, "I hate you!" but yelling about hating him would be giving him too much power when he already seemed to have all the authority, so she pushed the words back down. The oddity of it all was his hurtful actions had distracted her from mourning over the sudden losses of both her mother and beloved aunt, and then, so horribly the death of her brother. Her mother's older sister had died five years earlier. They had long been a family of primarily women, with the exception of her brother who loved the fact they all doted on him. Her own father died when she and Richard were children, and now what kind of family was she? Immediately after hanging up the phone, she began to worry she would be too cloying for Jason to tolerate. How would she avoid seeming desperate to hang onto her son?

Her walk down to the lake was restorative, and with her feet breaking the smooth surface of morning water, Grace thought again of Susa even as the distant relative swirled around in conflated memories with her mother, her brother, her aunt, her soon-to-be ex-husband. Whether or not her studies were simply a distraction, she knew she was using them to work through the unworkable agony of her human mess of this divorce.

Returning to the search, she understood exploring the mystery of Ezra and his letters would not hurt her in the way her own losses continued to plague her. If Susa had not loved her Ez, why had she kept the letters? Susa had remarried, however, gone on to have four more children with another man. And Grace was descended from one of Ezra's only three children, the baby boy grown and married a young woman, Grace's great-grandmother, a woman who outlived all the others, 101 years of age before she passed away in her sleep, resting in her daughter's house in the Catskill Mountains.

As Grace was considering her family ancestry, she looked up to see the cabin's roof covered in moss, wondering how long had it been growing there. It was lovely, like out of some fairytale, but she knew enough to realize the moss had to be taken off. Perhaps the roof needed to be replaced. There were all these questions and problems for which she had no answers, she thought as walked back to the cabin and opened the door.

Grace's recollection of her great-grandmother was fragmented with images rather than coherent with sequential episodes. What she clearly remembered was the woman's white, wispy hair knotted at the nape of her neck and the fact that, although the old woman was blind when

Grace knew her, it always seemed as if Grandma Dessie was looking right at her, she thought.

In truth, learning about her great-grandmother made Grace feel uneasy when her aunt first told her the stories. She remembered staring at the old woman to see if she was really blind; looking for some hint she knew her great-granddaughter was standing before her. Grace considered she might have been less fascinated with Ezra Cross if he had lived long enough for her to meet him, if he had not been a Civil War soldier, if he had not mysteriously disappeared. But he remained the enigma. Grace was only his descendent, but a thread connected them, and she was searching for threads.

Ezra's son Willie, the youngest, grew to marry Dessie, who had children and lived an impossibly long life, a blind seer, the inscrutable prophetess, connecting children and grandchildren to this Civil War hero.

What was Susa thinking when she heard about her husband, about the idea he would never return home? Grace imagined a shawl Susa knitted, because women were all gifted in those arts at that point in history, was draped over the young wife's narrow shoulders as she stirred the crabapples over the stove, the kitchen filled with the comforting smell of cooked fruit, but where was her comfort after the death of her husband? Did she already know the man she was to marry when Ez never returned? Were they secret lovers, friends before Ez had been killed? Was Susa relieved she would not have to make a choice between men she loved?

Susa still felt like a complete enigma. It had not immediately occurred to Grace to wonder about the wife at home when she first began reading the soldier's letters. What did Grace know about Susa? From Ez's letters, it seemed the young widow was at odds with her in-laws, moving out of their house after moving in briefly during the War.

Susa ended up losing the small farm she had lived on with Ezra before the War, unable to make the payments. How had she reacted? How had she gone on? Grace would have to go back to Ez's letters to discover the wife and children he left behind. The image of Susa's stoic ghost was beguiling even in the face of adventures of the battlefield of her spirited husband. It seemed likely Ezra's story was simply more compelling—the action and the violence of war more riveting. So much of our written history figured around battles and men.

There was a letter in which Ez admitted Susa was asking him for help, and he appeared at once hopeless in response, angered, and seemingly indifferent, missing the point almost entirely that Susa and their children were about to be thrown out of the house they were staying in for lack of payment.

After Bill filed for divorce but before her aunt left her some inheritance, Grace recalled the feeling of dread related to fears of poverty and all the lack poverty attended it. Her teaching salary was enough to sustain her she decided, but she had left teaching temporarily. She knew, however, there were jobs she could return to easily. The position of worry made her recall Susa and how she must have wanted to cry in frustration at those missives from her absent husband. Turning again to the letters, not for solace, but distraction, Grace read the letter dated before Christmas, 1864.

Kellys Creek West Va

Evening

Dec. 15/64

Dear Wife and children

As I am on picket and shall have to be up nearly the whole night and having a paper to send, I concluded to write a few lines to put in the side of the paper for to let you no that I am well and thinking of them, I hope this will find you well and comfortably situated. You said in your *last letter of the 5th you wanted me to tell you what to do. I did not say anything about it in the answer I wrote for I had told you in a letter previous all I could tell you good and I feel like one of old though he slays me yet will I trust in him. Where was Let burried you did not say in your letter, and who bought that house tell me in your next if you know perhaps, I can prevail upon him to let you stay--I must now close by once more asking God's blessing upon you all My regardes to all enquiring friends.*

Your Affectionate Husband

Ezra Cross

Since writing I have learned there is only 450 Rebbel prisoners at Loop Creek. Give my kind regards to Bro and Sister Jackson and all enquiring friends.

My Love to you and the children

Give me credit for this will you. I have burned the letters so I can not referr to them as you told me to but I can remember a great deal of them, so good night. May Angels guard you while you sleep til morning light appears

From your Husband

Ezra Cross

Grace noted this letter was more broken up in several places than most of the soldier's other correspondences. Ezra must have been interrupted many times during the writing of his missives. Imagining the man at a desk on his lap overlaid with a hardboard, Ezra dipping in his quill pen, Grace could almost see a soldier opening the flap of Ezra's tent and informing him of some particular problem: soldiers suddenly taken ill, a horse gotten loose, missing rations, a shot near the sentry, deserters discovered. Yet there must have been considerable time in camp for the composition of these letters, too.

She wondered if Ezra had burned his wife's letters. Was this a common practice due to the constant movement of camps and their inability to keep extra material with them? Grace made a note in her journal. Ezra's multiple closing signatures and interruptive lines were almost comical, but Grace reminded herself the soldier must have been disturbed in his musings and often hurried when he tried to conclude his letters to his wife.

Why the P.S. about the number of captured Confederate soldiers? Of what use would this have been to Susa, particularly since there was no context? But it spoke to Ezra's imperatives of the moment, the disjointed thoughts of a man moving between boredom and crisis. It was almost as if Ezra had momentarily forgotten to whom he was writing. Were there formal papers to be filled out, and he had inadvertently filled in the line about the prisoners in his wife's letter? Perhaps, on the official document, he had written some endearment to Susa? The deepening unfamiliar.

As she arranged her notations on index cards, she suddenly remembered Tim and the fact she had forgotten to see him on her scheduled day. Upset with herself, she called the VA to ask if she could visit in the off hours. After waiting an interminable time on the phone, the receptionist referred her to a charge nurse on Tim's floor.

Drained, the nurse was initially curt but then changed her tone and suggested the timing would probably be okay for Tim because he had been awake for only a short time, and no one had visited him for several days. Grace changed her shirt and grabbed a couple of books before heading out. All the way to the VA, she questioned whether her visits were for Tim or for herself. How careless. How could she have forgotten to go?

By the time Grace pulled into the full parking lot, having waited for a blue Chevy to pull out just in front of her, Tim was already asleep. By the time Grace reached his room, he appeared to be dreaming, and

Grace felt oppressive guilt as she stood at his door and watched him sleep for ten minutes when he, quite suddenly, opened his eyes and said, "I've bbbbeen wwwwwaiting ffffor you, gggorrrrgeous." He hadn't forgotten her, and he had forgiven her.

"Good to see you, too," she said unable to keep from smiling.

THIRTEEN

I shall try to take things by their smooth handle

I don't know what he wants from me. I couldn't be more alone even with the babies nestled against me. His mother speaks so coldly and sharply. When she stares at the children, it's not with the eyes of a grandmother; it is with a hawk's sharp eyes as if she would pounce upon them, tearing at them like a catched rabbit as if she could imagine the children are not her son's.

What was it about me made her shrink away? Her son nearly 30 before he married, yet she found me lacking. She watches my hands pare and core the apples. It is a critical gaze. She picks up a knife and begins paring more quickly as if in competition. I let her win. Her shawl is perfect, the wool tightly woven, and mine is ragged with dropped stitches and for that she judges me, and I try not to listen to her complaints over everything I touch. She picks up my children's coats and angrily hangs them in the closet in my room. I told her they will pick them up, and I'm trying to teach them to be responsible, but she says she can't wait for me.

There is no sense of warmth or family in this house with her. It is cold all the time no matter the weather outside. She complains if I try to light a fire, telling me the wood needs to be saved for the colder weather as if there was a limitation to the forests. If Willie catches a cold, I will never forgive her. He doesn't come home, and the money he says he sends never arrives, and I don't know where to look so her eyes won't find me or the children. George can't stay out of her wrath, always yelling at him even though he's doing nothing but being a boy, all limbs flying. I can't remain in this house with her any longer even if she let me and my babies stay on. Why can't Ez understand? George is old enough to pick up on her meanness. Quick like a jack rabbit, he avoids her gaze as well as her grasp. I try to tell him not to speak Ill of her because I know my Ez would not want to hear his son say such things, but, secretly, I'm in agreement and have a mind not to punish him when he curses about his grandmother. I almost laughed when he dodged her and she shrieked at him, grasping nothing but air. She saw my face and knew, however. Jennie seems to know no different.

Sometimes I don't know what I will do. It is good Ez doesn't know my thoughts, doesn't know how close I come. I peel the crabapples with a fury finding no other home. I throw the scraps to the pig and watch him devour the remains.

She approaches me from behind like a snake and hisses. "Your boy is crying; pick him up!" I hear no one but her voice and the long sentence with no love in this house; one that will never be my home. Even if Ez was here, this would never be my home. What would he say to her if he was home? Would he pick me up and carry me away or just go to his room, content to be the center of this household? Would he leave me with this unloving woman who stares at my children as if they were beggars or vermin? Would he demand we have our own room, my babies cooped up with me even though there are empty beds upstairs?

George outgrowing the pallet bed.

I feel such hate for this woman—and I know it's unchristian—butt I don't care if she's burdened or worried about her son. She never had a kind word to say to me when she learned about my brothers. Even Ez's father was soft spoken then and told me he was praying for them and for my family.

The space in this small house is not big enough for us. Even if it was a mansion, we could not live under one roof, but what choice do I have?

What was Grace to make of the irony or mystery of Ezra's uncertain disappearance? His letters home recorded his thoughts about gratitude: "I feel thankful to him who doeth all things well for leading me safe through the storme of shot and shell." The poet soldier had come through an alliterative storm, surviving the considerable odds some 360,000 of his fellow Union soldiers who didn't return could attest to, with 112 wounded in every 1,000 Union soldiers in battle, Ezra himself wounded twice, as well, but surviving only to fall, or be pushed, or walk off a train meant to take him home?

Layers clouded by time and mixed contexts: Grace did not know if she would find her way through such obscurities. What did it matter now he had been educated, had written rather lyrically to his young wife, had attempted to provide for his family sending his pay through an imperfect, albeit free (to Union soldiers) mail system, offering such promise but often found letters arrived late, not at all, or opened and empty? What did the "evidence" matter to Susannah? What the young woman knew was she had three children to care for with no money, no home, and a husband who never returned.

This line of questioning was leading perilously close to one where life was in jeopardy. What did any of it matter? Hadn't her students on more than one occasion bragged they had never read a book, only "tricked stupid teachers into thinking I've read?" Perhaps because her students had raised the question, Grace knew it mattered.

*

In Coleman's claustrophobic, musty classroom, Grace picked up her bag as her professor approached. "You were quiet tonight, Mrs. Storey. Was it my lecture or the topic? Admittedly, I have grown used to your relentless questions."

Attempting not to wince involuntarily, Grace looked up and asked Coleman, "Please call me Grace. And it was neither the lecture nor the topic." The idea of taking back her maiden name seemed most appropriate, but, as a writer, she had always loved her ex-husband's last name. The symbolic associations with Storey were not worth the continual reminder, however. There would be changes on all of her records, her driver's license: the thought of it exhausted her.

"Grace, then." *How careless of me*, thought Coleman as he remembered another student had casually mentioned Grace was in the process of a divorce. He realized he probably shouldn't have known this, and it should matter.

"Just preoccupied tonight. I'm truly sorry if I appeared inattentive or rude." Grace would normally have felt exhilarated Coleman was bothering to talk with her after class, but, at that moment, she simply wanted to go home.

"No, not at all, not rude. How is the abstract coming along?"

Not tonight, Grace thought, feeling vulnerable. "The work is going slowly, and—I keep following false leads," she said as she glanced over at a few of the graduate students exiting, eyeing her. She could imagine them thinking she was simply trying to improve her grade by talking to the professor.

"Of course," Coleman said, suddenly. "That is what we historians do. We follow false trails and begin again. Yet, the record of our movements, as well as what we discover becomes the history."

"I honestly don't know how many times I can do that," said Grace, revealing more than she wanted, her sorrow spilling out in the tone.

Coleman appeared not to notice her weariness, helpless to his own sense of excitement. His spirit was buoyant. "As many times as you need to. I've never sensed indolence from you." He had already come to appreciate her thoroughness in the research and the class discussions.

Grace looked up and noted most of the other graduate students had already left the room, and she was alone with the man who stroked his mustache either reflectively or self-consciously. When fiction writers sense life has become too unbearable, they can always have their characters leave the planet, thought Grace, become Billy Pilgrim among the Tralfamadorians.

"There are those moments when I would rather be reading Vonnegut," she said, surprised by her spoken honesty and the fact the thoughts she was hiding were now transparent. She wondered if Coleman would think she had just lost her mind, but he looked intrigued. While it was possible for an historian to conjure up the smells of the gunpowder, the artillery shock to the soldier's system as he sweated in his heavy, wet uniform, carrying the odors of battle, the spatter of blood from the man too close whose head had been ripped from his body, a cannon ball separating the inseparable, it was more likely the territory of the novelist.

History could document the deaths but the emotions? Could the fiction reach out and pull the widow from obscurity and elevate? Give her not just a voice but a protagonist's role for once? Allow her to climb Faulkner's tree with Caddy and her muddy drawers and jump back down, yelling at her brothers who were racing to tell their mother, step out of the margins and into the middle of the page with a bruised chin and dirt under her nails from digging up roots to feed her children, scarcely competing with the tale of her adventurous husband on picket with the Rebel soldier pulling his father's musket up to this shoulder to steady it, both eyes squinting to scope, and his trigger finger already cocked when another Union solider knocked the young Confederate to the ground with the limb from a nearby fallen tree, the branch all he had to prevent the shot that would have pierced Ezra's skull. Instead, the young Southern marksman awoke with a bandage wrapped around his head, his hands bound, a rope pulling him forward on his way to a Yankee prison, dysentery, and inglorious death awaiting.

At the edge of consciousness, Grace spotted Susa.

I am here, whispered Susa, her dress ragged and her hair matted at the nape of her neck, the thought of combing it out and untangling the twisted curls was a luxury she had nearly forgotten. I am here, too. Willi has been crying, and I can't make him stop. They are hungry.

Grace tried not to imagine all of it because the scene was fluid, her fingers reaching out to warn Susa's husband of an assassin's bullet, help Susa find a suitable home.

"Yes, we're grounded to actuality in history, however speculative, and it's sometimes frustrating when we come to those irritating gaps in information, in the records and documentation, however thorough we are," remarked Coleman, pulling Grace back to the classroom. "I'm a Vonnegut fan myself, and I'm not entirely sure whether we don't derive a truer sense of the Dresden bombing from Vonnegut's novel than we do from Frederick Taylor, but how do we judge the fiction without historical fact, contextual statements? They're not exclusionary."

Grace simply nodded, unable to have the kind of conversation that would either engage or enlighten. "I don't know Taylor's text; I'm sorry," she said after a moment.

"You should read it if you're interested in the bombing of Dresden." Coleman was missing the point, she wanted to shout, but she said she would read it, concluding the conversation while pulling on her coat, not taking the time to button it. "But remember, the historian has the records, the dates, the certificates, the logs. From this, we know with a degree of certainty."

"And their letters," said Grace. When all of the dates and numbers lined up, did she have Ezra and Susa? Was she looking in Ez's eyes at the moment he left that train in whatever way he left it never to return? Was she able to pull back the mourning curtain and see Susa in her home, finding her weeping or making a meal for her children? When did Ezra's and Susa's mystery become her mystery? Not simply a historical puzzle to be figured out, but the need for an answer.

Coleman moved toward her as if they were going to continue their conversation all the way to the parking lot, but Grace turned abruptly and said, "Good night," leaving Coleman looking puzzled, perhaps embarrassed by his dismissal. If she had remained a few moments longer, she might have told Jeff Coleman exactly what she was thinking and just might have said something she did not want to reveal, even to herself. The whole project—this going back to school to become something, someone else—suddenly felt like a mistake. The walk to the parking lot in the dark seemed endless, and she allowed herself a slow pace in those moments of nonjudgmental shadow. Here she could hide from whatever assessment others had of her.

As she shut her car door, adjusted her seatbelt, turned the keys in the ignition, she sat protected in the light above a street pole overlooking the lot, wondering why Coleman had spoken to her after class. He was not the kind of professor to engage in chitchat with his students, it seemed. In fact, he always appeared irritated by their presence. Some instinct told her that Coleman was attracted to her, but its absurdity as well as her own chaotic predicament pushed away the suggestion. Her curiosity about Coleman gave way to the surge of emotion she had been fighting to contain.

She forced herself to think about her historical research and came back to the absurdity of Ezra's death. Her great-great-grandfather had escaped all those horrors: four years of dysentery, rebel bayonets in hand-to-hand combat, horse's hooves in charges, the mini-ball shot from cannons thundering so loudly they obscured reason, the marksman holding his rifle from his position behind a rocky outcropping, the typhoid, the pneumonia, fevers, chills, a laundry list of contagious diseases, hunger, botched doctoring, germ infested quarters, dirty bandages on wounds, nearly drowning, falling, heat stroke, all to end by falling or being pushed off a train. To have his head removed from his body by the sharp iron wheels. All this, all this and not to be counted in the 360,000 plus Union dead. He was not a casualty of war but of heading home.

He must have been killed, accidentally or murdered, as he ventured between rail cars. Surely, he did not just invent a new life? She could not believe her ancestor had willingly deceived his wife and family by never returning. Why did he leave one car to stand in such a perilous space? There was no way to get at this, she thought, and then, quite suddenly, she was sobbing, loudly, inside a car with the windows rolled up, steaming them, on the hill overlooking the picturesque college town, knowing full well she was crying over her own losses rather than those of Ezra's and Susa's.

FOURTEEN

———

I hope and pray to God to repare me

Even when Grace wanted to sleep, she ended up in the tiny library study which had long been the hub of the cabin, expected in a family of readers. She sometimes woke early and then felt her way down the narrow stairs to the light before going over the letters, trying to make meaning from their seeming randomness. Her methodology varied from day to day, exposing her non-scientific approach to no one but herself. Some historian, she scoffed. She glanced around until her eyes were drawn to a particular phrase: "for god knoes I love my dear wife"—in a letter, and then she would pick it up, less the scholar than the shopper, her inability to show discipline. Even in the manner in which she read the Civil War correspondence disheartened her.

At 41, she was too old to be so unsure of herself, but all the while knowing the cost of tearing apart a life results in uncertainty. But if she were brave enough to try, perhaps she could rebuild another image. She turned back to Susannah, thinking about how she had rebuilt her life.

Fort Elsworth VA

Sunday, August 18th/'61

My Dear Wife

I again take my pen in hand to inform you of my health which is good at present and hope these few lines will find you enjoying the same great blessing of God. I received your letters of the thirteenth and was glad to hear from you about news of the children. You wrote that you had not heard from me in good while but I have written every week since I was in the battle at bulls run and sometimes twice a week and I no not the reason why you have not gotten them. I had written four letters to you between the one I got from you before I got yours of the thirteenth and so I was writing or rather I had just written and sealed another to send you when yours was brought into my tent and I grasped it with eager hands and tore it open and read it then brok myne open and said in it that I had received yours it made me feel bad to hear your sick for god knoes that I love my dear wife and children and to forget them would bee to forgetting myself for you are in my thoughts day and night and can not forget my existence for was it not for you and our dear children I don't know as I should have any greate desire save for the salvation of my country yet I have friends that I love I assure you but my family lays neares my heart than all the rest besides and I hope and pray God to repare me and mine to meet again on earth where we can enjoy one anothers society for years to come.

Now Susan, I don't want you to worry so mutch about me for I no it makes you sick as mutch as anything you can do. Bee of good chear dear wife and trust in god for he doeth all things well cast thy bread on the water and it shall be seen many days after so sayeth the worde and his promises is shure depend on him thou canst not fail make all thy wants and wishes known fear not his merits must pervail ask but in faith and to this is given it is now raining harde hear and has rained more or less for 3 or 4 days we were out on picket guarde Friday and Friday night about 4 miles from cape and when we were eating our lunch I told Fred Randall and the boys with us if you new where I was and what I was doing you would not sleep a bit that night. there is a boy in our company by the name of Philander Shaw and he is hear and well. I have not hearde anything from Rolly Randall or Reubin Wright yet but I don't think they are killed but mearly taken prisoners.

Give my love to your father and mother. Tell when I write to you it means them to. so no more at present. Let me hear from you often.

Ezra Cross to wife

"To wife." It was strange, Grace considered. Susannah's husband signed his letter, using his full name, as if the physical distance between them was growing more real, emotional distance overlapping geography. The letter, dated August 18, 1861, was pulled for inspection was longer than many of his others and seemed more repetitive as well. Voice behind the man with the "pen in hand" more desperate in "grasping the letter" and tearing it open. Noting the reference to the battles of Bull Run, Grace surmised Ezra had just been through hell and back and was trying to convince himself he would make it through the war.

How things must have felt so strange to him after those early days of the war when the regiment seemed to be marching to nowhere in particular, always getting ready, producing an unrelieved tension.

He had no idea, early on, he would be in the second battle of Bull Run or Second Manassas where 13,800 Union soldiers would become casualties in one of the bloodiest battles of the war. She also noted the unlikely prospects for survival of Rolly Randall or Reubin Wright, most likely killed at some point during First Manassas, a roughly five-hour battle in which more than 2,950 Union soldiers were casualties, the battle considered a Confederate victory, and McDowell discredited as a Union commander. Yet Ezra made no mention of criticism of his commanders in his letter to Susannah, Grace observed.

Look up names Rolly Randall and Reubin Wright, she wrote. There must be historical records in the counties of their births. Why did Ezra mention the "boy by the name of Philander Shaw?" Was the young man really just a boy? Grace's research, using National Archives and Records Administration (NARA), discovered a Philander Shaw born in Connecticut in 1821 and who died in 1896. There was a Lyman Philander Shaw and a Robert Philander Shaw, but the "boy" Philander Shaw seemed to have disappeared from the records, even from the genealogical ones, often the best bet for tracing the history of an individual.

She found Reuben Wright, a 21-year-old private in William Shaw's 115th Regiment of the New York Volunteers, who survived the war, and as a 77-year-old man was robbed and found his way into the newspaper account of the attendant's robbery at the Soldiers' and Sailors' Home in Bath, New York, published in the *New York Times* in 1920.

Suddenly, Grace felt sidetracked and like an imposter. What kind of historian was incapable of following a single lead to its natural or unnatural end? There were so many threads. And where was Susannah's voice in all of this, she wondered. Perhaps Coleman was right. There was no way to discover the woman's voice in all of this male-dominated history. She could feel defeat creeping up behind her, but she refused to turn to look, a stubborn quality which had been one of Jenna's many gifts to her.

Studying the map of an area of Virginia, in which the battles of Bull Run were fought, gave Grace little insight into the horror the men must have felt as they were engaged on the bloody fields. She needed a narrative; however, she loved maps. In fact, part of the reason she had decided upon history rather than English literature in pursuit of her doctorate had do to with the physical reality of maps and artifacts, the tangible effects of the past. Yet, even tracing the troop movements, along the lines recorded on the historical map, offered scant insight. Coleman would have told her she needed to understand the movements of the regiments first and then go into the details of the particular narratives. Although she was not sure he was incorrect, she knew the only way for her to proceed rested with stories. She returned to her source, to Ezra's letter, his wording in the letter dated August 18.

Headquarters 1ˢᵗ Vet. Cav.

Near Charles Town VA   *August 18ᵗʰ/64*

Dear Susa

You may be supprised at getting this so soon after getting the one I wrote at Hall Town Va but supprise or not I shall pencil a few lines just to let you no that I am well as usal and you can not be more supprised at my being near than I am myself for when I wrote before only four miles distin from hear I picted instead of being near today to have been at New Market or Harisons Burg sixty miles up the Valley well we have been up as far as Ceeder Creek 4 miles this side of Sleaves burg and forty-four miles from near when our army got their we found the Jonnies on fishers Hill thick as leaves in autom and well fortified they were estimated at sixty-five thousand. Strong our advance had three or four different skirmishes with them night before last. They received twenty-five thousand reinforcements under Longstreet making their force if our scouts tell the truth eighty-five thousand men conciquently we had to get back a peg or two but not until the sixth corps and Sheradans Cav gave Longstreet a brush. They captured 300 rebs killed 100 wounded 75 drove them into the river at front Royal and drowned 200 more so there is hundreds less to fight us their than was when they left Richmond. We lost 4 men killed 17 wounded. We must have an army hear today. Well Susa I am not at liberty to say how many but there is a right smart lot I reccon we have the greatest confident General Sheradan and believe he will lead us to certain victory so let the Butternuts come on and invade MD and Pa and NY the destroyer is on their track as sure as justice and mercy is administerd by God our father was it not for this hope or faith just as you please to call it that I have in God I do not no but I should give up in dispair but my faith and hope remains firm and unshaken yes I verily belive that the unforeseen finger of him who ruleth the heavens is directing this war and that the will do all things well and if I may judge according the signs of the times this war is near to a close yet it may raze a—

Ezra's letter was cut off at the bottom as if a page were missing. Of course, there would be missing pages, Grace thought, but this was the first instance of an absent page she had come across. And how symbolic—his life also missing a page. The one containing the description of his death, hardly a "good death" where he might have expired on a battlefield in the midst of glory narrative or at home years later with his grandchildren in the next room and his beloved wife at his bedside. What had Susa thought when she opened this letter? Was the page missing for her, as well, leaving her to speculate, to fear something had happened to her husband as he wrote these lines to her? But that made no sense since the letter was mailed; it had reached her, and Susa had preserved it.

Grace imagined the last page of her great-great grandfather's letter containing some personal reference, some intimacy Susa kept in her Bible by her bedside.

It was clear Ezra's religious faith sustained him, however confusing it seemed to Grace as Ez mixed pagan and Christian concepts seamlessly. Then a line struck Grace: "was it not for this hope or faith as you please to call it that I have in God." Grace could feel Susa's doubt through Ezra's letters; a doubt crept into his words fortified by Biblical allusions.

One line from Ezra to his wife opened up various interpretations at once enlightening or edifying, depending upon connotations of those words. The uncertainty made Grace think again of her love of literature, the ambiguous, the enigmatic, the unfathomable woven into a compact with the reader, finding meaning variously, altered interpretations with the silent dialogue between reader and the text. Sometimes she picked up one of Ez's letters and found Susa's voice, and then later, she would return to the same letter to find only the details of a man on picket duty. Always, however, there was the threat of a bullet, one already discharged, heading toward the man.

*

What should I think when you tell me about going out on picket? I imagine you sitting on a stump or log, brushing away the mosquitoes when a Reb comes up behind you whilst you wasn't looking' and then he raises his rifle. I see the bullet comin' at you and try to scream or call out to you, already knowing you won't hear me, won't hear my warning or heed my words. I try not to dream. I wish I didn't see the bullet. I wish I didn't see you sitting there alone with the mosquito buzzing about, you trying to swat at it instead of paying attention to the Rebel sneaking up behind you. I put your letter away, but I still see this image. I go outside and catch the chicken that stopped laying eggs and make George and Jennie watch the Willie while I'll try to kill it, the thing making a horrible racket, the head half off, its blood spurting out while it runs around like some demon, and I catch it again, my breathing hard, my heart nearly as hard as a stone when I hack at it again, finally killing the thing, plucking out feathers, the body still twitching with the memory of life, the blood on my hands and clothes in stains I think won't ever come out, and me, at this moment, hating everyone, everything, especially this dead bird that won't die; this image stays with me long after I have cooked it, cleaned up the mess.

What should I think when you write to tell me I don't write to you, though I do? I don't know where them letters go to or disappear to. I am so lonely and lonely for you. It is all I can do to get up some mornings, but the baby is crying, so I get him and forget about me for a little while again. George is a good boy, but he needs a father, so's he don't be disrespectful. I don't know where he heard them curse words. I don't forget about you ever, but I put you out of my head for a couple of hours just to get some work done because if I didn't, I'd be paralyzed with this grief and worry all the time and not just most of the time.

I worry our Jennie will grow up afraid of her own shadow because she sees me mournful or unable to provide for them. I try to be strong for her and George and for you, but I'm not as good as you, not brave like you was going off to fight this war, not brave like the generals, not smart like the President, not even good at knitting like your mother. I can't even write you a letter you receive and understand how I'm feeling and longing for you to come home. No one knows what I'm thinking—even the children.

FIFTEEN

I shall survive the pale motions of the dead

Johnny and his father Willem exchanged the briefest of looks but said not a word, the son grabbing a wooden bucket as if he was about to fetch water for the camp, the river only a half mile away, his father hauling the carcass of a dead dog out of the Union encampment, the dog Folly a victim of a stray bullet; the dog had hung around the camp long enough to have a name.

At the tree line, Johnny tossed the bucket aside and turned only once to see his father releasing the dog's tail as they broke into a sprint, the father keeping up with his eldest teenage son. The brush tore at their arms, their faces indifferent to the branches stinging, their legs independent now, running with a speed never imagined by the farmer, but his son was still pacing himself to allow his father to keep up, down to the riverbed; they jumped the bank, stumbling but not falling, until they splashed into the shallow creek, not stopping but following the river northward. They had calculated how long the disorganized commanders, mostly new lieutenants, would struggle with their counts *until it was decided someone had turned and run. The officers wouldn't be sure at first until all the dead were accounted for and calculating such numbers would not be an easy task.*

Johnny writing a letter to his wife, overwhelmed by the dead—not just accounting of them—scenes of the battle before his bloodshot eyes, the promotion new on the face of the man who gained what was lost from the ranks of the officers who had fallen. He wasn't sure if Johnny and Willem had been taken prisoner, fallen in the fields where they were not seen, or just missing. And when Johnny and Willem had run until their lungs ached, they stripped off their Union coats, revealing the civilian clothes they had on underneath their heavy woolen uniforms; if they were stopped now, they were farmers in sympathy with the North. Father and son kept running even though no one looked for them for a long time; miraculously, they made it all the way back. The sight of their farm, with its red barn needing paint and the barn door needing fixing, the weather vane atop the roof half off, all too fine for their weary eyes, but it was the sight of Ethel's startled face who brought them home. Willem died only a few months later in the arms of his wife, his foot race had killed the father but saved the son, who was sometime later dishonorably discharged.

*

The line from Ezra's letter—the one he composed as Johnny and his father disserted—would not leave Grace's thoughts as she considered it sitting across from her at the kitchen table; it waited patiently while she rinsed dishes then scrubbed a stain refusing to fade, having worked deeply into the enamel. The line walked up the stairs with her and floated near the window while she dressed, choosing a loose, white shirt and her favorite black skirt. It occurred to Grace her style was slowly changing in the absence of critique. A soldier who wrote poetry. Why not, "I hope I don't get killed, or I hope these ghosts don't get me." The reason the clause moved with her, she was beginning to understand, had something to do with whether or not she believed she was capable of surviving the pale motions of the dead herself, as her mother's voice whispered to her, *there are spiders in the house and the floors need washing.*

Her brother didn't say a word, which was very unlike him; he was always making long, detailed stories out of the most everyday occurrences, one with detours that became more intriguing he went along, his sister suspecting he began fabricating as his eyes lit up with discovery. How was it possible her brother was dead? The boy who banged his index fingers against a worn and deeply etched old desk in the virtuoso drum beat to *Anagodadavita* when they were both still kids.

Pushing the old car when he rolled into the drive, Richard afraid Jenna would hear him come in during the middle of the night, and Grace not telling on him. And then, in her stream of conscious, running rhythms of thought, she considered the correlation between T.S. Eliot's last lines in *The Waste Land*, "Datta. Dayadhvam. Damyata," and how silly the correlation seemed, revisiting words for their sounds rather than their sense while she simultaneously wondered about the idea of a possible connection, her brother still banging away in a furious dexterity in her mind, so absorbed in his rhythms she did not want to speak to him but, instead, stand outside his door and listen until the drumming ceased, and only then would she enter to tell him.

If she could speak to him then, knowing everything she knew at the moment, what would she say? How was it, the poetry of the moment worked its way into her soul more readily than prose? Was she really going to become a historian or, as she suspected, a writer who wrapped a guise around her like some black cape, enabling her to dig into mysteries without anyone asking why she was wasting her time? The study of history sounded solid, and writing of our passage sounded productive, unlike the years of attempts at fiction in which words found their way into corners in attics that had never been cleaned but were inhabited by bats, the smell slowly drifting deep into the wood.

She could record her family's history, but she had no entrance for the way in which her brother's illness and death left her. No, worse—she was disconnected in some kind of unreal stasis in which she could not move at moments. And when she finally moved, the unreality stayed with her like a shroud.

Perhaps her mourning was why Bill left, she considered, dusting every bit of wood in the cabin, moving books and relics from another era. Yes, he had grown tired of her sadness. It was a conclusion she had already reached but not incorporated. But if he had understood or even tried to comprehend what she was going through, she thought. He had other options. If he had wrapped her in his arms and told her he was feeling sorrow, too, or he would be with her through this time of sadness. Even if he could not have felt the pain with her, if he had only understood she needed time. That was not Bill, however. Bill was fun-loving and easy going, not one to suffer. Bill found a woman who would put him back in the center of the universe where he was most comfortable even though Grace had come to believe no one lives in the center because there is no center. She had lost her rotation.

As Grace picked up an old photograph of her father fishing, she remembered her mother dusting this same picture, the way she held the frame long before finally setting it back in place. There had been those pale motions of the dead for many years, she thought, but Jenna never carried it, so it deliberately hurt others, thought Grace. There was no possible way to move about her cabin without running into these pale motions. There were ghosts everywhere.

*

In the kitchen, Aunt Evelyn was leaning against a counter with a cup of black coffee in one hand and an unlit cigarette in the other. "So, I still can't smoke in here?" she asked her niece, who always replied, "The porch is lovely," as she handed the rough looking, bleached blonde—with the white tips splitting at the ends—an empty soda can for the ashes. Years ago, she had given her aunt an ashtray for the cigarette of the moment, but Evelyn said she preferred a soda can, so the ritual was repeated often enough neither of them thought of asking anymore.

Evelyn seldom protested or imagined she had a choice because her own mother, Grace's harsh grandmother, had always banished her daughter from the house when she "decided to engage in that filthy habit." Looking back, Grace recognized something puritanical in herself had been passed down like a bad gene from her grandmother and wished, more than wished, begged herself to let Evelyn back inside. She wondered if she could have forgiven Bill if he had asked her to do so.

It annoyed her thoughts of Bill kept interrupting her. If she had just let Evelyn smoke her lungs out in the kitchen or living room or whatever-the-hell room she felt like lighting up in, well, then Evelyn would still have died, but they might have shared another story or two while sitting together. Rationally, Grace knew there was nothing to feel guilt over in regards to her aunt, but if she couldn't stop death from visiting, then a compassionate niece should have at least allowed her aunt to be comfortable and warm inside the house rather than smoking outside. Strangely, she now missed even the awful order of cigarettes, recognizing without much profound analysis, she really missed Evelyn, missed her old connections as everything unraveled around her.

So, Grace replayed last conversations over in her head, considering alternate dialogue as if the whole scene had been something out of an

O'Neill play. She could manipulate the conversation, adjusting it at will, creating new endings and evoking altered emotions. The play's title would be *Pale Motions of the Dead*, adopting a line from Ezra. There were characters in abundance in this new play, ones who walked back and forth across the stage, but then they would all have to be without speaking parts, a few instantly recognizable, the audience baffled as to what was going on during the performance. The protagonist would know exactly what these ghosts were demanding, however, and it would be up to her to convey intention to the audience through gesture, through soliloquy, through exits and entrances. They would study this play in school after a few years on Broadway, the ghosts taking on the quality of old friends, ones you no longer have to explain yourself to or be too careful around.

For a few months, her husband's—she would get it right eventually—her ex-husband's footsteps were heard on the stairs at night, and Grace sat up in bed, nervously and intently listening, but she heard nothing more. One night, she went so far as to get a flashlight and make her way to the staircase, shining the light down, creating shadows, unnerving her further. Sleep evaded her all night more than once after the initial visit. The next day she moved around in circles, unable to find her balance. When she was trying to find a book for class, she heard him—didn't imagine she heard him but actually heard him—clear his throat upstairs. She froze, waited, but then there was nothing more.

She hoped it was Jason coming home unexpectedly although he had never cleared his throat in that manner. Grace thought about madness and sanity a lot after the incident or vision or nightmare. Following a particularly realistic dream in which she leaned against a railing talking to her dead brother, she woke to discover the dream felt far more real than the waking. She was still leaning against the railing and could feel its coolness.

After all, her husband was not dead but merely gone out of her life. The difference was not as dramatic as it should have been. Lying there alone, she sometimes wished him dead and then tried to forgive herself. Not really dead, she whispered. It was better not to think of him at all than to feel so weak and helpless she felt the guilt of a murderess in the middle of the night.

*

There was her father standing before her, what she remembered conjoined with stories told to help a child's imperfect memory of the man who patted the top of her little head when she wrapped her arms around his pant legs, not wanting to go to bed at night. Sometimes he swung his leg with her whole body attached to him, and she felt the clearest sense of freedom she was ever to know. He always seemed so gentle, but she never knew with certainty the sainted man of her dream-state memory was whom he actually was. The flesh and blood father had left a fishing cabin to his wife and little else, but Jenna never complained about him.

Grace knew it was Jenna who formed her image of the man who was her father. It was Jenna's descriptions she relied on to fill in the gaps left by time and distance. Leading up to Jenna and the friendship with her mother, lasting until Jenna's last breath in a hospital room with her daughter standing beside her, intoning comfort in order to hide panic, the doctor on the other side, checking for a pulse and shaking his head slowly, all prepared for this moment and completely unprepared for the effects of being left an orphan at the age of 41.

Would she survive the "pale motions of the dead" or those now dead to her? And the moment she recognized the question, saw its shape forming slowly, she knew she was going to survive at least long enough to contemplate the outcome. Long enough to feel incredibly foolish and self-indulgent because she was still focusing on herself. It wasn't the first time it occurred to her, but the first time she allowed herself to consider the idea at length. Bill had left because he was tired of dealing with death and loss and mourning. And he climbed into bed with a woman whose sexuality would appear to allow him to only exist in the present.

*

If I have to smile or cajole one more time to get some attention in this hellhole they call a hospital, I think I might as well be dead. How is it I survive? I survived that blast? I will never walk again on my own legs? That my legs are gone even if I still feel them? My face is not my face at all but some hideous, contorted mess? Losing my face is the worst, I think, because it was my identity; it is that loss my mother cannot bear, that makes my father turn to the window as if there was something out there of far greater importance than anything happening in this stinking room, that helped Katie decide we should "go our separate ways," as if I could choose my own direction or even propel myself at all. I can't really blame her, however.

My mother tries. God, she tries, but the look she wears—like she's been stricken with a terminal disease and my father already blinded in the corner? He was always a hardass. I don't know if I ever liked him, but I wouldn't have joined in the first place if I didn't love him, and I couldn't even tell him that. Of course, that was his legacy. I don't ever remember him telling me he loved me. That Kate can fall in love with another man and leave me only remembering her when she was naked and reluctant to get out of bed, her hair all tangled over her eyes. I get to think about all this over and over with nothing but time to remember what I can't feel.

The sound of a shell exploding is some distant abstraction—I didn't know it was a shell or even an explosion--no time for analysis or thought processes--unrelated to the sensation of awful warmth and sickening unreality spread over my lower body, swimming up my bloodstream to my brain as I lay there first conscious but unknowing, certain of nothing but death and then nothingness. As if the space between fighting for my life and landing in this place I'd rather leave through dying was nothing more than a disappearing thought, fleeting, blurry, nightmarish. Mostly unrelenting absence. Not even heroic. It doesn't matter what others call it. I know.

I recite my friends' names in the Humvee. There was a Tony. His last name? De Luca. Goofy smile with crooked teeth. I'm not even sure he was my friend, but we rode into death together. Why is there so little I can remember? Who was driving? Greg Falco. I must have known him. I don't even know if they were all killed or landed like me, blown out and limbless. Why don't I ask? Why don't they tell me? When the nurse comes, I see her look at me with pity and discomfort, maybe disgust. My face is an abomination. My body is absent. I'm already lost. But if I scream nothing happens except a needle, and I don't want to forget any more than I've already forgotten.

Here she comes. The volunteer who reads to me like I'm a child, but I am not a child. No man is so helpless. Forget it. Read to me. Don't leave, lady. I don't care if you're old or married. I'll whisper anything you want to hear if you'll stay with me in this stinking room that smells like my own piss. I'm not yet a ghost, but I no longer feel like a man. I don't know if I want to survive, but they never asked me. They never asked me. If I had been blown away a hero, it would have been more bearable than this.

She has a book in her hands. Her fingernails are painted like she's going on a date. Maybe I'm her date. I wish I was her date. I would marry her if I could.

*

"You're awake. Hi, Tim."

"Hi, ggggorgeous."

"You know I'm going to get a big head if you keep saying such things."

"Ttthere are wwwworse ttthings."

"Yes, there are."

SIXTEEN

———

Sleep on ye gallant dead

Ezra's phrases and letters began ordering her life. Writing down her favorite expressions of his, she had placed them around the house and realized they had become poetry for her. Lines floated up the stairs at night, drifted into the kitchen when she was cooking, blew outside when she walked down to the lake.

Raining and hearing it, she didn't want to wake. Somehow the sound of falling water had worked its way into her subconscious. It rained until she was up and out of bed, checking for leaks. Not the pleasant little sprinkle replenishing but a battering deluge pushing through crevices and underneath doors, damaging and staining floorboards, sliding through tiles on the roof, staining ceilings as the water takes on the color of old yellow wood.

Thunder rumbled, each time shortly after the lightning cracked, and attendant sound rattled dishes in the jelly cupboard. In defeat, she got up to watch the storm and mop the floor since it had become impossible to sleep, irritated Bill had never fixed the leaks around the door—he would have referred to the exterior casing trim as the problem—to keep the rain from damaging the floors. Now, there was no one to blame except herself. She stuffed a few towels at the base of the opening. From one gathering cloud across the lake, four violent bolts charged to earth simultaneously like the Four Horsemen of the Apocalypse; white, red, black, and the pale horse of death. What must the booming cannons in the Civil War have seemed like to those soldiers if this lightning storm was unbearable? This insubstantial house shook on its foundation, yet she was no longer afraid. Jenna used to tell her such tales as a child, stories of men split in two by lightning, and she remembered hiding in a closet, always cowering. Bill laughed at her fear when she told him about her childhood trauma.

"Don't be silly. It's just a storm."

"More people are killed by lightning than by." She stopped, always able to come up with something to rationalize her dread. Perfect. Rationalizing the irrational.

"So, buy a lottery ticket with those odds," he'd remark, standing in the doorway as if to challenge the Gods, and there she was, standing at the window, not challenging, not brave, or bravery born of immunity not from danger but from caring. She was waiting out the storm again.

There was something she had read likening the cannons to thunder. What text was it, she wondered? There must have been something hidden in those letters, something she failed to notice or analyze. Susa's voice seemed to be in the room with her sometimes, calling through the ages. Where were those particular letters dealing with the sound of cannons? It would be perfect irony to trip in the dark and fall, breaking her leg or neck while in search of relief from these fears, she thought. Probably a relief to Bill but not to Jason, so she made an effort not to trip because she felt she could will that kind of thing. "I cannot think about my brother, my mother, my aunt, my ex, and Riley, his presence more a part of my routine than any one person for all those years," she said out loud. Too much loss too quickly; she could have been a survivor of a war. "I am a survivor of war." Again aloud. Then corrected herself, as everyone is a survivor from those who came before. Always in the midst of a war. The absurdity of it. The real survivor of war lies in a hospital bed unable to write or walk again or even to speak without tangling his words. Grace had never asked Tim about his war experiences. It seemed presumptuous or cruel. If he wanted to tell her anything, Tim knew she would listen, but she suspected the stories of war were only glamorous from far off, the reality of it dirty and horrifying and dehumanizing. The war to Tim must have been the concept of blowing up in your face and taking your limbs and your heart. It was in this mood, sitting in the dark feeling around for a flashlight, she was struck by their tenuous connections.

Oh, the lights were now working again. Electricity changes everything. She was relieved she had gotten rid of so many boxes, making her way to the library with ease. Where was that letter? The one benefit of losing her husband, she decided, was there was no one there to criticize or complain about her midnight wanderings, her forays into history. No one to ask when she was coming back to bed or why she was getting up in the middle of the night again.

*

Camp Piatt

West Va   *July 13th/65*

Dear Wife

Yours of June 26th is received. Was glad to hear from you and Willie, would been glad to have heard from George and Jennie. I am glad that you tire not of reading my scribblin. I had made up my mind that you had, you wrote such shorte letters and I had also made up my mind not to weary you so with a long letter. I hope you'll not be *offended with the letter I finished on the 7th for I did not feel as though I aught to hear from you as often as once a week and had I not got a letter from you I should not have written very soon. Could you have blamed me--I think not justly. As to dying with home sickness God holdes my vital breath in his hands and he being willing I shall survive the pale motions of the dead. I have been afflicted and I am yet with uncomfortable comforters I have one the small of my back it is very painful but I grin and bear it. The same as I have to a good many other things--I had rather be in active service where I could smell powder than be hear playing band box soldier--for I could forage my living then--this I call a swindling. I have said it, so let it slip. there is no prospect of getting paid very soon. I have spent more than $13. Wish I could get along on nothing--would do it willingly. I cant say when we'll get dischd. Perhaps between now and the 1st of Jan/66. Perhaps not untill our time is out. I haven't heard from Pont, yet they can do as they please about writing again. So will it. If they don't want to hear from me, I don't want them to.*

So we are agreed. Perhaps I am saying more than I aught to if I be I am sorry; it continues very hot hear with frequent showers--I hope you'll not find yourself away on my account. Charley Helt is well. So is Whittlesy but I think the latter is unlearning every day. I am studying human nature at present, as far as I have got, I find it to be very deceitful defective and depraved.

There isn't a man in (an enlisted man I mean) our regt that feels satisfied with being kept hear if there was any more fighting to be don. They is all willing to do their part and trust luck but there is no more fighting to be don with rebels and for my part I am glad of it, but we all supposed when we enlisted that when th war ended and civil law was again established that we would be permitted to return to our homes and families not be kept hear eating wormey hard tac and bacon--there is several cases of the scurvy in the regt. It is getting late so I must stop and try to sleep for my head feels bad. Good night and write soon to please.

Ezra

*

One of the last letters he wrote Susa kept or the last one surviving the ages was in Grace's hands. She read it several times and heard his complaint, his longing, and his discouragement, yet thought him lucky to still to be alive after all he had been through. A few weeks after writing the last letter to Susa, Ezra would have been heading home when something happened. What? There were always the little mysteries in every letter beneath the largest one.

Who was Whittlesey to Ezra? What did he mean by Whittles "is unlearning every day?" Was the reference some kind of 17th century slang for getting dumber by the minute? And, after all of his experiences in war, was it any surprise Ezra wrote of human beings as "deceitful defective and depraved?" Yet, over and over, Ezra ignored battle descriptions and details of the conflict, asking repeatedly for Susa's letters to him, reaching out for home, for a woman's touch and compassion he did not seem to feel was there.

How was it possible such a descriptive, poetic soul wrote so little of the war itself? At times, Grace felt as if she were drowning in his letters without even the trace of war. He might have been saving Susa from brutal descriptions of conflict, censoring himself from the time he picked up his pen. Perhaps it was all he could do to keep from complaining about his fears and the horrific scenes of battles. There was always a reference to money in his letter: what he spent, what she could spend, where he sent the money, who was carrying his money home for her, questioning her about why she did not receive it. In the midst of war, the most pressing subject was still how much money they needed to survive.

Exhausted, Grace turned out lights in the library. The lightning storm was over. For some reason, she was thinking about Tim Fitzgerald at the V.A. again. His charge nurse told her on a recent visit Tim was having more difficulty breathing. She decided right then to go to the V.A. the next day regardless of the progress on her paper. Not formally making the connections, she knew Tim's suffering and hers were connected.

*

It rained all day, this time lightly but persistently, so the sun never seemed to surface. Living on water, Grace had come to think about rain in a different way. She already felt like she was swimming on any given day, but after an all-day rain that "goes by like a shadow," as Ezra would say, she needed to get outside of herself, to do something for someone else. She walked down to the lake and watched neighborhood children jumping off a nearby dock. It was far too cold to be swimming, but they didn't seem to know. The kids appeared unaware the weather was too lousy to be outside at all, but they were laughing and screeching, pushing one another over the edge of the planked dock. One of them shot up a hand to her. Waving back, Grace smiled even though she did not feel the amusement. The gesture was simply reminiscent of another era when she was a child, and her brother leaped off their dock ahead of her.

He was always the more daring, but he made Grace braver, she thought. When he swung from a rope and landed without killing himself, she followed even though her belly hurt for two days after landing on her stomach. She could still hear him laughing as soon as she stopped gulping water. All you needed was each other and an old inner tube on the water, something to cling to in the deep.

The drive to the VA went painfully slowly, not simply a matter of perception, but a truck had overturned the night before and taken out the guardrails; the state was already replacing sections of railing, and traffic was backed up for at least a couple of miles. Cars were crawling. Really. The speedometer read 10, no, 15. Her foot rode the brake rather than the gas pedal. The word brake again. She knew why so many students had difficulty with it, spelling it break—all those myriad homonyms in the language. She recalled Ezra's unintentional puns in his letters to Susa as she passed an overturned orange cone. Waiting. Susa waited for her husband to come home. How long the war must have seemed—endless by its 4th year, but only to a people who expected peace from the beginning. Grace wondered what Tim thought of the peace experienced by the majority of people in the country while he was losing his limbs? The seismic shift in thinking from the seeming state of grace to perpetual war still unbalanced the sane, the Richter scale between the living and the dead.

By the time she got to the VA, it was later than anticipated, and she was a little concerned Tim would be too tired to visit, but he surprised her with his exuberance.

"It's abbout tttime," he said as she entered the room with a bouquet of fresh flowers she picked up. She set the flowers on the stand next to his bed.

"Nice," he remarked, and she thought he meant the flowers, but she was not entirely sure.

"I didn't know you were waiting for me," Grace smiled at him, realizing he was just a little annoyed, only picking up on the sarcasm indirectly. She wanted to plead her case about the lateness and more frequent absences. She wanted to tell him she thought of him like a son, but Tim was nothing like her son, and the sentiment would have been a lie. Maybe getting your legs blown off makes you an old soul, she considered. She did not know if Tim liked her as a friend, but she knew he usually seemed pleased she had come to visit.

"I'm sorry," Grace said.

"Fffor wwwhat?"

"For not bringing something better than flowers," she remarked.

"Llllook, it's only you and mmmme, darlling, sssso llllose the apppology. Wwhoss said IIII don't like ffflowers?" He smirked as if he was using one of his old pickup lines, and some part of Grace was oddly flattered a young man would flirt with her so shamelessly, but then she reminded herself he was helpless and lonely, and she could look like a crustacean. It would not matter to the young man waiting in a hospital bed he would never leave.

"WWWhat's nnnnew, bbeautiful?"

"Thanks for the flattery, but I just brought some reading material. I don't have anything new or exciting."

"You have nnnno idddea. Mmatter of opppinion, I guess. To me, wwell, you cccould bbring a list of chores. WWWhat's on the agenda?"

She noticed Tim's stuttering abated somewhat after he had been speaking for a while. "I brought a Hemmingway short story."

"Noooo. Nnnot him. I gggot toooo much of old Errrrnest in ssschool."

"Okay. Well, I bought a new book for myself, and it's rather long, but."

"The lllonger, the bbbetter. WWWho?"

Grace adjusted the pillow under his head and turned his neck slightly, so he could look her way more easily. "I've got David Foster Wallace's tome *Infinite Jest*." She pulled out the thick novel and set it on the stand which was crowded with a box of tissues, a food tray yet to be removed, and a nurse's chart of some kind. "It's certainly something a little more substantial than the usual fare." For an instant, she wondered if Tim would live long enough to hear the entire Wallace story.

"I'mm all ears." He made her smile and he knew it. She tried not to feel sympathy for his large, damaged ear and face, but she did so, before placing a chair close to his bed, no longer trying not to look at the misshapen side of his head curving inward. Yet, sometimes, when they were talking, she forgot for a moment how badly injured he was. She began seeing the other Tim, the one who moved athletically, confidently, not just his body suffering.

"This might take a while," she said as she flipped through nearly a thousand pages, causing a puff of air to escape.

"In ccase you dddidn't nnotice, I'm nnnot ggoing anywhere."

"Point well taken." They had grown used to each other's slight sarcasm. She gave him a critical overview of the novel because it was a crazy read, realizing Wallace's prose was all over the place like some, "heat maddened, summer fly," as she recollected a line from the poet Roethke.

"I'llll hhave to remember that llllline."

After a couple of pages, she asked, "Is this too hard to follow?"

"Nnnot unless you expppect to quiz me."

"Promise. No tests. No questions, except those raised by Wallace, of course, which are largely unanswerable." She noticed Tim seemed more relaxed lately when she was reading, and his vocalization problems diminished somewhat after she had stayed for a while. It was as if he needed to get started like an engine recharging his brain. She settled into reading, stopping occasionally to see if Tim was growing tired, but he appeared to want her to continue, his eyes taking it all in, eager for much more than all the words she had to offer him. After twenty pages—and the print was small—her voice growing hoarse, Tim was still wide-awake, intensely so.

"I ddddig this guy's wwwork," he said. "Thanks for bbringing him.

"You do realize, at this rate, I'll be reading this novel to you for a year."

"Pppromise? Tttthat hhusband of yours don't know how llllucky he is."

Surprised, Grace resisted the overwhelming urge to confess her husband had left her, but laughed instead. She knew Tim was serious about making sure he had a friendly face around for a year. She promised herself never to burden him with her own troubles.

"Promise," she responded with the same tone, thinking about this commitment in a way that hadn't occurred to her before. It was not just a matter of stopping by the VA when she felt the need to volunteer any longer. There was a time when she considered community service would help take her mind off of her own worries, and then she was considering how this young man was changing how she thought about him, not just herself. Yet, she was aware it could be dangerous to get too close. Perhaps, for humanity's sake, more perilous not to.

"Who's your favorite writer?" She stopped reading to catch her breath.

"Wwwhoever I'm rreading or llistening to at the mmoment."

"That would be Wallace then."

"That wwwould be you."

Grace put her hand on his scarred one without realizing what she had done, but she did not take it away. Wanting him to get well so desperately, Grace let his pain flow into her. He smiled with his thin, burned, and somewhat repaired lips. She remembered all of the stories about transferring health from one being to another. For an instant, she imagined she was one of those supernatural beings, and she willed her good health into the young man.

"If I fffall asleep wwhile you're still here, wwake me. I've been wwwaiting for tttoo long for you to come to dddrift off now. Unnnless

I'm dddead. Thenn lllet me ssleep."

Grace nodded. She could not believe the way he had of still trying to make a joke in such desperate situations. "If you fall asleep, it will be because you need to rest, and I'm not going to wake you.

"SSSometimes you ssssound like my mother."

"Probably a good thing," she said, feeling just the slightest sting.

"Bbbut then, I'm nnnnot attracted to mmy mother."

Grace could not stop the flush showing across her cheeks.

"You're bbblushing!"

"No, this is just how I look when I climb the stairs instead of taking the elevator."

"Nnnnot again. Is it wwwworth it?"

"You're always worth it." Grace began reading again, and Tim stared at her in the way a man stares at a woman he is in love with.

After a few minutes, he fell asleep, and she did not wake him. She wondered if Tim would really rather be dead as she watched him, his chest rising and falling in such irregular rhythm.

Don't die, she said, *please, don't die,* in a voice he could not hear.

SEVENTEEN

The day goes by like a shadow

The day goes by like a shadow, my husband Ezra writes to me from some dangerous place, and I see his shadow everywhere, standing over me, not a protective shadow, but one sometimes condemning, turning a stern eye toward my weaknesses. *I wonder how he can know if I am weak when he does not see what I do every day?*

Could I have been a soldier like Ezra? Would I been able to shoot someone? He never writes about killing anyone, and I wonder if killing has changed him. Will I recognize him when he comes home? If anyone tried to hurt my children, I believe I could kill, too. I wonder how many men my Ez has killed. How many times has a bullet whizzed by his head, missing him and hitting the man behind him? I'll drive myself crazy with such thoughts, but there is no one to talk to, no one to tell me Ez is fine, tell me and the children will survive. I don't know how long this war is going to last, but it seems like forever. How long I can last, but my little ones' eyes tell me there is no choice here. I got no more choice than Ez.

Some days Grace missed her classes, her students, the energy of the high school, even their boisterous profanity. It was always lively. She had inhabited a world with shadows for these few months; shadows where ancestors speak, and family departs whispering in the attic no longer there. Holly called, and Grace thought, at last, a support, a friend, an advocate, but Holly had terrible news. Holly could not talk, at least not in her normal voice. There was a wailing rasp at the other end of the connection Grace did not recognize. It was a few minutes before Holly could communicate in a way Grace understood what had happened. Jack had left her friend. Stunned, Grace initially had no words of comfort.

But she told Holly to stay there, and she would come to her. Hanging up the phone, Grace tried to come up with something comforting for Holly as she drove. All the way there, she was thinking about this exodus—it seemed too many men everywhere were leaving their women and the energy drain from sadness was profound. It hardly mattered her idea was hyperbole because it felt so real. It was all she could do to move her hands slightly and press her foot to the accelerator.

Taking a deep breath when she pulled in the drive, she knew that she didn't want to go inside. Paralysis, and she was stuck in her car at the end of the driveway in this lovely, older suburban community where there were bicycles leaning against maple trees and soccer balls lying in the neatly mowed grass. Grace gave herself a pep talk to be strong for Holly, at last taking hold of the handle to open the door of her car. Counting the steps she had to take to reach her side door, automatic garage door already opened, so she stood in the dim light waiting for an answer. Then it occurred to Grace: Holly, too, likely felt paralyzed inside and could not open the door.

Stepping in tentatively, she called out, "Hello. Holly?"

After only a few moments, Grace found her friend in an alcove off the kitchen with a cup of cold coffee at a Formica table. Holly had been crying, her face red and eyelids swollen.

"I don't want anyone to see me like this," Holly squeaked.

Grace put her arm around Holly's shoulders tentatively, as Holly dramatically pulled her in. They held one another wordlessly for some time. When Holly stopped shuddering, she looked up at Grace. At the moment, Grace wondered if she looked that way when Bill left. As Holly spoke, Grace couldn't believe what had happened to her, not Jack leaving, but the physical transformation. The voice nearly inaudible and strained, like a lost child trapped, forced to watch a horror movie. It was too awful to bear, but Grace nodded her head and tried to comfort, telling her friend, tell her she would survive this, too, although she didn't believe her own words.

"How do you do it? Keep going and working and just keep doing all you are doing?" Holly asked, remembering at last: Bill had left Grace just six months earlier.

And Grace realized she was supposed to have the recipe, the antidote to this poison, and she refrained from yelling at her friend. Part of her wanted to ask, "what the hell do you expect from me?" She didn't, of course. Swallowing those words, she forced something inane, like, "you'll make it. You're strong and beautiful, and you have your wonderful children, and you're an amazing teacher with so many gifts and people who love you." All of it was true, but it still felt shallow. Grace just kept offering compliments until Holly looked like she could bear the next ten minutes or at least expected less.

The really awful part was Grace felt better after comforting Holly, even though she did not feel sincere in all her words. Still, she wanted to believe Holly felt better because Grace was able to help in some small way. Stroking the top of Holly's head, Grace recognized on an intimate level the idea there are other failures, other marriages ripped apart when one of the partners does not see it coming. There were those worse off than her in a thousand ways. Isn't the human condition, she thought, to hope you're not at the very bottom of the pile of suffering humanity. Not always cynical, Grace thought if she didn't know better, there was no hope for anyone.

Holly suddenly launched a litany of broken promises. Jack had failed her, the teachers at her school were too busy to care, the students were immune to human suffering except their own, and "we all fail each other. I don't know how I'm ever going to trust anyone again," she stated emphatically after several moments. By the time she was done speaking, it was nearly dark.

Setting down a cup of tea she had made for Holly, Grace promised to see her again soon. She would e-mail her lesson plans and fill out the sub request. Thank God she's so organized, Grace thought. It would be an easy day for the sub with a pre-made test to hand out.

"Come back to our school," Holly said suddenly. "Why are you trying to get your doctorate anyway?"

"I can't return to high school, at least not yet, but I'll come back to see you, I promise." Grace hugged her friend again.

When she left, she turned again and vowed to bring bagels the next morning, but Grace was considering the fact this kind of emotional support was going to be too heavy, and she did not have enough reserves for herself and Holly, too. The journey through divorce is exceedingly lonely with many old friends suddenly feeling too uncomfortable to stop by. Maybe she could help Holly, and perhaps, herself without feeling fraudulent.

Let's be honest, she nearly said out loud on the way home. She did not believe she was able to help Holly any more than she could help herself in this redefinition process, knowing suddenly why she had ventured into historical waters rather than literary ones. It was not Holly's crying unnerving her; it was her voice, the shrill almost whisper falling from her mouth like a foreign object. Grace did not recognize her friend any more than she recognized herself.

The following Saturday, Grace drove up to see Tim at the VA; his mother had been sick and hadn't been able to visit him for a while. Dr. Malakar mentioned to Grace, Tim was not doing well that week, and she certainly did not feel like the right person but, apparently, she was the one person he claimed to want to see. Opening the door to his hospital room, Grace tentatively stepped inside. It was strange she felt like she was getting stronger, partly because of her connection to Tim.

Odors in the hospital were enough to depress anyone, as if one could detect each unpleasant odor, identifying the infection, disease, antiseptics, medications—all working against each other. Tim looked like he was asleep: his eyes closed and the sheets pulled up high around his legless torso. Grace wanted him to be awake. She brought a book titled *Guys Read*, thinking he could use a break from the expansive and difficult prose of Wallace. It was funny, she thought, at least her students used to believe so when they read the short essays and memoirs. Just as she set the book on a side table, Tim opened his eyes.

"Foooollllld ya, dddddiddn't I?"

"Hi. I guess you weren't sleeping, after all."

"Ccccan'tt ssssleep aaaannymore; ccccannnn't ttttttalk either. Bbbbbrainnnnnn damagggged, ya know."

"Your brain seems to be working pretty well, and you've got your usual sense of humor, I see."

"IIIIII'm a regggularrrr ccccommedddian. CCan't dddddooo standup anymore."

Grace shook her head at his ironic punning. "Standup comedy?

You sound just fine to me. I think you're amazing. Maybe you'll invent another comedic genre. I brought another book if you'd like me to read."

"WWWWhich one? Www're not dddone with WWallace yet."

"No. I'm saving *Infinite Jest.* This one's called *Guy's Read.* It's a collection of memoirs and short essays by guys for guys."

"Then I ggguess I qqualllify." After reading Lloyd Alexander's "The Truth About the World," Tim made a snorting noise like laughing. "Heeee's rrrrrighttt aahhhhbout the wworrrld. IIIIII cccannnn't ddancce eitherrrr."

Grace wondered if this was the best book to be reading, with lines like, "Life is ruled by unfair and malicious fate, filled with injustice, humiliation, shame, despair, tears and woe, misery undiluted. Naturally, I became a writer. I didn't know how to dance, anyway," but then Tim told her he loved it.

"MMMy kkkinddddd of wwwriter," he said. She gave him a drink of water through the straw. "TTThanks."

"You don't have to thank me."

"KKate lllleft me, remember. WWWorse ttttoday. TTThinking abbbout it mmmmore."

"I'm so sorry." Recognizing how insubstantial this remark sounded, Grace thought about telling him she, too, had been on the receiving end, but she did not. She also refused to tell him she already knew about his girl, having heard his confession to his mother on the first day she met the family. "That was a ridiculous remark I made," she said, surprised she spoke out loud.

"Wwwwhy?"

"Because it feels so much worse. Because saying, 'I'm sorry' doesn't help in the least. She should never have left you." For an instant, Grace thought she might cry. "Hhhey. Wwhat's wwwwrong?"

She was so close to telling him about Bill leaving and the mess Holly was in, and all of life felt unfair. Goddam tragic. Then she recovered from her own wants and needs. "Kate has no idea who you are if she could leave you." She suddenly hated Kate even though she had never met her, the young woman's face morphing before her.

"Whewww. Ttttanks, I ttthink. III mmmean, thanks. KKKate ttried, bbbbut it was too hard. IIIII ddddon't really bbbblame her. Lllookk, II dddon't think I have llllong for this wwworld. I'm alllready ssssome kkkkinda ssshadow."

They were both silent. His stuttering was worse, Grace thought. She read almost half the book before he fell asleep. For a few minutes, she sat and marveled at him: his will to live in spite of his horrific injuries which had taken a portion of his brain as well as part of his body.

He is remarkable, and she knew she was growing too attached. She did not ask the doctors for his prognosis for survival, knowing it was not her place or right, and she tried to maintain a professional distance even though she was just a volunteer. Professional distance had disappeared a long time ago, however. Grace had ceased trying to define their relationship; she just knew they had one.

Cleaning up the area around his bed, Grace took the trays to the kitchen before leaving. All the way home, she thought about Tim with his generous wit and gracious personality trapped in his mangled body. What did he look like before the IED exploded in his face? Did his handsome face match his wit? Was Kate madly in love with him or just "fooling around" when he went off to Iraq? She wanted this Kate to be madly in love with Tim and regret her decision to leave her solider forever. Thinking about Tim still loving Kate just made Grace sadder. She wanted to open the door and let him out of his hospital bed. Not considering assisted suicide, Grace was thinking of the magic of letting both his spirit and body free again.

*

Dr. Mary Cardillo met Grace for coffee at the old Randall Hotel turned into Sally's Coffee Shop, the building hugging the corner on the way out of town. As usual, Mary, an adjunct professor at a community college, was animated in talking with her friend. "So how is the research coming, or shouldn't I ask?" Dramatically tossing a cashmere shawl over her shoulder, Mary leaned forward.

Grace recalled the beginning of their friendship years earlier, dropping off their sons at a daycare center, Nick just a few months older than Jason. Although Jason and Nick had moved into separate circles, their mothers had remained friends, the bond altered but closer than simply one of mothers of sons. With Mary, Grace felt she could be herself or all of her various selves.

"I don't know. I'm not as confident as I should be," said Grace as she sipped the coffee tentatively. "It's not as if I haven't spent the time or the effort, but I feel like I continue to slip into a fiction, trying to." *How did taking coffee become such a social conditional?* wondered Grace in the space between breaths.

"Fill in the history? Of course, it's natural. We're all tempted to make the connections fit neatly together or find links where none are to be found."

"Maybe I should be writing a novel."

"As if that would be easier! Maybe for you, but I'd rather write ten biographies."

"Marilyn told me she was thinking about writing a novel based on her seminar paper."

"Marilyn? Who's she? What did you do with your hair? Something's different; I like it." Mary reached over, lightly touching her friend's hair where it met her shoulders.

"Oh. Yes. I cut it, and Kelly tried to talk me into adding a few highlights, but I told her I wasn't ready yet, so she lightened it with a lemon juice concoction." Grace ran her hand over her hair, smoothing it.

"Not that I didn't like it before. I mean, it's gorgeous. Who were we talking about? Marilyn somebody?"

"Remember I told you about her. The woman in my seminar class who always has the right answers and the wrong words in her papers. She's writing a novel; she told me she's only teaching for source material. I guess she hasn't found any yet." They laughed.

"Well, then I don't like her," said Mary. "Why is everyone always saying, 'I think I'll quit my job and write a novel.' Or, 'I should just write a novel.' While the reality of it is most of them don't or couldn't. This idea they have may be nothing more than a momentary electrical impulse across synapses, and as soon as the pen is committed to paper or the keys clicking on the keyboard, something awful happens. Those words supposedly bursting to get out are now sitting on the page or the screen, looking like earthworms after a two-day rain. They've drowned and nothing is moving."

"Lovely image. I didn't know you felt so strongly about it," said Grace smiling. "It's good I haven't finished anything, I guess."

"Sorry, you know I didn't mean you. You, however, will write a novel or a history—who knew you wanted to be an historian? How did it happen anyway?" Mary took her first sip of the latte, the foam coating her upper lip just like on the commercials advertising milk. "I love this coffee." Only then licking her upper lip.

Grace considered bringing up the coffee story she had read about Julio Alvarez's coffee plantation turned home for orphans, but was already exhausted by this leap before it could leave her lips. "This is your kind and generous way of saying I'm not an historian, am I?"

Grace's stomach was growling with the acidity of the coffee without food. At the moment, she recalled a story she had written years ago, and it struck her the theme was too familiar—the story about a young farmer who waited to die as the tractor he had been riding on slowly tipped to crush his chest.

She told Mary the genesis of the story evolved from a news clipping about an incident in a neighboring county, but she did not want to leave the young man for dead, so she began her fiction: He was plowing along the slope while his wife was in the hired man's house— not baking pies as people assumed but adding numbers, bookkeeping for the farmer because the hired man's wife was better with numbers than the farmer's accountant had been. The hired man could see the distant storm moving in, and he wanted to get out of the weather before it hit, soaking his clothes to his leathery skin, and he pushed the envelope. The deep green John Deere tractor went over quickly, but slowly enough the man knew what was going to happen before it struck him across his breastbone, crushing the bone and leaving him not enough air to scream or yell in terror or fear or regret, the tilled earth soft enough the blow did not kill him instantly.

She had wanted to save him—both the real, flesh and blood, young farmer and the character in her story, but when she wrote those words on the page, she knew there was no way out for him, so she waited with him, listening as his throat filled in blood, choking him while his mind raced, unable to pray in its terrible panic. Why wasn't he on the slope near the road where someone in a passing car might have seen him? and gone for help? Why was he only twenty-seven?

Suddenly, there was Tim again. Why wasn't he in the car behind the one blown up? At least in her writing, she could alter outcomes.

Grace felt a momentary breathlessness as she silently witnessed the tractor tipping on the paper, knowing she let it fall with the keys but could not stop it, could not stop the tractor from crushing this perfectly healthy man even though he sank part way into the newly plowed earth, allowing his death only to be more agonizing, slower. Why was it taking so long for him to die? And then the writer bent down closer, kneeling in the black topsoil to listen, as if the dying could deliver some message of wisdom, but his eyes were glazed and bulging then, and all she heard was a dog barking--a high-pitched, incessant yelp in the distance. He tried to reach out with his free hand, but she knew it was useless; he, too, heard only the dog at the end, his young wife unaware in the kitchen that her life had changed, ended just as drastically.

After the funeral and the well-meaning wishes, donations from the women in the church she attended, the farmer's wife would have to move, find another life, support herself and the baby growing inside. The terror of beginning again was sitting on the window ledge with the cooling pie.

When she had created the silent nightmare on a rural hillside, Grace turned away from the farmer, the summer heat, and the slow strangulation of inhabiting loneliness again.

"Hello? You look like you're a thousand miles away right now." Mary leaned toward Grace and adjusted the collar on her shirt. "It was turned in—your collar."

"Ah. Thanks. I was just thinking about, too much, I guess," sighed Grace.

"We'd be absolutely fine if we just stopped thinking so much."

"A fine thing for a college professor to say. Sometimes I can't really imagine myself completing this, to be honest."

"No," said Mary. "Of course, you will. I think you'll be successful as an historian. I'm just not sure you want to be. Why not English lit? It's not as if you weren't good at teaching literature. I just don't want to see you spend all this time on a book, paper? and then change your mind, get frustrated, I suppose. Honestly, Grace, why history?"

Grace shook her head. "I thought it would be less painful." Oh, no, Grace thought, now I've gone and admitted it.

"Are you talking about the level of difficulty?" Mary couldn't help but betray a slight offense.

"No. No. The introspection required with the study of literature. History seemed, I know, it sounds ridiculous now. History seemed to allow me a little emotional distance. But even though the reasoning is flawed, I'm intrigued with it now, becoming obsessed really." Grace suddenly thought of her students who complained about the literature she taught. "Why do we have to read about everyone dying? Why does this stuff always have to be so depressing?" She could hear their remarks repeated. No one ever asks a historian why it ends tragically. Of course, everyone dies, she thought. They die in the historical texts just as in the novels.

"Grace, obsession is necessary. We'd never complete anything of substance if we didn't become a bit obsessed. You're going to be a wonderful history teacher, and I think
you shouldn't give up. You've raised an original question about the Civil War, and one I think worth investigating. That's tough enough to do, so don't get discouraged."

"How can we not be discouraged?"

"So where is this going? I heard a 'we' in there, I believe."

"Not just the two of us. I mean all of us. Why discuss writing history or literature at all when the readers are dwindling down to a handful?"

Mary laughed uncomfortably. "I promise to read your historical paper, document, fiction—whatever it turns out to be even if I don't like where it has led. There. We're set."

"The last two readers in the world."

"It can't be as bad as that. And this from a high school English teacher!"

"I don't know, but the scary part is the cultural shift."

"All you have to do is get a job in which you require your class to read your work. Mine is required second semester." Grace realized Mary was being as honest as she was.

The waitress, a middle-aged woman with a deeply set voice, set the check in the middle of the table. "Anything else, girls?"

"No," Mary replied to the waitress then turned to Grace. "Let me get this."

"We'll split it."

"Don't fight over me, girls," said the waitress as she took Mary's empty cup and left the check on the table.

"Delightful woman. How about I let you get the check when you finish your dissertation."

"So, you're paying for another three or four years?"

"Since you put it that way, we'll split it," Mary said, fumbling in her purse for the change. "It's this embarrassing thing about women. We always have to struggle for change."

"But at least we keep track of it," said Grace, recalling the way Bill emptied his pockets of change anywhere they happened to be even when they had next to nothing in the way of money.

"Do you ever think you're writing about history and suddenly find you've gone off track; you're inventing as you go? I'm not even sure it is history I'm writing. I feel like I'm not leading my course of action but following where the letters lead me."

Mary shrugged perceptibly. "If you preset your course, you wouldn't be a historian at all, the biases would be so apparent. Follow the letters, and if you also happen to write a novel in the process of writing history, where is the fault? As long as you don't try to pass off fiction as history. You need to make that delineation."

"Would you be tempted to fill in the missing facts with fiction?"

Mary hesitated. "No, I don't think I would, but that does not mean I'm a true historian and you're not or any such nonsense. It is simply my brain doesn't work in those ways. I'm always looking for the puzzle piece, trying to finish it. I can't imagine creating the picture and then cutting it up into little pieces of the puzzle."

"I thought I'd start at the end and work my way backward."

"Well, it's is a bit unusual for historians. We tend to work chronologically," Mary smirked in the way she could without seeming condescending.

"Suppose the fiction ends up truer than the history? There's this line in Walker Percy's novel *The Moviegoer.*"

"I've never read him but tell me. I love it when you find a way to get us sidetracked." Mary readjusted herself.

"'I picked up a yellow scrap of paper–or newspaper—and read of an election, and in the article, I distinctly caught the smell of history far more…pungently… than from the metal marker telling of the French and Spanish two hundred years ago.' When I read that line—at least its approximation, I had the sensation of living then, not just the time markers but the physical sensation of having passed through that election, the newsprint on my fingers, the Southern summer heat, the whites keeping out black Americans from the polling places, from the restaurants, from proximity even as they were in the same spaces, the racial divide widened by fear and suppressed guilt over slavery. And I knew it as if I was there in a way I could never have known it by reading a paragraph of factual data from the history."

"Then you haven't read your history very well, I suppose."

"The comment isn't meant to belittle the work of historians."

"Oh, I'm kidding," said Mary, looking at her friend's dejected face.

"We historians know veracity is subjective really. Who's narrating? The perspective colors everything. And I didn't mean the pun," she said, pulling the cashmere wrap over her shoulder and tossing it around the front, looping it once at her neck, instantly casual and elegant, thought Grace, acknowledging the fact she could never wear a shawl in such a dramatic manner. Mary simply was born looking like a college professor.

"I don't think I have read the history as critically as I should have," was all Grace responded, keenly aware she lacked a certain professorial deportment. "One of my friends from high school, Janet Walls, sent me a book she had picked up on a recent to trip to Charleston. I had written her about my decision to go back to school and my paper topic."

"Love that city. Go on."

"Reading the first few lines, I was struck by how ridiculously biased they—the accounts—seemed from this Southern perspective, but it made me think about my own biases, assumptions I had come to regard as fact. We all have these biases and assumptions coloring how we view the world."

"Those books are candy to historians. We love coming across various other perspectives and weighing them against our own worldview. Do you remember the name of the book?"

"It was a compilation of articles written for the centennial of the succession. I remember the way it began: 'tumultuous events led up to the secession of South Carolina, but the act itself was performed in an atmosphere notable for its dignity and decorum.' *The Civil War at Charleston* is the name of the work, I believe."

Mary laughed. "I love it! As an English teacher, you know how politically charged diction can be."

"And I thought about how my view of the Civil War, of everything would be different if I had been born in the South instead of the North.

Maybe I took the wrong approach with this seminar paper. I probably could have done a better job if I had looked at the historical significance of semantics." Grace felt defeated rather than excited by the prospect.

"Perhaps, but it's not what you wanted to do, so I'm not sure it would have worked out so well. You chose this topic for a reason; give it a chance to work." The tone in Mary's voice indicated she was moving on, ending this discussion as if it was just beginning. Grace wanted to ask her friend what she thought of the general who gave the order in battle that was fought and lost, the historian collecting all the primary documents, the numbers of dead and wounded, the details for the battle lines where men marched and where numbers of them fell.

What then? Grace wanted to ask Mary. Was the general thinking of his son who was in another regiment, purposefully giving a delayed order to avoid his son's regiment being called to the front, all the battle lost because a man loved his eldest child, the one who looked like his dead mother, far too much?

"I'm sorry, but I've got to run; I've got a department meeting, and I can't be late to every single one," Mary said, lifting her soft leather briefcase to her shoulder. "Call me."

"Yes. Thanks. It was good to talk about it with you." Grace waved to her friend and sat back down more from inertia than resolve, pretending to finish her coffee, holding an empty cup. On the way home, Grace dialed Holly on her cell. Holly still could barely speak, but they worked their way through a brief conversation.

"How do you do it?" Holly asked after a few moments.

"It's a disguise," said Grace, looking for troopers along the side of the road as she held her cell phone behind her hair.

"I need a disguise," said Holly so softly Grace could only guess at her last words.

EIGHTEEN

In regards to locking arms with anyone

Wearing her white, poet's shirt, the one Grace had picked up proudly at an end-of-the-season sale, she felt dressed to tackle the project that had been sitting around, abandoned for a week, while she tried to decide whether or not to continue, the reluctant historian began reading the letters in order of their dates.

Not until April 16, 1865 did Ezra give way to seeming suspicion of his wife's infidelity, but there it was on the last page of the letter, accusatory then apologetic—was he right or wrong? Grace found his remarks both poignant and troubling, coupled with those he had written about Lincoln's assassination.

*

Kellys Creek W. Va.
Sunday, April 16/65
Dear Wife

It is with an aching hearte and trembling hand I seat myself to acknowladge thte recept of yours of the 3rd. I was glad to hear from you and I hope this may find you all well--trouble it seams never comes single but is meeted out to us on every hand--I have felt for a week or two back joyous and buoyant at the good news of the success of our armies but today my heart is clothed in the habitments of mourning at the sad news of the murder of President Lincoln and Secretary Seward on the night of the 14th. I feel that our nation has been smitten with an awful clamity and that the greate center lightes around which we revolved hath by the ruthless and cruel hand of an assassin been put out. This may be a wicked thought or desire but I would to God that the dead could be brought back to life. How sad it seames I had looked for a speedy peace I firmly believed that Abraham Lincoln could see his labours for the last four years crowned with a glorious offing. Ah, how true it is, man that is borne of woman his dayes are ffew and full of trouble. I do not know as it will prolong the war a moment or that is any differently than it would have been had our Chief Majistrate been permited to dictate the tearmes upon which it should be settled but how degraded and preverted is man from what God designed he should be-- and I pray God to give Andrew Johnson wisdom to guide him to rule aright as he will now become the Chief Majestrate of an American people—that our present and still unhappy difficulties may be brought to a speady and honorable close.

I do not know what to say to you about our affares for my every hope seams to be crushed when just within reach yet all I said to you in a letter not long since I don't mean to give up the ship but try try again- - I pittey you from the bottom of my heart and wish I was their to find some place in this sin cursed world for you and children to stay overnight at least--bear up under it as well as you can don't worry yourself to death.

Here Grace stopped reading momentarily and made a few notes. It was too awful to know that Ez's speculations about Johnson proved to be in error. He was right about the "center lights," however. Of course, Ez had no way of knowing immediately Seward had not been killed but only wounded. Grace wondered how long it took for the details of the assassinations to reach the men in the field. Johnson was hardly the man to have the wisdom or strength to guide his country at such a time. Would anyone have been able to follow Lincoln without looking like a disastrous leader? It was a wonder a Southerner had been the man to attempt to lead his torn and bloody nation after the South's defeat, but it was the last paragraph that struck Grace, the one in which Ez's letter turned from the nation to the possibility of his own broken house.

Susannah was homeless, most likely because she was unable to make payments. "Some place in this sin cursed world for you and the children to stay overnight at least." Ezra's words resonated, revealing in his response to his wife her words to him. She must have begged for help from her absent husband. If she panicked, there was an impression made upon her husband but no offer of a solution to the problem of destitution. Their mutual helplessness was blunted only by the time it took a letter to reach its audience.

Ezra's pay, it seemed, did not always reach his wife during those long years. Was she writing to tell her husband she was leaving him or simply letting him know she would do whatever she had to do to keep going? What was it she had to do? Was the threat of leaving him and marrying another buried in her lost letters? Why "sin cursed world?" Ezra's anger rolled into the syllables all these years later.

The historian's reaction was physical with her stomach rolling along with Ezra's anger, the nausea kept at bay through strong will alone; empathetic, she considered this young couple, both of whom must have felt betrayed by the other yet trying to hang on. Grace fingered the letter resting on her lap and began reading.

Fall to the ground without your heavenly Father notice. This will shield the soul from the cold blasts of the world. It is true we have but little to hope for from the world but I've my hope for greater things from God--I do not know but my pitty will be cold comfort for you under the present stringent necessity but could I do more than to sympathise with you I would to it. Money would buy you friends if I had it, you'd soon have the meanes of purchasing, but a friend in kind isn't bought with money, and bougten freidnship dosent last long for when your cash is gon, your friends are gon, they don't go according to the Golden rule (be you to others kind and true), but act according to their own selfish inclinations proving the depravity of the whole human race.

Some are more so than others, and I am led to exclame in the language of the Scriptures (What is man that thou art mindful of him or the Son of man that thou art visited upon him) but God's wayes are not like man's wayes. He is of long suffering and merciful Holy, just, and Pure and in death we shall rest in peace if we rest in God--I think you must have misunderstood me in regard to locking arms with anyone. I did not understand it in that way nor did I say you did but said I believe these wordes (be careful that you don't lock armes with any one) It might not have been word for word but ment the same However it was so long ago that I had forgotten all about it and perhaps shouldn't have thought of it again I hope you was not offended with me about it.

Grace picked up her pad to write a few notes, finding herself nearly as angry as Susa must have been when she read the lines from her husband buffering the accusation with weakly paraphrased lines of scripture and rationalization. Because he had "forgotten all about it and perhaps shouldn't have thought of it" was no reason to dismiss his wife's hurt or anger at the insinuation of infidelity or at least the admonition against the temptation of it, Grace considered. Here was Susa's voice in the absence, alone, homeless, tremulous with indignation at the accusations, but, strangely, not without hope for she continued to write to her absent husband too long at war. I must be careful, thought Grace; this was so tempting to project her own feelings of anger on this young woman of another time, another mindset. Perhaps she simply was so used to being admonished she expected it. She wondered how historians remained so objective.

The letter called Grace back.

I should feel bad if I knew you was—I am well in body but sick at heart—I wrote a letter to Mom on the 11th if you should go there this summer read it – it will do you good—I hope you will excuse all misstakes and forgive all carless thoughtless expressions in my letters. May he that noeth the sparrows fall watch over and protect you my dear family is the prar of your

Unworthy Husband and Father

Ezra Cross

PS. Write soon and tell me all the news for my heart is able to bare it. Suspence is quite as bad as reality-- I am on picket.

Ezra

For the first time, Ezra had signed his name as "unworthy." This appellation seemed to betray wrongdoing either in form or substance. It was possible Ezra been unfaithful or simply unfaithful in his familial duties. Was this moniker reflecting the guilt of a husband unable to provide for his family due to the distance and impossibility rendered by war? Had he been accusatory of his wife, knowing she was simply desperate to find a home for her babies, and the guilt he carried was too much for him to acknowledge? The pain exposed in the letter was palpable and as much about the fears for his marriage as for the death of President Lincoln, Grace noted.

He knows. How can he know? Sometimes I don't know myself if I've been dreaming this. Jennie is too young to remember, but George is so quick, I must ask Will not to visit again or look at me the way he does when chopping the kindling for us. But him coming around to help makes it possible for me to think I might survive this war. Even if he never touches me, Ez knows, knows what I'm feelin'. I know that he knows, so I must not think of this man or want him to come round again. It was so nice to have him helping with chores, though. And he has good eyes, kind eyes, a solid-looking man even if his foot is mangled. Why am I thinking about him at all? I wonder if Ez is ever thinking about another woman. I guess there's no time for women in wartime. Or perhaps, he has been with other women, those women who come to camps. How can any war last so long? It almost seems like men don't want war to end. Is his life exciting or just in peril? I don't know if I'm angry or just scared.

Grace held the next letter, arranged by date, to find either accusation or apology and discovered the letter held neither unless it could be inferred through the double meaning of, "then is it a wonder that we should feel that justice aught to punish the guilty but wish not to make ourselves notorious and become a lot of desperadoes and we use [lynch] law but hope justice and [mercy] may go hand in hand." Grace could imagine Susa searching for something more in those words seemingly meant to express the soldiers' indignation at the murder of Lincoln.

Kelley's Creek, West VA
Thurs. Eve. April 20th 1865
Dear Wife

I have just finished reading the account of the assassination and death of our late President Abraham Lincoln-how depressed my heart teares of sorrow for the greate and good man fill my eyes Am I foolish to weep for the noble dead I feel that I am not. We all feel that we have lost a friend second only to Washington and could you look in upon our encampment you would see the men gathred in groopes covering same

Respectfuly,

Ez to Susa

Time and again, Grace found Ezra's letters to contain contradictory and seemingly disconnected statements. Here, he had penned a note, "hoping it may find all well at home," after writing about his response to her not having a home. Was he unaware of the effects his words had on his waiting wife? Perhaps, his inability to alter her circumstances, his sense of powerlessness to protect her and his children in any way, was more than the sane man could stand, so he wrote and denied her state of affairs to himself. Were Ezra's accusations the result of his guilt over Susannah's circumstances? It was the question she wanted answers to but was unable to find any definitive proof. Was it simply he could not bear to think he had failed her by not providing for his young wife and children? Grace reluctantly began considering the idea her ancestor might have gone off to war willingly, enlisted before he had to

171

in order to avoid inevitable family conflicts related to poverty. And what did these impulses say about his failure to arrive home? It was too hard to think of at the moment, but suspicion had begun to creep into her musings about Ezra's disappearance.

NINETEEN

———

It has so much the appearance of home

Marilyn, who was breathing heavily from trudging up three flights of stairs walked into the classroom with Grace. "I didn't take the elevator. Hey, I've been wanting to ask you something."

"Go ahead."

"Why did you leave a secure teaching job in a subject you know well? I mean, starting all over again seems kind of impulsive, if you don't mind my saying so." She did not even flinch at the accusation.

"I think I was trying to reinvent myself."

"I do that every day I get up," Marilyn said as she adjusted her raincoat over the chair, trying to keep it from slipping off onto the floor which it did as Coleman handed back their paper abstracts. Leaning over the paper conspiratorially, Marilyn asked, "What did you get? Your grade? I don't think the bastard likes my thesis." She pushed her paper toward Grace who looked down and saw the red C underlined. Grace shook her head as she turned over her own paper, revealing an

A-. She was relieved but not pleased, yet she did not know what she expected. Certainly, not an A+. So, I'm continuing, she thought, almost as uneasily as if she had failed the paper. Marilyn's face grew red, and Grace could see she was trying to stay calm but wanted to storm out of the room. Coleman never looked at Grace during class, so she began to assume she had been mistaken about his interest in her, as if anyone could be interested in her, she thought.

"What am I supposed to do now?" asked Marilyn, loud enough other graduate students noticed, looking over at her. "How can I continue in this program?"

"Talk to him. Maybe he has some suggestions which would allow you to alter the paper slightly."

"Slightly! It's a C! I might as well have gotten an F. I'm going to ask the son-of-a-bitch to explain himself. 'Why?' I'll see you, or maybe I won't be back!"

At the end of class, Grace got up with the other students and turned to Marilyn. She realized she had nothing more to say about a grade on a paper. Marilyn had stared at Coleman with hatred for the entire lecture but he appeared not to notice.

Coleman glanced up at her but then turned to the young woman raising her voice with her eyes flashing, approaching him. What he said to Marilyn, Grace never knew, but Marilyn suddenly turned and left the room in a hurry. Then Coleman walked up behind Grace.

"I wanted to discuss your paper with you," he said nonplussed by his encounter with the angry Marilyn, whose notebook could be heard hitting the stairs, echoing in the stairwell, along with Marilyn's curse.

Grace looked toward the door and wondered if she should go after Marilyn to help her but stood immobile.

"An unhappy student," said Coleman. "Not a very good paper, I'm afraid. She'll adjust or she won't and will decide to stay in the program or not," Coleman continued impassively, nodding his head toward the space Marilyn had occupied.

"I know I have a lot of work left to do," Grace said a bit nervously, feeling defeated and uninterested in being conspiratorial with him.

"Of course, but it's promising." Coleman adjusted his glasses on the bridge of his straight nose, and Grace could not help but notice the discolored indentations in the skin of his nose where the glasses hung too heavily. "I was genuinely surprised by your paper, expecting, well, expecting a less scholarly attempt, I suppose."

Looking stunned and then feeling her face reddening from the complimentary insult, Grace said nothing as Coleman tried to correct himself. "It is really quite excellent. By the end, I was thinking about the voice of the Civil War widows as resources lost to our American story."

"Thank you." Grace had enough courage to continue. "Sometimes I feel like the speculation is too narrative, too ahistorical."

"Yes, yes, there is that aspect, but also something compelling and worthy of exploration." Coleman was standing so close to her now she could see the tiny hairs at the end of his nostrils. If she backed up as she wanted to do, it could be taken as insulting, so she stood taller, projecting confidence. Coleman then leaned back against a sturdy classroom table, bracing himself with long, thin fingers; Grace noticed the man looked as if he never ate or cared to. Perhaps he survived merely on the consumption of historical texts.

"You have to be careful, of course," he said after a brief interlude in which neither of them said anything. Grace waited for the admonition. "You have to take care your narrative does not overtake the search for the factual information. The temptation is present with every good storyteller to invent what is not readily seen or easily uncovered. That is not to say, however, a good historian is not also a storyteller." He was already thinking ahead to her dissertation topic which he would approve.

"And when the truth has disappeared in a vapor of time? When all the trails are washed away in the torrents of rain?"

"Suddenly poetic?" Coleman asked or rather stated.

Grace winced.

"I didn't mean that exactly. Speculation from factual information—primary and secondary source documents—is a technique requiring a craftsmen's touch, but speculation from dreams or fantasy—another domain entirely." Coleman picked up his worn leather briefcase and moved toward the door with her.

"Yes. There is a danger, I suppose." Grace sensed another kind of peril and could feel herself retreating.

"I'd like to continue our conversation over coffee, perhaps?"

"Thank you, but not tonight. I've got to get home." What did she have to get home for, even she wondered? "I promised a friend I'd stop to see her." It was almost truthful, Grace told herself.

"Yes. Ok. Well, have a nice evening; perhaps another night then?" said Coleman, looking less confident than he had moments earlier.

"Yes, of course. I'd be happy to," and Grace retreated all the way to the shadows of the building, avoiding the light until she reached her car.

If she called Holly, then it wouldn't be a lie. "Holly? Are you up? I'm sorry. No. No, go back to sleep. I'll stop to see you tomorrow. Right now? Yes. I'm driving. No, I don't see any cops around, and I don't mind listening." Grace held her cell phone all the way home.

*

Before Coleman walked in, Grace sensed the intake of air as the door opened. She still could not believe she had agreed to meet him for dinner rather than coffee. He was wearing a gray cashmere sweater which had the desired effect but seemed too calculated, thought Grace. I'm not being fair, she reminded herself. She wished to be less trouble to him but could not avoid it.

"I'm sorry I'm running late. Another meeting, I didn't think it would take so long," Coleman said in one breath as he stretched out his hand for her to take. She hesitated, wondering at the official handshake, but shook it as if they were just meeting.

"It's no problem, really."

"I see you've been writing," Coleman stated, looking at the journal in her lap.

"Nothing really."

"Nothing?"

"Well, just a few ideas I had for organizing the paper."

"Good. And that would be?" Coleman pulled a chair next to her at the table in the corner although one was perfectly situated directly across from her.

Believing she had groaned out loud, Grace looked embarrassed then was relieved to discover she had not actually made a sound. "I'm not quite ready to talk about it yet," she said, pleased to have wiggled out of what would prove to be an irritating discussion with Coleman suggesting all the reasons she had to adhere to a chronological ordering.

"Better to discuss it now and find you have room to turn around, if necessary," he said, smiling, leaning over suddenly as if to kiss her when sensing her restraint, he altered his course and reached for a place setting on the other side of the table. "I'll save the waitress the trouble." He congratulated himself on his deft maneuver to sit closer to her.

"Kind of you." There was no turning around, thought Grace.

"Listen, I know we're both divorced, and I like to get this baggage out of the way quickly, so we can decide whether or not to proceed."

Ugg, thought Grace, hoping it would not continue in this forced and clumsy manner. "What do you want to ask?"

"Did your husband leave you, or was it the other way around?" As Grace scanned his face for signs of irony, the waitress came up.

"What would you like to drink? Can I take your order?"

"Gin and tonic." Coleman spit out without looking at the waitress. She noticed he seemed to take in only the presence of certain people.

"Ah. An iced tea," said Grace, deciding to wait before ordering wine.

"Lemon?"

"Yes, please." The waitress left, and Grace saw Coleman was staring and waiting for a response. "He left. Why do you ask?" She looked around her wondering if anyone could hear them.

"Because I left my wife, and I just hope you don't see my circumstances as a problem."

I do, thought Grace, but she measured her words instead. "Perhaps we should start with a lighter course."

"Oh," said Coleman smiling. "I see where you are going. It is just I prefer directness, and I don't like to waste my time—or anyone else's—if there's an insurmountable issue."

"I'm not as comfortable with the approach, and I don't want to waste your time, but I'll try to answer a few questions honestly."

"Good. Why did he leave you?"

"Bill?"

"Your husband."

"Oh, for a younger, prettier woman."

"Younger, perhaps, prettier, not possible."

Grace couldn't help smiling. It had been a long time since she'd heard a compliment like that. "Did you want to tell me about your ex-wife?"

"Yes and no. Keeping in a literary vein, I'm no Rochester, and she wasn't the woman in the attic, but she was disturbed."

"Like Bertha."

"Pardon?"

"Bertha Mason—Rochester's wife in the attic and her illness are speculative or rather dependent upon your point of view." Grace was already thinking about Jean Rhys' Creole protagonist in the *Wide Sargasso Sea*. "I'm sorry about your wife." Grace couldn't tell him she also identified with the wife he left.

"No need to be. I tried for as long as I was able. Are you going to keep using these literary references as a history teacher or, for that matter, whenever we have dinner?"

She was taken aback by the second part of his question, but she proceeded. "I guess I haven't completely changed my way of thinking."

"Since we've gotten that out of the way, how are you ordering your paper?"

Grace wondered how long his patience lasted, recognizing she was not ready for this conversation. "Non-chronologically."

"On what basis, then?"

"I'm cataloging the evocative phrases and using speculation based on the diction found in Ezra's letter."

"I don't know. It sounds intriguing, but I still have reservations this will descend into a feminist polemic not acceptable for this project."

"It won't." Grace wondered how she could find a civil way of ending their conversation and exiting.

"Look. I'm sorry I just stated my concerns so directly. I've just read your last paper, and it was very well written and offers a scholarly and original historical perspective. I'm just not used to such creativity in my graduate students' writing, but I rather wish more of them were as creative as you. I did not expect to approve of your paper, yet I was surprised. There, you have my confession. It probably still has too many metaphors in it, but when I find a student's paper that keeps me up all night reading, well, then."

Just when Grace was ready to exit and abandon any relationship with her professor, he said something lovely. It cheered her on the way home.

Although it was late by the time she arrived at her house, her mind was too active to get ready for bed. Instead, she went directly to her library with the mass of papers and letters spread out across the floor. Then she went to the kitchen to make a cup of tea, knowing it would keep her up beyond the reasonable. As she walked through the rooms of her little house, she could almost hear Jason's feet running up and down the stairs as a child, could hear Bill calling for her to come and see the pike he had landed, could go back further and see her mother folding towels on the dining room table, handing her a stack to put in the linen closet.

Nothing was the same, but her house made no allowance for the changes inside her.

TWENTY

———

When the billows of life's

tempestuous sea are raging

Camp Sullivan

Sunday morning, Feb 28th/64

Dear Wife and children

You will see by this that I am in camp again. I got here about 4 o'clock this morning and my furlow is not out until 12 tonight. I had looked in an almanac; I should have stayed at home until last night but I am here and what can't be cured must be endured. But let me see. I promised you in the letter I wrote from Baltimore to write you the particulars about a fight our boys had in camp. Our company and the company of another regiment—the 15th and the 21st—started out with one of the boys tossing something into the fire. I think it was a letter. Someone said a remark to the soldier and the next thing you know it was bedlam. The only thing broke up their hitting each other with bloodied noses was word that the Johnnies had sneaked up the gap 30 miles distant on our side of the river. We encountered a party of

Mosbeys and Stewart's cavalry and a fight ensued, resulting in the loss of two killed on our side and eighteen wounded—15 taken prisoner. The loss of the Johnnyes was 175 killed. How many wounded is not known, and scouting parties have since brought in 23 more Johnnies. The boys made up their fighting, shaking hands after, knowing their real enemy.

No one at this time.

From one who love his wife and children
Ezra Cross

Grace thought about the idea Ezra seemed to lose the irony of the fight in camp preceding the fight with the enemy. She could picture the soldiers exhausted and tired of being confined to the encampments, ready to let loose on anything when the Confederate soldiers gave them an opening.

Before the phone rang, Grace knew it was Bill. "Look. I called because Jason told me you are going back to school to try to become a college professor? I didn't believe him at first."

Grace could hear the word "try" echo, but she held her tongue momentarily.

"Are you there?"

"Yes," said Grace icily.

"Do you really think that's such a good idea? I mean, giving up a secure teaching position for uncertainty, for the uncertain prospect of a job you may not get? You've got tenure and Jason to think about. You're not really at an age when that's practical. College positions are hard to come by and easy to lose."

She knew exactly where Bill was going with his fear: she might ask for or be granted alimony. "I'm not seeking alimony; I told you already."

"I know. You've said so. It's just, I think this is foolishness, and

182

we have Jason to consider." Grace wondered how much Jason figured into the equation when he was beginning his affair with Beth.

"Fortunately for me, you no longer have a say in what I do or don't do." Grace hung up the phone, her temples pounding with the rush of blood. She had never hung up on Bill. The phone rang again, but she did not answer it again, allowing the message machine to screen calls for her, but it was only a telemarketer asking if she wanted the latest update on some internet server. She wished she had said something harsher to Bill. His lecture was impossible to tolerate now they no longer shared any love.

The worst aspect of Bill's call—it fed into her doubts about herself and the idea of moving on, but what were the choices? All right. She did have a choice, and she was choosing to do something challenging, something that might take her to the unfamiliar. She turned again to the letters.

What if all her speculations about the lives of Susa and Ez had been wrong? Grace wondered in a moment of near panic. It was possible Susannah no longer loved her husband; it was even possible Ezra was not killed by a train at all but simply got off the train home, tossed down a paper with his name near the tracks and kept walking. A mangled corpse had been found with Ezra's identification papers nearby. Was it really his body? A vanishing act.

Was history a vast vanishing act? The collective vanishing of one person and another and then whole civilizations, cultures, neither ghosts nor spirits but absences disappearing in a black hole. She came to no firm determination about the disappearance of her great-great grandfather. Even after reading and rereading the letters--those brittle primary documents almost a torture at times—conducting research at the historical societies in those small towns and villages, later speculating, each consideration turning down a different dirt road leading off into a field without footprints, without even the broken blades of grass a native American guide could read. It was as if Ezra Cross had just marched off like the good soldier he was for the duration of the bloody, monumental war. His actions changed everything; he marched out of sight, and off his page but also off the pages of his family's.

There were no Social Security numbers back then. A man could change his identity as easily as in a fiction, more easily even. All he needed was the means or, perhaps, merely the impulse to do so. At length, not at first or even after completing the first draft of the paper, Grace decided—because she felt she had to come to some conclusion—Ezra did not desert his wife, however; there was too much love in his letters home; even his sometimes desperate, accusatory tone expressed love. So, she kept at it. In some ways, she found herself envying the men who could disappear and launch their lives again, unencumbered by the past.

Sprawled across Grace's desk were books held open with pencils, a fork lying across two pages, a stapler as a makeshift paperweight, and a coffee cup with the stains darkening by the hour. Yet for all the disorder in the room, Grace's writing was still orderly, she thought, wondering at her need to find the right word, the right angle for each perspective as if arriving at the solution to a complex mathematical problem.

On her favorite reading chair sat David Foster Wallace's book. *Infinite Jest* looked up at Grace, mockingly, indifferent to her growing despair. It was the work itself not the author providing the criticism of women writers and their insufferable nesting instinct. Grace could hear *Infinite Jest* in all its swelling prose--wild--expansive, untamable, the way a little boy enters school unable to sit still, tipping his chair, dropping his pencil, while his female classmate carefully sets her

Number 2 pencil in the proscribed indentation designed for writing implements on the desk, the child secure in the fact her pencil would not roll or stray from its ordered place until she had chosen to reach for it—such sexist behaviors and motivations collected over a lifetime. There were those little girls, Grace reminded herself, however, the ones who bounded into the classroom, had to sit in the corner or the principal's office, mouthed off unladylike, and she loved them all.

While considering her writing not her methodology, Grace had this terrible epiphany—of course, there was no woman Shakespeare; of course, there weren't a lot of men who were Shakespeare either. She also felt she knew why there were no women who were James Joyce or even David Foster Wallace. But there was Virginia Woolf and then Jean Ryes correcting the story—of one woman alone and another of Rochester's mad wife—inventive, significant, but, perhaps, not wild, or nearly so expansive. Even in her attempts to write about Susannah and Ezra, Grace was aware of the need for order, for the tidy arrangements never really existing in life.

The phone rang again. "Mom. I just wondered if you're doing okay."

"Yes, I'm fine. What are you up to today?"

"One of my friends is visiting. I think I told you about Ajmal. We're going hiking in the Adirondacks—with Dad."

"Sounds cool, but you know, people get lost, so stay on the trails. Cell phones don't always work in those mountains."

Jason laughed. "Yeah, I know. Hey, listen, I really called about you."

"Me? Why?"

"Well, I just wanted to say I know Dad's being a real asshole to you."

"Yes, he is," she couldn't help smiling at her son's assessment.

"But I think it's because he feels guilty. I mean, he is acting worse because he's the guilty one. He knows what he did to you is wrong. Does that make sense?"

"Perfect sense."

"I'm sorry, Mom."

"Hey, you have nothing to apologize for."

"Yeah, it's just—"

"He's your father. I understand. Being with him or visiting him is not betrayal on your part, got it?"

"Thanks. I mean, love you, Mom. And I think you going back to school to teach history is a cool idea."

"Love you, too." They hung up, and Grace stood looking out at the lake for a while, not quite able to move.

Part of her hurt when she thought about her son off having a good time with his father, and part of her felt an old joy, too. They should do things together. What she really needed at the moment was another distraction, and she knew right where to look.

History seemed to offer possibility, delineation, and the speculation a search had an ending, a certainty against the mad genius of gargantuan novels rushing headlong into what exactly? The scarcely manageable form, not of the novel but life, threatened to overflow the pages, crash into other texts, and then flood the streets of the still panicked. Yet, here Grace stood looking at the boxes neatly stacked, the shelves with labeled bins and the ordered words marching across the page, but marching into some other realm.

It was in this order she found yet another entrance. Ezra's letter, dated August 8th, 1864 attested to his desire for home and family in almost irrefutable terms.

Dear Wife,

I could not resist the temptation to write a few lines to you tonight as I find myself so comfortably situated for this evening finds me seated at a table with a nice white clean spread on it, a nice pitcher of cool water right beside me, a carosean lamp to give me light, two beds in the room, one a high post bedstead with a nice bed on it made up by some lady of taste for the pillows are large and clean white cases on them and a beautiful worked spred on the bed. The other is a low French bedstead neate and tidy in appearance with a good clean bed with two nice large pillows and large bolster. On one lay one of my comrades sick, Sergeant S. G. Case, and I am sitting up with him. I think he has got some kind of fever, but I hope he will get along without having a regular course of fever. Yet the family appears to be very kind to him, and one thing I hope is that if I should bee taken sick while I am in the army that it may bee my fortune to fall into as good hands as he has. I do not no as the lady of the house would like to have me search her house looking under her beads, and see what I could find, so I will not, but I will venture to say that everything is nice and tidy and everything in its place. It looks verry much like home indeed. All that is lacking to make it a reality is my Susa and my children. Then it would bee home. Sure, you could not beet me out of that for it has so much the appearance of home that if you and the children were here, I should say home at last--now I will tell you what I have been reading this evening. It is a work and course of lecture by the Rev. Dr. Al Fletcher to the young, but it will bee good for the aged and middle aged to read and ponder it in their hearts for it speaks of God and his son Jesus Christ the Savior of the world. The first lines that my eyes rested on when I opened the book were these

> *Jesus is all my soul can crave*
> *My refuge and my fort*
> *My health my strength my life in death*
> *In war my Victory*

He is my light and liberty
My refuge and my fort
He is my salvation and my shield
When Satan throws his darts
And adders and lions you shall tread
The tempters wiles defeat
By grace you'll break the serpent's head
And tread him with your feet

From yours truly

Ezra Cross

Grace wondered what had happened to S.G. Case, the soldier who was being cared for by a civilian family. It was almost certain he died since Ezra never mentioned him again. Death was casual because it was so common. A solider dying in battle was one thing, but the likelihood of dying of disease, of infections, of a bad heart, those were deaths the chronicler would have scarcely mentioned unless the dead man was a singular friend. Strangely, Ezra didn't appear to have many friends in camp, but perhaps this was an error, too. Maybe he only wrote what he wished his young wife to know.

The letter brought her back to the man and another appraisal. If he was not in love with his wife and family, his prose and recitation of scripture, as he remembered it, seemed too convincing not to be honest. And if he loved them, how could he have been any other man? He was a father and a husband who wanted to come home. Grace began to consider how she valued words as evidence or truth and how naïve she had been. Of course, a man could write something dishonest and go undetected.

Was he deceptive with himself? Again, she knew there was evidence of both. She had to trust her ability to read behind and between the lines to understand what they revealed. The letters allowed various interpretations since Ezra contradicted himself sometimes within the body of one letter. She could almost see the young soldier writing this letter next to the kerosene lantern. A historian collected evidence, and this was evidence, she thought before wondering about the letters Bill had written to her in that ancient time of their young love.

What she saw next, however, was Ezra Cross heading home.

*

As Ezra Cross boarded the train home in his civilian clothes, trading his Union blue bummers cap for a nondescript slouch hat, and carrying a wad of greenbacks stuffed in his jacket as well as pants pockets, he moved around looking for a seat in the sea of returning men, men with haggard faces, men who had grown old in four years or fewer, depending upon their service to the Union, all changed men, thought Ezra as he found an empty one next to an ancient ex-soldier. There were no longer any boys to be found, all having grown roughly by the experience or dead in unknown lands. But he could not sit down. For how long now had he been sitting, just waiting after the war was already over for orders to move or be released? Conditioning prevented spontaneity until this very moment.

Initially, he hadn't intended not to go home. He hadn't decided to leave his old life until the present moment slapped him cold across the face. He found himself moving forward, forward until he reached the rear of the train where he opened the door. The train had slowed for something on the tracks he could not see, the machine lurching forward again like a stubborn donkey. Whether it was Susa's accusatory letters about money, her destitution, and his years of helpless guilt, crammed into another emotion entirely, his being unable to care for her or for crying babies, he did not know; family now strangers, a wife who felt like a petulant child, parents who seemed as remote as the miles between them, friends who had gone to war and were not returning; the world had changed and was reshaping itself; whether it was for all of these reasons or ones he could not yet define, Ezra stood for an instant longer on the gangway between cars and then waited as the train slowed almost to a stop.

Jumping, he was unhurt, executing an athletic, calculated leap, as the train began to gather steam again.

After rolling over several times, he stood and looked up at the passing faces of ex-soldiers who had awoken to the sight of the man leaving the train, straining their necks, opening their eyes wider, wondering what he knew, they did not, turning around in the last car to follow the now stationary man set against the backdrop of their disappearing futures with their eyes wide as the locomotive shuddered before it gained momentum and chugged away, the steamy breath of the engine dissipating into the air as Ezra Cross disappeared from their view. He walked away John Lincoln Fuller, a pseudonym for the man who was in process, who was without past or responsibilities or relations or old wounds or jealousies; the clothes he donned altered him even as he vanished into civilian life another man, the paper he dropped coming to rest beside the tracks.

Don't ever look back, he told himself.

TWENTY-ONE

As if affrid we would disturb the Sacred dead

There is more of God in the way he touches my hair when he leaves me than the sermons the preacher gives us from the Holy Scriptures. I know William wants me to be his wife, and I'm willin.' If Ezra's killed in this war, I will be damned forever even if I pray every day he returns unharmed and strikes me down. I hear the hollow echo in the cave of my thoughts. Now, I'm even sounding like my Ez. He is still my Ezra, but it is so long and lonely. I'd be truly wicked if I weren't so full of sorrow. If I think about William, then I am damned. I can't but help think about William. If I wait for Ez, I might not be destroyed but my children will suffer. I am looking at my little ones, tucking the covers around them, then stoking the fire. It is warm in our little cabin for the first time in a long time.

*

Standing in front of her bookcases, Grace began hauling out everything until the middle of the room was a sea of books, papers, artifacts seemingly unrelated, shoes, clothes, albums, boxes. I can do this, she thought, intending to begin sorting out the untidy mess in her life, beginning with the library where she spent most of her days. If her life were ordered, if not chronological then at least ordered, she could begin to make sense of it all, she speculated, tossing out papers and books with the bindings broken.

The cottage had been her sanctuary, neat and orderly until Bill dropped off the boxes from their house in town, the memories and articulations of another life lived with Bill. He had thrown in the marriage certificate as if she would have wanted what he discarded. She crumpled it and then considered she might need it for legal reasons, smoothing the edges again and placing it in the box marked *legal.* She was glad she wasn't home when he stopped by, the note on the door as cool and indifferent as if it had been delivered by a mailman. No, not cool or indifferent, Grace corrected herself. The nasty note containing the struck-through line still stood out. And there was the implication of wrongdoing in the phrase, "You're never home."

Grace,

You're never home. What are you doing all day?

~~I was going to throw this stuff out~~

I thought you might want these boxes.

Bill

She wanted to write a note back to him.

Bill,

You left me.

I'm sure you wanted to throw out these boxes as you did our life together.

Grace

But the fantasy was only that; nevertheless, it made her smile as she pulled the note off the door. There was a lifetime of stuff accumulated and filling up the cottage, overwhelming it, burying it with other lives. *I can do this*, Grace thought, tossing items into the various boxes she had labeled but not without stopping to examine each item, taking her back to the moment, it had been given value, now in the process of becoming lost.

An oversized, mounted black and white photograph of her father's high school graduation ceremony stopped her momentarily. The girls were all in white in the first two rows, their hands folded in exactly the same manner, their feet neatly and tightly together in their white shoes. In the third row, second from the end, stood a group of boys in black robes, her father looking about the age of her son, the boyish face with the mischievous eyes staring out at the world before he would conquer it. He offered no evidence of foresight, no indication he would die so young.

There was no possible way Grace could throw away this photograph, so she made a new box marked VALUABLE PHOTOS. Digging into the boxes, she came across a hand-tinted photo of her Aunt Evelyn wearing three strands of pearls. Grace realized she had never seen her aunt with her hair cropped and curled tightly about her head—long before she felt the need to color it, wearing pearls, so the occasion must have been a significant one, perhaps a college graduation. It was placed in the VALUABLE box—already too much in that category. She considered the fact she would never find enough room in her cabin when everything was marked VALUABLE.

Just then, a movement caught her eye—something darting across the floor between the stacked boxes. Sitting on the floor, Grace didn't remember jumping up but stood looking tentatively around. A mouse-- I'm being foolish, she thought as she sat back on the floor but decided against the risk of having the mouse run across her leg or foot. After moving a few of the boxes with her foot, she saw another little gray creature scurry around the obstacles and then another. Oh, no. An invasion! With her heart racing, she pushed the old coats out of the way to find the buried broom and took it out to chase away the mice becoming brazen in their adventures through the camp, having found a way in was easier than finding their way back out.

After several minutes and out of breath from swatting at rodents, scarcely breathing during the attack, Grace sat clumsily, half fell in a chair, pulled her feet up and started laughing. It was either laughing or crying, she told herself. This was so perfect, she thought, chaos everywhere. She remembered a set of traps were under the sink where Bill had put them after he purchased them, telling her "camps always get mice. There's no way to keep them out." Why didn't she know about things like this? It was absurd to think dealing with mice was exclusively the territory of men. Now it would be her territory.

Like some cartoon villain, she baited the traps with peanut butter because Bill told her it worked better than cheese. Before her second trap was set, she heard the terrible snap and the death throes. She didn't dare open the cupboard door under the sink where she had set the first trap, suspecting the location was a place of entry. It would have to stay until she'd worked up her nerve. The mouse problem certainly couldn't wait until Jason came home. Finding her old gloves for bringing in the wood, she opened the door and picked up the mouse by the tail. Its head was flattened and certainly did not look threatening. Grace felt a wave of regret she immediately dismissed by tossing the tiny carcass in the garbage and taking it out to the garage.

After setting the other traps, she climbed into bed only after shaking out the sheets and blankets, then tucking them under the mattress. She crawled into the enclosure and pulled the covers up to her nose, alternately fighting off crying and laughing as she wrestled with sleep, determined she would have some but saw her dreams and waking merge in the gallop of scratching little rodents, an invading army of miniature yet daunting proportions. Susa must have dealt with mice, Grace thought, covered up to her eyes. Susa wouldn't have been scared because rats and mice must have been commonplace in every country house at the time, but the soldier's young wife would not have liked it, Grace was sure. The more she thought about Susa off by herself in the world, the greater admiration Grace held for the young woman of her imagination. Mice would not have defeated her great-great grandmother who was far stronger than that, so the rodents would not defeat this generation of women either.

By morning, Grace had determined the exterminator would have to be called if she were ever to sleep again. Roy Phelps had answers immediately.

"You ought to get rid of some of these boxes," said Roy.

"Well, it's my plan," said Grace.

"Mice like places to hide. You have any cats or dogs? Because this stuff wouldn't be too good for 'em." The exterminator seemed like the wisest man she had ever known as he went about his business laying out the green lumps of poison. And, for an instant, he made her remember one of Bill's qualities she had appreciated. "They like the taste of it, and they go off and die." Then Grace felt horribly cruel again, like a monster for her use of poison. "No dogs, right? asked Roy again.

"No. Not anymore," said Grace, thinking of her beautiful dog Riley who had passed away not so long ago. Riley had loved the camp for the time he was able to enjoy it before his arthritis prevented him from jumping into the lake, the camp when it had been a place of solace, a place where Jenna, who spoiled them, indulged Riley as well as Grace. "I need to store some things," she said, looking helpless, giving Roy an opportunity to appear gallant to the woman and to get some business for his cousin simultaneously.

"My cousin Doug's got a public storage place on Route 13." He gave her the number. "He'll even load up for you."

"Thank you. Thank you." Grace almost felt love for the scruffy looking man for helping her get rid of mice and solve a storage nightmare in one fell swoop, but they didn't become friends after all. He wasn't at all like some character in a movie. Not heroic but practical, and Grace realized she rather liked practical. The VALUABLE photos were not going to the storage facility, however. There would just have to be room for them all somewhere. In turned out, there were more than valuable photos in the box which became two then three. She had reduced the number, however, and had to take solace in her scant progress.

In trying to discover what was once there—a flesh and blood man and woman—but was now diaphanous, Grace imagined herself a character in a LeGuin story in which she tried to determine what is almost but not quite at the surface, the trace of writing left by water on the shore, the almost decipherable but impossible to read text embedded in the intricate lace collar. She tried to remember the words stitched in Sara's lace collar.

She wondered if they could be heard if she listened with a trained ear. The contemporary woman was searching for the answer to the woman left behind and the man who disappeared after a terrible war. Even following all the hours of research, the letters, the stories told by an aunt, the answers remained cryptic, just below externality.

TWENTY-TWO

Tell me all the news for my heart is able to bare it

She caught her breath as she wondered if this had all been part of some "progress narrative." Grace had been thinking about Virginia Woolf but not because the British writer had committed suicide, or perhaps she had thought of Woolf for that reason initially, she admitted, but then had moved beyond the tragedy to Woolf's literature, the richness of her narratives. And as Grace stood on the steps of the Lincoln Memorial waiting for Jason to return, she remembered a line from *Mrs. Dalloway*, "she always had the feeling that it was very, very dangerous to live even one day," and she knew she was stuck on the line but trying to get past it. Scanning the steps, she looked around for her son.

Jason bounded up the steps toward her. Their Thanksgiving trip to Washington, D.C. had been planned for months, with Grace finding ways to keep her son close even as he was rapidly distancing himself from his mother and his boyhood. She noticed signs of shaving, and it saddened her, ridiculously, of course. Asking him to give up a weekend of partying at college was no small sacrifice, she noted. The Memorial had been at the top of her list of sights to see and was far more impressive in actuality than she had imagined it. She wondered how she had never been to the nation's capital before this. The steps appeared easily surmountable in a photograph but were physically intimidating as she took several long breaths near the top. Halfway up, she had turned and sat down, out-of-breath, looking out over the reflecting pool, the visitors and citizens mingling below.

Jason jumped down beside her. He sat still for a moment. "Quite a sight, huh?"

"Incredible," Grace said, trying to disguise her need for more air. "Look at all these people from all over the world," she added, nodding in various directions, too tired to raise her arms for an instant.

They both looked around to watch individuals and groups of people sitting on the steps leading up to Daniel Chester French's 20-foot-tall sculpture of Lincoln. She was too exhausted to appreciate the scene just yet.

"Where'd you think they're all from?" asked Jason, standing and ready to bolt up the steps.

"I don't know. You're not going to ask them, are you?" Grace was suddenly concerned her impulsive son would create a commotion on the steps of the monument, perhaps fall himself or cause someone to tip over backward down the steep steps.

Jason leaped two steps to an Asian couple. Grace could see him gesturing with his hands and talking. The Asian couple turned their heads to look up at her and waved, the man with enthusiasm and the woman with a quizzical look on her face. Grace returned the gesture, slightly embarrassed but secretly proud her son was so bold and friendly. There was no way to stop Jason, she thought, he would talk to everyone whether she wanted him to or not. Watching her boy move from couple to couple seated on the steps, Grace thought about how like his father he was when Bill was young. It was Bill's most winning quality; she considered at the time. The brightness of the day, reflected in sharp glinting points of sun off white limestone and marble, as well as the pool below, hurt her eyes. She held her hand like a visor up to her forehead to shield her eyes and gazed at the overwhelmingly magnificent scene. There seemed to be people from every country in the world seated on these steps with her, all stopping to rest and contemplate the achievements of the 16th American president or perhaps their own accomplishments in arriving there at that moment in time.

"I'm never going to complete my dissertation," Grace said suddenly, taking in the expanse—from the bravery of her son to a Chinese couple at her immediate right. They nodded and smiled politely, trying not to offend the crazy American woman, she thought. When he would finally return to his mother, Jason would not know, at the moment, she intended to go back to her high school job as an English teacher. Maybe history was not the course for her after all.

"Don't worry about it," Jason might say, she mused. "I never thought of you as a historian anyway." He would look at his mother's face. "Hey, it's a compliment, Mom."

"Thanks, but I wish you loved history rather than found it boring. You're so young and have all this time to invent your own," she would tell him. She would not be a failure in the eyes of her son, but Grace wrestled with the concept, believing she was somehow giving up if she did not persist in her efforts. What did he know about "one-word" days, those awful days when all of the effort produced nothing but one-word edits feeling like defeat?

"Hey, Mom, are you okay?" The flesh and blood Jason was standing in front of her again, having leaped the last two steps.

"Yes. I was just thinking."

"What? Sorry, Mom, I was just looking at the little kid over there. You think he's going to fall off?"

"Oh. Where? No. There's his mother. She's got him, I think. People are so careless with their children. What was I saying?"

"Probably you think I'm immature." Jason moved toward the unattended child quickly then caught him before he fell. He picked him up and set the toddler back down on the step before moving back to his mother.

"No. You're definitely not immature, and I think you just might have saved the baby a nasty fall. I don't believe his mother noticed." Grace got up and looked directly toward the woman.

"Mom. It wouldn't do any good. Maybe there will be someone to save him the next time, too."

"I just worry because I want a good life for you."

"I've already got a good life," Jason said. "I think coming down here was a great idea, especially when I get out of doing extra work."

Grace laughed. "I guess this means I'll have to mow the lawn when we get back."

"You know, I'll do it if you want me to, but it's a little late to mow the grass, probably have snow on it when we return."

"I know. No, you have to go to school. You want to finish up the fall semester with a good grade point average."

"I'm doing okay," said Jason.

"You're doing better than that," said Grace, smiling. "It's just I never knew there was Myosotis in our yard until your father stopped mowing it and they grew."

"What?"

"Myosotis. From the Greek word for *mouse*—those tiny blue flowers are considered weeds and cover the ground like reflections of the night sky."

"You're such a poet, Mom. Don't mow them then. Who cares? It's your place now." Jason reached for his mother's hand, and she stood again. They climbed the steps together.

"Yes," she said, noting secretly he had said, "your place," and she could let her lawn and weeds grow wild with blue Forget-me-nots. "Let me sit a moment. I'm afraid I'm out of breath."

"Hey," Jason said, dropping down beside her. "Want to hear a joke, or kind of one."

"Sure."

"I was watching TV the other night, and some guy is talking about a woman who thinks she found Jesus in a piece of Cheetos."

"What?"

"Yeah. This woman claimed this little twisted corn chip resembled Jesus on the cross, so she contacted the news people, and they ran the story. It reminded me of a Bill Murray joke, one he told."

"And?"

"And it goes something like, the shortest joke in the language is, 'Jesus, cheese whiz' or is it 'cheese whiz, Jesus.'"

Grace laughed simply because she was with her son. "We're a pretty screwed up species. Looking for answers in all the wrong places."

"Sounds like a song," he said.

Grace started humming, "Looking for Love" on the steps of the Memorial, and she thought again of her historical search.

"Mom?"

"What?"

"Stop dieting."

"What are you talking about?"

"Seriously, you're getting a little too skinny. And if I notice, it really is too obvious."

"I'm not dieting."

"Then start eating again."

Grace was surprised but had thought about the fact food didn't seem to taste as good as it used to. Unless Jason was coming home or Mary and Holly were sharing a meal with her, she didn't spend time making dinner anymore.

"I will try to be more conscious of it," she said, her son's concern touching.

"Thanks. C'mon. Let's go see this great old man," said Jason holding out his hand to pull her up.

She was stretching now, looking out over the Capital, when she turned to her son at the top. "Yes, we've come all this way. Let's visit Mr. Lincoln."

"Hey, Mom. What happened to you when your chin got all purple?"

"What? Oh, well, I fell on our front steps."

"Was there ice or something? I mean, what exactly happened? No one hit you, right?" In the back of his mind, Jason was concerned his father had struck his mother.

"No. No ice. Why are you asking me about this now?"

"I don't know. I was just thinking about climbing all these steps, and I don't want you to fall again."

"Really, I'm fine or I will be." Grace wrapped an arm around her son's waist before releasing him. "I'm seldom that clumsy. It was just a slip when I was carrying the groceries, so I wasn't able to catch myself."

"I don't think you're clumsy. I just think, well, maybe you should be more careful for a while."

"Why didn't you say anything when you first saw me with my

hideous bruise?"

"It wasn't really hideous. I guess I didn't want to embarrass you."

"And now is okay?"

"And now, you don't seem upset about it, so, yeah, I think it's fine to ask about it."

Grace wrapped her tall son in the quick hug only a mother could get away with on the steps of the Lincoln Memorial. On the white mountain, Grace understood her son was worried about her in a way she often worried about him.

Inside the monument, Grace and her son stood looking up at Lincoln who was forever composed and thoughtful in his stone grandeur as they imagined he had been in life. Noticing the stillness around her in the crowded but hushed space, Grace felt the people communing with Lincoln in a way she had not imagined. She could hear him below the surface of her breathing. A wave of certainty flooded her, giving her permission. She had to finish her historical paper wherever it led, she knew. Even the restless Jason was silent for a time in the hallowed chamber. Standing there with her son and Lincoln, she thought of Ezra again and his love for his president, of Tim and his love for his country, and all of the sacrifices made.

But her certainty inevitably turned to disquietude when she and Jason walked through the National Gallery of Art. As soon as they passed the heavy glass doors, Jason was ahead of her. She lingered in the East Wing Mezzanine where a temporary exhibit of the Spanish painter Luis Meléndez, who had a habit—or necessity—of painting over other works, recently revealed by infrared lighting, was displayed. As she studied the lines behind oil paint strokes, Grace thought she could see another life, not just another surface, the one the painter had longed for. She wandered alone in the Gallery, knowing Jason would find her again. By the time she came across Magritte's *The Human*

Condition, she was prepared for the surprise but still found herself with a tremor. The painting she had used for years in her creative writing class was like an echo in front of her where she could hear her own voice as she stared at this painting of a painting, a bit like glimpsing immortality. She recalled Magritte's work found its way into Howard Nemerov's poem and spoke to her students as she wrote about visualizing uncertainty—the concept made tangible.

Even after leaving the Gallery, Grace continued to think about the other paintings, the ones hidden beneath surfaces. Jason had raced ahead up in the Tower, into and through the hall of Modernist collections, ready to move on. Whatever Lincoln seemed to answer by whispering to her in his Memorial, from his gargantuan throne, the day before was again turning to enigmas in a still life painting.

TWENTY-THREE

Perhaps I am saying more than I aught

So, tell me, Grace, Marilyn wanted to say, but started with, "Are you interested in Jeff Coleman, or am I imagining something going on between you two?" Marilyn probed as they descended the stairs.

"I don't think so, but I'm not at all sure he has any interest anyway. So, yes, you're imagining things."

"And if I weren't?"

"If you weren't, I wouldn't be interested. Something about a divorce leaves you feeling raw for a long time."

"I'm so sorry. I guess I shouldn't have brought it up."

"No, don't be sorry. I have a friend who's going through a divorce at the same time, and it's such a strange phenomenon; she's lost her voice or the way she used to talk. She speaks in this strained whisper now as if she's becoming someone else. I have to remind myself to whom I am talking when we are together."

"God, you're such an English teacher! 'To whom'—no one says

that," Marilyn remarked. Grace sighed audibly. "Sorry. It's not an insult; it's just if you're going to hang out with us history majors, you have to give up some of your English teacher jargon or formality. Remember, your ex is not feeling that way, and it wouldn't hurt you to get back into the mix, have some fun. Dating someone does not necessarily indicate any kind of commitment," Marilyn said as she threw her head in confirming nod. "But, by the way, I'm glad you're not seeing Coleman. He's such a bastard," she said before heading to the parking lot. "Can you imagine having sex with that dick—sorry for the intended pun."

Double-entendre, Grace thought, but said only, "It's okay. I'm fine. Good night." Have some fun, Grace was thinking but didn't say, as she caught the door with her free hand, balancing her books with the other and looked out over the campus in the quiet evening. How strange it sounded. For an instant, she was back in her own history, young again, starting college and discovering the world, but then she felt all the years of her life catch up to her, tumbling around then weighing down on her.

There were only finite possibilities in the world, and she felt as if she had run out of them. In the middle of class, she thought she had noticed Coleman looking at her again. Their first "date" had ended awkwardly but honestly. He admitted he'd been out of practice, and she had no desire to help him, but his gesture was rather sweet. He still has no idea how old I am, she mused, smiling at the trick she inadvertently played by looking much younger than her years. It was a gift from her mother's and father's genetics, both of whom who always appeared ten years younger than they were. Even at the end, Jenna could have fooled most people about her age, passing for Grace's older sister.

By the time Grace got home, it was dark outside without a star to guide her. Well, she corrected herself, there were a couple of stars not covered by clouds, but she couldn't have navigated by them. She fumbled for her keys and let herself in, dropping one of her texts in the process. With her coat half off, she pulled one arm out and reached into the undersized refrigerator for a soda. My addiction, she thought, as she heard the phone ring. Her heart skipped a beat because she always worried a late-night call might be Jason in trouble or in a car accident. She fumbled for the lights before picking up the phone. Her cellphone was too deeply buried in her purse for a quick retrieval.

"Oh. Yes?" she said tentatively into the receiver.

"Grace. It's Jeff Coleman. Sorry. I hope this isn't too late to call. I thought of a book that might interest you."

"Yes?" Grace wondered why it was so important for him to give her a title at this time of night, but she got out a pen and note card to jot it down.

"The title is *This Republic of Suffering: Death and the Civil War* by Drew Gilpin Faust. Reading your précis made me remember a line in Faust's work." Coleman hesitated.

"Oh. What's the line?" Grace asked, trying not to sound slightly irritated and already thinking about the play on words, not wanting to tell him she had already read Faust's incredible work. She could hear Coleman shuffling papers and waited for several moments as he was not prepared to provide it immediately; she imagined him fumbling through his papers.

"Yes. Here it is. There are a couple of lines I wrote down, thinking of your seminar paper: *But for those Americans who lived in and through the Civil War, the texture of the experience, its warp and woof, was the presence of death.* Your passage about Susannah living with death reminded me of this, and her use of metaphors, of course. And here's the other line resonating from Faust's work: *And if they are survivors, they must assume new identities.* You seem to be exploring the concept, examining the wives of soldiers."

Grace suddenly forgot her annoyance and listened attentively. Ezra abruptly came to her as if in a new guise, someone else's great-great-grandfather. "I'll pick up a copy of her book. Thanks. You've got me intrigued. Faust, the Harvard president?" she pretended as if she was not sure without understanding why she was keeping her knowledge from him.

Coleman cleared his throat loudly. "Yes. The same. Look, I've been wondering. I was thinking we could try dinner again sometime. I believe I came off as a little forward or awkward last time."

"Umm. No."

"Oh. If I am out of line, here, just let me know. I thought we could talk about your paper, keep it professional. I won't ask you any more questions about your personal life."

Grace flicked on another light in the library. "No. No, not at all. I mean, yes, I'd like to have coffee or dinner after class. This isn't about the reasons I need to drop out of the program, is it? I know you still have reservations about my background in English literature and the program."

"What? Of course, not; I thought we'd settled the question. Listen, my words didn't come out right." Coleman made an inarticulate noise into the receiver. "Sorry. I'm not usually so graceless." They both laughed. "I just detected a common interest, rather interests."

"I did say, 'yes.'" She could feel his relief through the phone line.

"Thanks. Great. Good. How about after class on Thursday?"

"Fine. I'll see you then."

"Well, okay then. Good. I'll see you Thursday."

Grace started to laugh again but caught herself, realizing he was done with the joke. "Yes, well, good night."

"Have a nice evening." Grace heard Coleman say as she hung up first, slightly concerned he might still be talking when she set down the phone. Standing in the tiny library surrounded by letters from the past, notes, and with no knowledge of future, Grace wasn't sure if seeing Coleman was more depressing than seeing no one. It wasn't she didn't like Jeff Coleman or even that she found him utterly unattractive, but the prospect of beginning a relationship again seemed about as arduous at the moment as rock climbing. She picked up the receiver and dialed.

"Jason?"

"Hey. Mom? What's up? Everything okay?"

"Yes, I mean, nothing, really. I just wanted to hear your voice. How's school going?"

Silence. "Fine. Uh. Mom, I'm kind of busy tonight. I've got a paper to finish before morning."

"Sorry. I won't keep you." The silence extended well past seconds.

"Mom? What is it?"

"I know. I have to stop calling for no reason."

"Hmmumph. I'm not going to die at least not for a long while."

"Not funny."

"Yes, it is."

"Okay," Grace laughed uneasily, in relief.

"Hey, if you're on the phone, one of my buds can't go home for Christmas until after his basketball tournament. I thought I'd bring him home for a few days over break. Sound good?"

"Of course." Grace was aware she sounded too excited. She didn't want to scare off her own son. It was hard not to hold him to close and drive him further away.

"We might go into the city for a few days, though."

"But you'll be here for Christmas?"

"Wouldn't miss it! Listen, I really got to go. Nite, Mom."

"Good night, honey."

She wanted to talk with him all night, but a few sentences would have to suffice. Grace smiled at the thought of kids—even grown ones—in the house during the holidays. She stretched and rubbed her sore shoulder before turning out the light in the library, saying goodnight again, this time silently, to her absent son, and moving on to those other absent but yet in the land of the living: Holly, Mary, her Aunt Gretchen and Uncle Charlie, her nephews Kevin and Dustin, Tim, before moving to the dead, whispering to Jenna, to great-great-grandfather Ezra, and great-great-grandmother Susannah, to history, as she picked up Garcia Marquez' *One Hundred Years of Solitude* to read before bed. I'll be one hundred years finishing this book, she thought, as she started to read, "Many years later, as he faced the firing squad, Colonel Aureliano Buendia was to remember that distant afternoon when his father took him to discover ice," and then she knew she would be up half the night searching.

*

Moving his thumb and broken index finger over the Greenbacks in the pocket of his unfamiliar civilian clothes gave Ezra a feeling of well-being such as he had not experienced in a long time, perhaps ever, he thought, for the moment, a rich man. With his mustering out pay stuffed in his overcoat, he waited for a train home, the train that would take him at last to Susa and little Willie and George and Jennie. Would he recognize the two older ones, he wondered, knowing full well he could not possibly have known his infant, who was now a toddler, running around mother's skirts. The image of his wife's soft skirts billowing about her girlish thin legs struck him with an impossible tenderness such as he had not felt for such a long time; he acknowledged the ache of it, like an old longing.

Whistling of the approaching train reminded him of the loneliness he kept tamping down during days and nights that had become years in a war somehow, impossibly, finally over. It wasn't the ending he had anticipated with parades and rejoicing, but the quiet turn in the earth, in men's faces, in temperature of the air signaling a change in season, in the atmosphere he could smell, allowing him to register the fact he was at last and indeed going home.

As he boarded the train, another man, probably a soldier like himself, a little younger, jostled him getting on, the younger war-weary man nearly losing his balance. It was only when Ez caught the man from nearly falling, he noticed the man's false leg, a product of shrapnel that hit, or the result of the work of a poor or overworked surgeon in the field.

The younger man nodded in thanks but said nothing before making his way to a seat. This young man was lucky to be alive but without his leg, how would be go back to where he was? Of course, no one went back to where they were. Ezra could hardly believe his life was about to change again, and he was grateful, for the first time, for the transition from war to peace was gradual not abrupt. He had time to shed his other skin and become a husband and father again. He had not been a tender man for so many days and nights. When he looked around him at the other men on the train, a quantity of them already sleeping, he was struck by the hollowness of their faces; perhaps some were coming from prison camps; he wondered at their extreme gauntness. Not a one was unchanged.

Ez expected to sleep on the train and wake upon arriving, but the motion stirred something in him that would not allow quiescence, or perhaps it was the sensation of expectation he could no longer hold back which made him get up and walk down the aisle to a door. The passageway between railcars was empty, unlike the crowded car rumbling sullenly with weary men. He pushed the door and stood in the open space between compartments, allowing the experience of seeming freedom wash over him. The odor of cut grasses and shrub brush was more powerful than the thick, smoky skin the air wore around the engine.

Ez smiled for the first time since he could remember, thinking about buying a little plot of land and working the fields with George a helper at his back; the little girl would be tagging along after her mother, he imagined, and Willi, his dear little boy, he would not recognize now, would run up and hug his pant leg. Seeing this picture so clearly, he needed no photograph to imprint it in his mind.

For just an instant he allowed himself to experience great, uncontainable joy he would not permit to surface during the duration of the war or even when he first learned he was going home. At that juncture of reflection, longing, the transcendent picture of his family together, he was jostled ever so slightly from his foothold by the engineer applying brakes as a startled deer froze in the tracks, the fate of man, animal, and machine joined as Ezra Cross was thrown, with no time to consider how to take the fall or what terrible thing he had done by his precarious movement but allowed only less than a second glimpse at boundlessness. Less time than an almost escaping "Oh, no," and then he twisted impossibly, his neck broken, his breath and conscious thought knocked clear of him, a shot as quick as a flash of lightning charging through.

*

Tim moved his head slightly, waking. *Grace has forgotten me, I know it. But what did I expect? She was going to fall in love with a piece of a man? What the hell did I think would happen? She was too old for me anyway. She's old and beautiful. Give me a needle. Give me a needle. Give me a needle. Please, give—me—something, God. Just a way out. In my dreams, in my thoughts, I don't stutter. I am whole.*

TWENTY-FOUR

———

Will be good to read and ponder it in their hearts

Grace read over her preface again:

Preface

At its center—caliginous and cold or a solid core boiling at the speculated 11,000 degrees, the earth remains a mystery but no more so than the end of one soldier's life or the thoughts of a woman waiting for the return of her soldier. Science cannot answer the meaning behind our journeys. The historical record of Ezra Cross' letters to his wife Susannah during the years 1861-1865 attest to not only the heart of the hand-colorized portrait of the Union solider but to the idiosyncratic husband, father, and son who were divisible aspects of one man. Ezra's letters are at once symbolic of the broader social, cultural, religious, and political context of a young America during its horrific Civil War and highly individual, so, by reading and analyzing his letters, we come to know both the lieutenant in the 1st Veteran Calvary New York Volunteers and the voice of Ezra Cross, the farmer, as he sits on picket duty contemplating his fate.

But for his wife Susannah and the spouses of the other Union soldiers who left home seeking honor and the glory by saving the Union, initially, retribution and justice later, their words have been as much the work of imagination as history, the primary documents of the women frequently burned in the flames of campfires as the men packed up, saving room in their breast pockets for a scrap of paper with their names for identification purposes in the event of death. The letters of their lovers and wives were lost. Before considering how to find the voices of the "waiting" women, we might ask why it is we should listen for their voices; what those voices might contribute to our understanding.

Are not the records of the men sufficient? How does our understanding of history change through the introduction of other perspectives? In recognizing what voices of the women might offer us, what insight into our history, we proceed. If we are to find the stories of the women during the Civil War, we must first read the letters of the soldiers and consider the spaces between. And if we are to have a better understanding of not only the Civil War era but who we are today, then we need to weigh more than the lines drawn in battle, more than the accounts of fathers and husbands, brothers and sons.

For the women back home awaiting word from their men in the field, there were the inevitable misunderstandings due to lack of any means of communications other than sporadic letters, resulting in problems of every degree, from the mundane to the severe, as witnessed in this example from Ezra's letter dated February 2nd, 1862:

> *You did not seem to understand me about the purchasing of the village lot belonging to Doctor F.D. Girdley. I do not feel prepared to meet an expense of that character at present and will only say that I should not be willing to buy it. I am sorry to*

In the space of a few lines, we can discern Ezra first implied Susannah is ungrateful for a gift (sorry to find that …[it] did not take your fancy) and then surmise she may never have received it (let me know whether you received the picture and the watch). The space between the question and the answer was often weeks and sometimes longer, with both the letter writer and those who received those missives making speculations based on imprecise, imperfect understandings or, rather, misunderstandings.

There were lost letters; money and watches that never made their way home; lieutenants from other companies who had their own families to feed. And in the first sentence of this excerpt lies the question, not simply about a misunderstanding or misinterpretation of directions about a property, but an insinuation Susannah may not have had a place to live.

"Home," while it meant salvation to men on the battlefield, may have been a rather tenuous condition for the women worried about how to pay their taxes, manage meager budgets, provide food in the absence of funds. Home was not the abstract or ideal waiting intact in the distance but the reality of coping in the face of tremendously difficult and often strange circumstances.

During the Civil War years, women who were not used to farming were suddenly farmers. Women who did not work outside the home had to think about finding other means to support their families in the event the Army's pay never arrived. What these women did during this period in history was no less daunting in terms of holding the Union together than the "hard days marching" of the soldier. They were actively engaged, as were the men, in changing the face of the nation.

The initially discouraging task of finding the woman's voice and her prominence during the Civil War is much like finding her voice and influence in any period, as the official record has traditionally analyzed civilizations through documents collected and centered on the event of wars and the domains of men. Who writes history and from what perspective does matter. Of course, the "victor" writes history, but if we allow it, the ruined, those left on the battlefield, those who had no voice previously in the pages of a text should be heard and considered, the "wife," the former "slave." The approach to how we examine historical events has to allow room for voices previously unexamined or unrecorded if we are to better understand not only our American history but ourselves.

What Ezra Cross was doing and thinking during the American Civil War seems clear if we believe the evidence of his own words and the war records. Although somewhat contradictory, alternately contemplative then banal, devoutly Christian then superstitiously pagan, political then apolitical, Ezra emerges from the primary documents he left behind, not only as a Union solider but as a complex, intelligent man who provided us with one piece of the puzzle that is our heritage even as he carried with him into death the mystery of his last hours.

Susannah, like the wives of most soldiers, wrote letters that were destroyed as the men moved between encampments; yet slowly, painstakingly, the young woman emerges in a portrait only visible by analyzing the small brush strokes found embedded in the language and letters of her husband. Deciphering the codes of language, in search of a second voice, is admittedly speculative but allows us entrance into history that can only be found through the wives and mothers on the home front. Susannah Rummer Cross loved and mourned her brothers, Edgar and Let, it is certain from Ezra's letters, and she looked to her husband—even as he struggled to survive through a horrific war—to provide for her and their children is also clear through the words of Ezra. His words betray she felt misunderstood, sometimes guiltily, felt overwhelmed, patriotic, isolated at times, and also, part of a larger community of sufferers. This is not merely speculation but historical evidence with some degree of authority based upon the inferences from these primary documents. She was most of all a survivor who would nurture the future in her children.

Finally, it may be stated we know something about Susannah Cross because after the deaths of her brothers and husband, after being turned out of her in-laws' house, disowned by her father, after losing her own home and finding the condition of poverty and want to be semi-permanent, she does live beyond the War years. We know this not from letters but from her progeny.

Susannah began the Civil War accepting her husband would make the most basic decisions for her and ended this period managing to decide for herself what was necessary to ensure a present tense for her family, for George, Jennie, and Will. Her voice may be found through echoes in the letters of her spouse as it is in a church chorus singing a hymn, the voices of her children, grandchildren, and her great-grandchildren, and the impossible march into an uncertain future. Although carried on by her children and grandchildren, Susannah Cross Hendrick's voice became both individual as well as indistinguishable from the countless voices of the women who mourned the dead in the Civil War, representatives of the America that attempted to heal a wound which would never completely go away.

After reading her words again, Grace felt conflicted. She really had no idea what Susannah Cross Hendrick really thought or wondered or even how she possibly survived with any authority or primary evidence. Everything about Susannah was inferred from Ezra's letters. She did not know if Susannah gathered her child, Willie, in her arms and wept openly or sternly told George and Jennie of their father's death, George already knowing his time in the home of another man, who had replaced his father, was limited. Jennie weeping but afraid of the burden on her mother. Willie only sobbing because his mother was upset.

Actually, Grace knew nothing of why Ezra Cross never came home. Whatever conclusion she reached would be mere speculation or conjecture. Whether he was murdered by another ex-soldier looking to start again with a bigger roll of greenbacks or careless in slipping from the train, drunk, perhaps on whiskey or on the giddy freedom he must have felt at the end when the soldiers were finally released, mustered out, and on their way home to wives and children, mothers and fathers who had spent every day praying for their return.

That is history, she supposed. Speculation, uncertainty, malleable, depending upon whose voice related the past. Not simply records and time lines. Our human story takes into account our lack—not knowing even if we have all the clues laid out before us. We can follow the clues and fill in the spaces between words and documents. Is it fair or honest if we do? Is it accurate if we don't? Grace jotted down those words.

*

Then, she was standing at her cabin door with Jeff Coleman, the dim yellow porch light producing the kind of romantic ambiance one sees in movies when he leaned over to kiss her. He was less awkward than a lot of characters from the movies, but his movements were still awkward. Dinner had been pleasant but not producing the kind of conversation leading to any permanence or love. In spite of that, Grace might not have moved her head slightly and touched his lips if a large moth had not flown in her face at precisely the right—or wrong instant. Instinctively, she reacted, dodging him and the moth, without pretense.

"It's not going to work out, is it?" Jeff took a step back, his hand still on her arm, before releasing her.

"I." She realized she liked Coleman but not enough. The emotion and everything it implied were swift and ruthless.

"Look, just don't say, 'It's not you—it's me,' so I don't feel like a gag from a weak Seinfeld episode."

"No. I'm sorry. I won't. Then, you wouldn't consider friendship to be in the offering?"

Jeff sighed. "I've already got plenty of friends." He knew it was the wrong thing to say but couldn't help himself.

"I didn't know you had a quota."

He sighed. "As a matter of fact, I do." Then he laughed. She smiled.

They stood there dumbly for a moment longer. She was ready to say goodnight and go in when he stepped toward her again. "Now, I'm the one who's sorry. I don't know why I'm such an unbearable ass sometimes. There isn't a quota. I was just hurt, to be honest."

"All right. I understand." She decided not to let him off the hook entirely.

"I think, maybe, if I hadn't been thinking about you in another way, we might just have become friends."

"It's not too late to change course, is it?"

"Yes, I'm afraid it is. I seem to end up falling for my best student."

"Oh? Then, I'm glad I didn't get too far into this before finding out about your next one." Rather than bitterness, they both experienced the sudden awkwardness of dating—or attempting to—finally ending in relief it was over.

"Fair enough. Good-bye, Grace. Become a great history teacher or go back to teaching English. You will do well either direction you choose."

"Good night, Jeff Coleman. I will," she said as he turned.

As he reached his car, he suddenly looked toward her again. "If you change your mind, I could still be persuaded, but there is a time limit on this extended offer."

Grace smiled but was firm. "Good night, Professor Coleman." It was definite.

It turned out Professor Jeff Coleman was an interesting man but not Grace's William Hendricks arriving in a white car. Of course, she was not Susannah, either, and she wasn't looking for another husband, just companionship. She had meant it about the friendship between Jeff and her, but friendship between a man and woman who were looking for a partner was always a more difficult balance than it would seem. What one person needs is not necessarily what the other is willing to accept.

Surprisingly, Jeff still gave Grace great recommendations later when she needed them. He even called a dean at the college she applied to in order to convince them to hire her. She only found this information out accidentally, after she was already teaching in Boston.

Although she knew they clearly weren't right for each other, it is not to say they both hadn't hit a nerve.

TWENTY-FIVE

———

I begin to feel like a caged bird and long to get free

Grace woke up feeling optimistic, went to the library to read and mark passages in a few more texts, and then got into her car to drive up to see Tim at the VA. When she got there, Dr. Malakar accidentally bumped into her at the elevator. She held it open for him, the elevator door hitting her shoulder in the process. The shoulder was still sore, maybe arthritis, she thought, although she hoped she was too young to inherit the disease that had nearly crippled Jenna at the end.

Malakar was one of her favorite doctors because he actually talked to the volunteers and seemed genuine in his concern for patients. They exchange pleasantries as the doors shut. Dr. Malakar has beautiful eyes, thought Grace, and a thick Pakistani accent, but his English is excellent. She recalled telling him she was an English teacher, so he often joked with her about his grammar. Typically, she told him it was flawless even though it was not.

"I'm heading up to see Tim Fitzgerald," she mentioned, just to remind him of her connection to the hospital. It was unnecessary, but there was an awkward moment or two in the elevator when you are riding with just one other person and the compulsion to speak becomes overwhelming.

All morning, she had been thinking about Ezra, not Tim, when she read one of Ez's lines making her sad. In the middle of the library, the letter began weeping. It wasn't even his last letter, only the second to the last one she read.

Camp Piatt, W.Va.

June 25th 1865

Dear Wife

I am so lonesome that I don't know what to do with myself. I am all most homesick. I'm so lonesome, hear we are shut up in camp day after day only two passes given to a company at or in a day and they are only for two hours.

I haven't been out of camp since we left Kelly's Creek and I begin to feel something like a caged bird and long to get free--talk about prisons and penetencearies. I never have been to either but it seams that any place where man can move and breath would be preferable to being domineered and playing band box solider if I live to get home I believe I shall know enough to stay there and I will tell you of things I durst not write, don't let it excite your curiosity for it may not be so interesting after all. I wish with all my heart that the authority at Washington would discharge us now that the war is over if their was any need of our staying or if there is any more fighting to be don I am willing to stay and do my part of it but as it is there is just as much need of a regt of armed soldiers at Chenango Forks as there is of me hear, and if I had no one to care for but myself it would be diferent but I have a family that is dear to me and should like to be with them.

Ezra

Grace held Ezra's letter as if it was her only connection to him. It was not so very different in tone than the others, she thought, considering what it was making it more heartbreaking. He had written it shortly before he died or was killed, the historian never knowing the truth of the moment.

"I wish with all my heart that the authority at Washington would discharge us now that the war is over." Ezra's plaintive tone could be felt in the line, all the more poignant because she already knew he would never return home. She realized she was not a very good historian as she thought about how she had grown affectionate toward her Ezra, wanting to protect him, wanting to put him in the arms of his Susa. Even his spelling errors were becoming endearing, sacrilege for an English teacher to admit. And what was worse, she thought of Hamlet and his pun on the word *"seems, Madam, I know not seems."* What kind of historian thinks in terms of literary allusions? Ezra's letter suddenly made Grace want to connect with Tim.

When she found herself in the VA hospital again, thinking about Ezra and Tim as if there were no distance between them, all in the infinitesimal space, the elevator door opened and Dr. Malakar entered like some heroic figure out of romance novel. Indulgently, she allowed herself to think of him as this character in some ridiculous but chivalrous fiction. After all, when she entered the hospital now, she was no longer struck by the smells, the antiseptic covering of death. Tim no longer reminded her of death.

"Good afternoon, Dr. Malakar," she said.

"Good afternoon," he responded officially, killing off any silly dream of another kind of conversation with him.

Malakar cleared his throat. The elevator stopped at his floor. Pressing the hold button, Malakar turned his head, first checking to see if anyone was around although the door was closed, and there was no one else; he said, "Oh, I'm very sorry." The kind, thoughtful Dr. Malakar touched his right temple, looking down for a moment before taking a gathering breath. "He died last night. I'm sorry. Terrible injuries, that young man." She could see the guilt on his face because he knew he should not have told her. He shook his head and turned away, exiting the elevator as the doors were already closing with two other visitors getting on, staring at Grace's drawn, pale face.

She missed her stop but felt there was no stopping now. Instead, she traveled to the top floor, and a group of young physicians got on, laughing. They looked at her and were suddenly silent, lowering their gazes in unison. By now they had learned to see death on the face of visitors. As they descended again, she tried not to think about what to do next. Was there a next?

The physicians got off, and a nurse wheeled a patient onto the elevator. The young nurse was joking with the patient who was flirting with her in return as Grace rode up and down, the floors passing by with the bells and lights suggesting entry and exit as synonymous, people coming and going as one, but she continued to ride.

She did not know how long she remained on the elevator, but after some time, she caught the door and exited, unaware of the floor she was on. It's not supposed to end like this, she thought. Damn it. Nothing turned out the way it should. At least in a fiction, she could have allowed Tim a miraculous recovery, wheeling himself down the hallway to greet her. It was not impossible to create such a scenario. Before she could think about Tim, she had to get a hold of herself and where she had been set adrift.

This was why people drank and ran their pickup trucks into electrical poles on the side of back roads, shot up in an abandoned building, tied weights to their ankles and walked into the Ouse, screamed unrelenting into the night, cursed words never meant for human ears, made quick incisions on each arm at the wrist, rigged a shotgun to release the trigger with the barrel tilted to meet the chin, she thought.

One of her students wrote about cutting herself in a journal. Grace remembered reading the words three times before gathering up the notebook the teen had decorated with photos of girls with black spiked hair streaked with red and purple. Explaining to her student the reasons why she had to report the sacred trust, she waited for the girl to exhale, the breath drawn in lasted long enough for a deep dive, and she twisted her mouth, met her teacher's stare, and pushed up the black sleeves of her shirt for Grace to see the tangle of lines where the shallow slices had scarred over, saying, "If I really wanted to kill myself, don't, the fuck, ya think I would've by now?"

*

Grace leaned against a windowsill surprisingly dirty for a hospital setting, she noted even in this exorcism of grief as an uncontrolled torrent rushed out like a purging. No one bothered her or asked her to move. They were used to death and the physical reactions of the living in this place, she knew.

And she stopped analyzing the moment and let go, the wail beginning with a long, deep breath, as quietly as possible until she was exhausted, spent, finding herself on the floor next to a wall beneath windows, not quite remembering how she came to be holding her knees to her chest in an approximate fetal position. There should have been someone walking up to put his or her warm arm around her shoulders or kiss her forehead gently as her sobs slowed then subsided, but there was no one, not even the child she imagined with the chubby little soft hand. Where Grace would remain, trapped in floating pain, unless she rescued herself.

In front of her field of vision was the image of David Foster

Wallace hanging himself. Perhaps it was the fact choice was involved that made her act. Suddenly afraid, she reached out as if she could touch his hand, stop his motion, watched him remove the rope from his neck and place it on the ground. But it was Tim she wanted to save more than herself, and no imagining could change the outcome.

Finally, she decided to return home because there was no good option. Breathing in rhythm again, she was self-consciously aware of each breath, but she no longer cared it seemed contrived or typical or even clichéd because she felt as if she were just waking. Her chest was tight and aching; her eyes burned as if they had been open in the wind for days; her head tingling with the sensation Jenna used to call *pins and needles*. She recognized, because of these physical discomforts, she was fully alive and remembered even from her position that Tim was not. She considered it selfishness she felt his loss so horribly because she wanted him alive for her, too. She knew. She loved Tim and loved the idea of fairness even if it did not exist.

The next move was hers although she was no chess player. Determined not to participate, her thirst forced her to look up and calculate the distance to the vending machine. There was a nurse looking at her with a face revealing concern mixed with disdain. Aware of the nurse studying her, Grace nodded, indicating she was okay even though she was sitting on the floor, and her hand searched for a couple of crumpled dollar bills in her jeans pocket then pulled them out as she pushed against the tiles, launching herself into life again.

At the end of the hallway, there were four passageways coming together as if her fate lay in one direction or another, so she followed this train of thought and choose the path away from the Voluntary Service Program Manager. Something told her she should begin again, but she simply could not. Her grief was like lead, dark and heavy, and she was not reborn or reinvented, coming out of the fetal position.

Grace followed the only choice she could at that moment, moving away. She turned once, looking back toward the room where Tim had been.

Counting the steps gave her time to recover, or perhaps allowed her soul a period from which her mind had burdened it. She suddenly wished she had been a mathematician. Such pure certainty until, of course, you get to the advanced levels where the abstractions centered around infinity. Her heart rate slowed, becoming more regular with the rhythm of her shoes on the hard, hospital flooring. Up 286 steps in a wing she did not typically walk through, she recognized nothing—senses stripped down—except pungent, clinical smells. A desperate need to flee rose as instinct for survival.

Grace felt no certainty about anything, of finishing her doctoral program or becoming a history professor, but she had enough determination to try to look forward even as she continued looking back. That is history. Being able to look back and take surfeit of the past, making her think, if not satiated with living, at least connected by familiar rhythms. She longed to be connected again. She missed her exchanges with Tim, her relationship to Bill, to Jenna, to Richard, to Evelyn, to Riley, even to being in the classroom teaching. Anger arose, as if Tim had no right to leave her. These self-centered feelings washed over her indulgently, soothingly, as she thought of the young man as the bravest soldier she had ever known before admitting to herself she had not known many soldiers. Yet, she believed even if she had known thousands, she would still find Tim remarkable for the way he lived in the face of such cruel circumstances and pain. And she realized it did not matter if we sob and carry on and pray and curse or beg. All of it changes nothing. Loss and life are relentless, the propulsion to move if not forward then in a continuing circle of living and dying. All of it is this horrific but wondrous chaos we organize into history with timelines, chapters, and stories. There must be some relief, and that relief was found in the familiar even if it meant listening to one's own breathing. The stories, however, allowed her to reflect.

Looking up to discover she had found her way into the visitors' coffee shop; she took a seat near a back window. Instinct told her fainting would not be helpful. Probably low blood sugar. She was acutely aware she should not get behind the wheel of a car yet.

A hospital volunteer, who wore a crisp uniform well, and wore her hair in patted tight gray curls on her head, asked if she could get anything for Grace who must have looked as if she were in need of something strong. Grace wanted to tell the woman to sit down with her. It was tempting to ask for her old life back, but she wanted Tim's life to return. Could you please rid all of us of this fear of death surfacing as panic? No, she would not say it out loud. Then she knew she probably would not take her old life back anyway. She was no longer the same woman who had fallen in love with her husband and marked her days by the high school students' moods, so she ordered black coffee. Then changed her mind, remembering her low blood sugar.

"Sorry. Please. Could I have sugar and cream, too?" The bitterness of the coffee seemed acceptable or more appropriate, but the cream and sugar were necessary.

"We don't have to check you into a room here, do we, dear?" asks the volunteer, looking concerned. Grace's face was pale and her hands shaking.

"No. No. I'll be fine." But she was not fine. The coffee had probably been sitting in the coffee pot for a while, but at least it was hot. She burned her tongue on the first sip. Was she still looking for a human savior even while her rational brain told her there was none, at least not the kind where miracles intervene.

Grace wanted to read to Tim again. Even though she had always considered the idea she was doing him a service, she fully understood he was helping her, too. I went too far, she thought. Although she only meant to volunteer, help a little, take her mind off her own troubles by assisting someone else, something had happened. She never meant for this, for any of this: not for the hole collapsing inside her for a young man she had never met until stepping forward to volunteer. Not for the friendship turned almost into love.

Now she had no choice but to mourn Tim, and she had grown into a powerfully reluctant mourner. Strange because suddenly, it was as if Tim was not gone at all; in fact, it appeared as though he was whole again—before the I.E.D. met him—and waiting for Grace. Although, his girlfriend should have been the one at his door.

He, too, was going to be walking around with Grace the way Jenna, Richard, and Evelyn still wandered into her rooms whether she wished or expected them.

A woman at an adjacent table reached across the expanse and touched the index finger of a man with whom she was seated. He looked surprised but then smiled. This reminded her of a scene she had experienced in the airport. "I don't know anything," she said almost out loud. The couple looked like they were still dating. Grace could not imagine really dating anyone ever again. She knew she was disinterested in Coleman; there was no spark for her. On some level, finding love again would be vastly different and far less romantic, but what she did know was she could never love Coleman.

Grace attempted to measure the distance it would take to determine whether it was her fault or just poor chemistry with the professor. It was not about looks at all and never could be. Perhaps her thinking would change with time. Would she ever tell Jeff Coleman burning her tongue was a relief because the physical pain momentarily balanced the psychic pain? She could have talked to Tim about that because he would understand. Would she discuss historical dates and timelines around the dinner table with Jeffrey Coleman? No. And if not, what would they talk about? She would have never fallen into a routine in which they were mired in historical theory or the reign of the Ming dynasties. Even if he promised to discuss American history, she did not think she would want to converse all evening about the logistics of battlefield decisions by the generals or answer for her random ordering of the chaotic world. She was still trying to decide if she could forgive Coleman for leaving his wife because she "was not the woman in the attic" but "crazy," according to him. Suddenly, Grace experienced feeling far more curious about the former Mrs. Coleman than she was about the professor. Grace could envision herself as the woman locked in the attic while Jane Eyre waited with her hands neatly folded in her lap, Rochester walking into the room with his pained, romantic expression. Everything was supposed to end with Jane and Rochester getting together after all they had suffered, but their liaison, too, was not right—just the suffering part.

Despite her reluctance or anger, curiosity reemerged like some hungry fish out of water splashing beneath the surface again, but the emerging figure was not a different human being, just one who had experienced too much loss too suddenly to recognize surroundings. Slight relief. Grace was breathing easier. She did not try to analyze what caused the altered breaths earlier, but knew she was not suicidal, or as her poetic ancestor would say again and again in those letters, *I'm yet in the land of the living.*

If she thought of Tim, he was alive for her. She did not care how egocentric it sounded. Maybe she could convince herself he was fine and leaving the area, just as she was about to do. What Grace understood with certainty was she had to keep moving, even if time was not linear at all, she would do whatever it took—even tricking herself with lies.

Grace got up and began walking until she found herself free from the maze of a building and driving home, aware she was speeding. She was conscious of working at controlling her impulses in her present state. She had the feeling her brain was manipulating the phenomena Tim was sitting in the car with her. The dread at the tip of her brain was a constant. Must be daring the troopers to pull us over, she thought, but none were around, their radar silent. Tim is silent, too, but she felt he wanted her to drive faster. "Sounds crazy," she told him, but she could not stop racing.

"What do you want from me?" she asked him out loud, aware she sounded mentally ill. Yet Tim had stopped stuttering, ceased talking, just sat quietly beside her. Without turning her head, Grace could feel him, which she knew was not a good sign for either of them.

"You will have to go, you know. I cannot do this." As if he heard her, Tim disappeared, and she felt the weight of his loss again. She had asked him to leave. "I'm sorry," she said. "I'm so terribly, terribly sorry," but there was no answer.

Grace felt really scarred.

TWENTY-SIX

They is all willing to do their part

When Grace pulled into the drive, it was already dark, and she fumbled for house keys in her large leather bag, jabbing herself on a pencil deep in the mystery of her purse, breaking the tip and her skin. Perfect, she thought, examining her hand under the interior lights of the car. She seemed to have a knack for injuring herself as if to distract from mental anguish. Feeling sorry for herself before she realized Jason was home, the car they used to share pulled up on the lawn now covered in muddy snow. It was too dark to see anything other than the outline, yet she could recall exactly how everything looked. Her son's presence changed everything.

She was so glad her son was home again, but she could not let him know it immediately. There existed an impulse to be strong in front of her gown boy even though she was aware he would stay but a short time. Not wanting to appear desperate or needy before him, she resolved to try to control her emotions.

"Jason?" was all she got out before she heard it, before she saw the little intruder: a yelping noise preceded the pup racing around the corner to greet her. There was no time to think, protest, or debate with the flurry of paws around her feet, nearly tripping her at the doorway.

"Mom? What do you think?" Jason said proudly as if he had presented his mother with the gift of salvation.

"Oh, no," was all she could say as the pup leaped at her, mouthing and pulling her short boots when she bent down to pet his smooth black coat. She looked up to see Jason had not yet puppy-proofed the library, several books sprawled across the floor, a pair of his socks wet and obviously dog chewed. She was glad Ezra's letters were already filed away. Grace had long ago given up worrying about tidiness, but the pup presented a type of disorder which seemed crushing in the moment.

"He's going to be a great dog, you'll see. Oh. I'll clean up this mess. Promise. Don't get upset, Mom. Mom, are you okay?"

Already exhausted, physically and emotionally, Grace felt the hyper state in her car had already passed but the thought of training a puppy seemed impossible at the moment. Jason misread her pained expression. "Look, Jason, it's not that I," before she could finish, her son was already trying to convince her of the wisdom of his impulse. "He is going to be a great guard dog. You'll see."

"Honey, I don't even have enough energy to drag myself to my bedroom. How am I going to look after a puppy?" She wanted to cry again. Not a dog, she thought. Too much energy required when she felt she had nothing even for herself. She felt as if she was not ready for healing or giving. Nothing left to give anyone. The dog was already looking at her with intelligent, little black eyes; however, his head cocked to one side so endearing it seemed staged, even artificial.

"You'll get used to him."

"And how did he come to be with you?"

"Some girl—Melanie—was giving away pups at Antonio's."

"What? A pizza place? Who's Melanie?"

"She works there. Brought the pups in a box. She said her father was going to drown them or something, so I said, 'Give me that little guy.' He was the smallest one in the bunch. He doesn't look it now, but he'll grow up to be a good watch dog. I thought you could use a dog. You need a dog, again, Mom."

"Him?" Grace realized she sounded too incredulous. "The runts don't usually fare too well," she could not help commenting, determined not to get attached to this little animal. What was her son thinking?

Jason overlooked his mother's obvious annoyance. "This one will. Look at him. He's smart; you can tell already. He'll be housebroken in no time."

"Oh, Jason, how am I going to?"

"It'll be fine, Mom," her son said, sitting on the floor with the pup, wrestling with him. The puppy then peed in excitement, pee spraying the wallpaper, as well as the wood floor and Jason's pant legs. Jason broke out laughing while trying to shield himself. "He got me!" Grace knew she would have been furious with anyone else putting her in such a position. Something like anger wanted to rise but was dissolving before it was even recognizable.

"Damn it, Jason," she said, trying to stifle laugher. "I told you no puppies."

"Sorry, sorry, but I know you're going to love him. I'll clean this up. Don't worry. He only pees like this when he's excited."

"Well, that's good," she said, sarcasm evident.

"He'll calm down, and you'll see. Well, maybe not right away," Jason said, still laughing.

"No. Not right away." She was suddenly trying not to laugh, too, but hysterically so; fatigue, recognition of being in over her head, manifested as laughter.

"See," said Jason, "you're already cheered up." And, of course, he was right. Although Grace was not feeling cheerful, her mental and emotional positions had been altered. Jason added, "I think," qualifying his optimism. "Will you keep him? I mean, I hope you will. I can't take him back."

"Yes, of course, I'll keep him." Chaos is sometimes necessary. The pup was more nervous than Grace at the moment, drawing her back from the darkest place where she had been living for quite a while and might have continued to inhabit for some time if this little messy miracle had not peed all over the entrance to her house. She sat on the floor, not caring about how her life would be transformed by this pup. Then she wrapped her arms around the slobbering little mutt, pulling her son into the embrace with one arm.

"Mom, Mom, what's wrong?" Jason asked, initially pulling back, nervous.

"Tim died," she said, realizing she was crying again.

"Oh, God. The injured solider in the hospital?"

"Yes. He's gone. All willing to do their part," she said with evident sarcasm tinged with bitterness."

"What?"

"'Willing to do their part'—a line from one of the Ezra Cross's letters about soldiers going to their deaths for their country."

"Oh, no. I'm sorry, Mom." Jason sat on the floor with her, the puppy jumping between them, licking their faces and biting at their hands. "I know. I know."

Then the pup let out a sharp, demanding bark.

"I think he wants to go outside. I'll take him."

"No, it's fine. I'd better get used to this." She pushed herself up with effort, but then stopped crying, focusing on the demands of a wild little pup. "We need a leash."

"Happen to have one," Jason said pulling out the short leash from his coat pocket. Normally she would have cared very much about the fact she had plopped herself down on dog pee, her clothes all in disarray, her hair snarled at the back of her neck, but at the moment, none of the rest of it seemed to matter.

"I'll go with you. Let me get a flashlight." Jason disappeared, and she rubbed the pup's ears. He nuzzled against her as she adjusted the leash.

"Goodness, you are a cute little thing," she told this intruder.

Then Grace, her son, and her new dog made their way down the dark country road lit only by the narrow beam of light. "How did you know?" she asked before they reached the bend in the road.

"You needed a dog?"

"Yes, that I needed both you and a dog right then?"

He laughed. "I didn't. I just felt like coming home, and I stopped for a pizza. I really never intended to bring a dog home. If you'd have seen those puppies in the cardboard box and heard the story about how Melanie's father was going to take them all out and drown them."

"Who is Melanie again? Do you know her?"

"Not really. We went to high school together, but it's not like we were friends or anything, just a classmate. I know you would've picked him out, too. But I'm sorry about the timing. I guess I wasn't thinking, just reacting."

"No, your timing was perfect. It's good you were—." Grace slipped her hand through the crook of his long, right arm. Normally, her son would have pulled away gently, not wanting a clingy mother, but he let her hold his arm. The contact with her son, the yelps and gentle huffs of the pup trotting beside them, and the sharp cold air caught her from freefalling.

TWENTY-SEVEN

———

I will tell you of things I durst not write

Grace packed away the letters belonging to Susannah Cross, wrapping Ezra's words again in a white ribbon as Susa had done all those years ago. The letters composed by Susannah's husband had been lost and found, read with love and anticipation, and reread with a scholarly eye, catalogued and analyzed. Now they, too, were part of history if we are willing to consider what they told us.

But she also knew there was a story beyond the letters, important history remaining outside of textbooks and artifacts. There was no letter detailing Ezra's disappearance on his way home after the Civil War. There was no missive explaining how Susa accepted her great losses and found a way to continue, to rear her children who would grow up to have their own children and grandchildren. There was no letter offering understanding as to how she or any of us healed or did not heal after such catastrophic rifts in our nation. These were the questions of life which Ezra alluded to when he created his line, "I will tell you of things I durst not write." But, of course, he was never able to or willing to tell

Susannah of those things. If he had made it home to her, perhaps in time, he might have gone to unearth those "things" too terrible to put in print.

Grace imagined Susa's letter not to her husband but to her missing brothers.

*

Dearest Let and Edgar,

I'm sorry I haven't spoken to you in so long. I guess you know I been trying to sort things out, take care of the children, and I married a man by the name of William Hendricks a year after the funeral.

My new husband don't have a silver tongue like Ezra, and he's got a mangled leg from a terrible accident on his family's farm, but he's a good, strong man who's kind to me. He tol' me he'd raise Willie and Jennie like they was his own kin. George is growing up and says he don't need no father no more. That's what he says to William, but William is good to him, too, and says it is God's will he should marry me because my young son has his name. I don't know if I believe him about being God's design, but I know William Hendricks has given me back hope I'd lost in the wilderness of Ez's death and the death of you, my brothers. I won't go on and on about William because it might pain you, but I wanted you to know I found a way to keep going.

I shouldn't tell you this, but William looks at me sometimes like I was the most beautiful woman in the world. I remember when I was young, you tol' me I was the prettiest girl in the county. William has tol' me this sentiment on more than one occasion. I'm embarrassed but secretly pleased my new husband thinks I'm a fine woman, and Let, you tol' me never to settle for any man who wouldn't treat me good.

Still, I can't help feelin' such sorrow now and then that I wonder how I can swallow my own spittle. I wonder if Mr. President Lincoln knowed what he was asking of you, of all of us, but I guess he had no choice, and he paid the highest price. I can't tell you I'm happy all the time, but the ache in my heart comes and goes, making me not so much forget as distance the pain. At times, I feel so light, like right here and now, I might just fly up to see all of you—Ezra, too. I don't know what he'd say to me, but I have to believe he'd still want to see me.

I suspect he'll forgive me when I get a chance to tell him my story.

*

I leave off thinking about my brothers for a time. After I've pulled the quilt up to my chin, the room so cold at night and William already snoring, I let my mind return to my Ezra. I move a little away from William on the bed, taking his hand off my hip.

My dearest Ezra Cross,

I hesitate to speak to you because I feel so bad. I think you should know Willie knows he's your son. I saved all your letters for him, Jennie, and George to read someday. I never was a good letter writer like you, so I hope you got a few of mine that let you know how much I cared for you even though I never had the knack for words, couldn't make them sound pretty the way you could. I wondered if you read them over and over like I read yours. I hope you wasn't disappointed in me like you was the time when I couldn't learn writing better when you tried to show me. I read your letters, sometimes putting my finger on each word, imagining your pen on the page.

I think of this when everyone's out working the field or still sleeping in the morning, the frost on our breath, the chill crawling under the door, me tryin' to find in the words to ask if you still loved me, if you love me even now in the place you are. I hope you wasn't sufferin' when you died.

I wish you was thinking' of me, but not so much you have no eternal rest. I'm praying, but I'm not sure what prayer means anymore. Don't think badly of me, but I'm not certain the Lord has a plan at all.

If he hears our prayers, he don't seem to react much to them.

There's something else, Ezra. I married again. I know'd you won't be happy bout it, but he's a good man and respects your name in this house. Reverend Goodell tol' me it was my duty to provide for your sons and daughter and marrying again was both expected by our community and natural in God's eyes. I don't honestly knowed how me and the children would have got on without him.

I don't always feel right about it, but if you could have seen me doin' chores before my new husband came along, maybe you wouldn't be angry. I nearly kilt myself chopping kindling one morning—sent a wood chip flyin' into my chin like a strong punch. I woulda laughed 'cept it hurt so bad I just sat there tryin' to get back my senses. I was scared most of the time you were gone. I never knew if me and the children were goin' to be turned out again. I guess you knowed from my letters. Thinking I might have caused you pain even at the end keeps me sad now and then, and the children seem to notice, so I turn my face and try to be looking forward.

I did find something' I'm good at, Ez. I can make things grow. Our little farm is givin' us a bounty, and Willie and George and Jennie are growing up like tall strong weeds that can't be pulled. Jennie's a flower, and the boys, well, they're going to be strong as the oldest trees. Jennie looks like me, I think you'd say, only she's so much prettier. As far into the future I can see, I don't know how they turn out, but they are running through fields invisible to me from my poor sight on this earth. There is one other thing to tell you. In my heart, you'll always be my Ezra, and I'll be your Susa.

*

Graced paused and realized how much she admired Susannah. Even when someone left—whatever the reason, that person remained part of the other's life forever.

TWENTY-EIGHT

I remember love

Reading a news article online about robots in combat, Grace immediately felt anger, thinking about Tim and wondering if those ground bots might have replaced Tim and his fellow soldiers trapped in a vehicle when it hit an IED. If only her friend had not been in the ill-fated SUV not so very long ago, but then she learned 2,000-plus robots "deployed" as ground bots were rather "stupid," unable to do much on their own, meaning a soldier's life would still have been on the line, pushing out ahead into uncertainty, being terribly maimed through combat experience.

She could envision Tim making a joke about ground bots' ineptitude. Behind his sarcasm, however, she was sure there was sadness, as he would wonder the same question she formed. Tim would always want his old life back even in dreams, even in death. If only, he must have thought. If only he had never signed up for what he could not have known. If only he had returned whole and ready to tackle the next adventure, not from a hospital bed but from an SUV or motorbike.

Sitting at her kitchen table, holding a tea bag in hot water, Grace imagined those little robots with big eyes clumsily marching ahead of live troops before their mechanical wheels hit an immovable obstacle. As if in a movie, she could see those bots fall over, piling up on top of one another as if in some horrifying comedy routine.

She desperately wanted to talk to Tim about ground bots, realizing not long ago she had fallen in love with him, partly out of loneliness but also because of who Tim was. Turned out, she did not fall in love with her professor but an injured soldier. In a moment of wakeful dreaming, she saw herself nursing Tim back to health, the way imagination lifts us temporarily before dropping us back down with sickening thud.

For an instant, she could see herself making breakfast for Tim before he waltzed into their cabin and wrapped his arms around her. She might have had that kind of love even if she was too old for him.

Sammy was nudging her away from the computer, so she got up to take him for a walk, thinking about where she had been and wondering where she was going. Grace learned of a new fatal attack on three American ground troops in Afghanistan when she returned. Her computer alive and talking: a video report of casualties of the recent bombing. It was matter of fact, so much more so than the lists of the dead and wounded during the Vietnam War era when the numbers were overwhelming. The television was no longer the only messenger of war news as we march from one battle into another, always another. There would be many more maimed young men, but none were Tim. In fact, each casualty was an individual who affected so many other lives.

*

I was Tim Fitzgerald, trapped in a mangled body far below the surface, swimming out of long-ago frozen gullies, leaving an almost imperceptible trace: carbonate imprints on rock and earth. I still remember the feeling of arms and legs—the feeling of blood rushing through my body not out of it. All the clarity in my soul trapped and rattling around in a stuttering echo well. I remember not being able to articulate even the simplest phrase. I tried to make them laugh with my eyes. Then, where water once coursed down, down, where lungs are aching, eardrums bleeding, my saw-edged spine nearly invisible as it circled round and around, I became shape neither angel nor devil, wings floating on a current that swelled, neither angel nor devil, assuming the semblance of God's messenger at the periphery. I still remember. I remember a face, a woman's face. A woman I might have, no, a woman I came to love. She read to me. Then further back, a girl's face. Then my mother's face. A boy's face, my own. I remember. I remember love.

*

Thinking about Tim at the strangest times, Grace felt as if he were often standing near, his shadow free of physical constraints and pain. There were things she wanted to tell him but hoped he knew. Knew more than she could imagine.

So, the call finally came. That call. The one she did not believe was possible at the moment it shattered her reverie five years after she had tentatively waded into the waters of history and finished her Ph.D. She picked up the receiver. Without the money her aunt left her in order to explore a new career, none of it would have been possible.

Her cell phone was in her purse where she couldn't hear it or see the messages. Apparently, she had turned off the ringer and hit buzzer by mistake. Then she was talking to a professor with a strong Boston accent. "Yes," she wanted to tell him before he finished speaking. She hoped she sounded articulate in setting up the interview, later finding out she was more than convincing, after fielding questions from the stern-faced committee—another time and place in the not-too-distant future—when Dean Alwes offered her the job. She would be teaching freshmen, he said, an introductory course, but it could be a "tenure track, not an adjunct position." She could make of it what she chose. The opportunity was there.

The new job meant benefits and some modicum of security if such a term were still relevant in the contemporary educational environment.

The irony of looking for security when she had deliberately given it up was not lost, of course. Alwes mentioned the importance of continuing to publish, the fact being a requirement some found difficult to handle, but what was such a stipulation after everything? She avoided sarcasm or even telling him how much she loved to write—or of her relief, even joy publishing was the burden he thought he was placing on her. Alwes had read only excerpts from her dissertation and a couple of her published articles but apparently approved. It didn't hurt she had already published a number of papers while she was still in her doctoral program.

Just like that, Grace accepted the job offer without calling Jason. Only after she said yes, did she mildly panic and attempt to text her son before giving in and calling.

"Honey?"

"Mom. What's wrong? You never text. What going on?" Jason sounded nervous. "I didn't have a chance to answer your text before you called."

"You never answer your phone, so I tried texting first. I've taken a job." He's right, she thought, she never texted, never actually wrote anyone LOL or OMG. Something was different, and it surprised her.

"Great! A college job or high school?" She heard his hesitation.

"Yes. Yes, college."

"Where?"

"It's a liberal arts small college in Boston, well, actually in Norton,

Mass."

"Oh?"

"Wheaton."

"I've never heard of it."

She laughed. "Well, you're going to hear a lot more about it, I suspect. I won't be living here any longer." She wanted to talk about her new job but thought she had better get this decision about the house out of the way. "Are you okay with this? My moving?" Was she all right with this decision? She wondered. The cabin had been her parents' gift to her. It had served as more than a home; it had been her sanctuary and security, the one place where she found peace. Agitation and guilt resurfaced over letting go of even that part of her past, part of herself. But, one thing she had learned about history is, you are forever connected to it.

"Are you kidding? Of course I'm okay with it. Yes. I just want you to be happy." Jason was relieved for her, for himself. She could hear the energy in his excited state. Sammy jumped up on the chair and nosed the phone, trying to get closer to Jason's voice. Grace pushed the pup's head down gently, but he persisted.

"Apparently, Sammy's excited, too," she said before adding, "it'll mean some big changes. You can stay at the house as long as you want, though."

"So, you're not selling it?"

"No. At least not now—maybe never. I don't know. If I can get by without selling it, I'd rather not." Although she tried telling herself she was keeping it for Jason, she knew the reason was far more selfish.

"It's okay with me if you do, though. Are you renting it out? If not, maybe I'll come to stay in the summer. You don't want to leave it unoccupied for too long, with vacant house insurance and everything."

"I know. But how do you know about such things?" She laughed.

Grace hadn't even thought about insurance on an unoccupied building or renting out the cottage before this. Something else she would have to attend to but not that night. There were a lot of decisions she had not completely thought through, but then she was feeling hopeful for the first time in such a long while. She could get a neighbor to look in on the cottage for a while, at least until she decided what to do with it permanently. "I guess I haven't quite decided yet," she said.

Jason heard her doubt. "Maybe you should sell it. You know I plan to move to New York—the city after I get a job there."

"New York City can be dangerous." As soon as she said it out loud, she realized how ridiculous it sounded, and she knew she didn't mean it, but she still felt helpless about offering no protection for her son in the wide world. He, too, had already faced so much loss, and there was more to come. Always. For everyone. Inescapable.

"Really? Mom, I know. Probably any place can be dangerous if you're in the wrong place at the wrong time, and you're going to Boston! Good city, by the way. I happen to like New York's energy." Jason's words made her feel silly and old. She could almost picture his head turned quizzically to see if she was going to be all right or not. She knew she sounded more ridiculous when talking to her son than when she conversed with almost anyone else on the planet.

"I know you do. You're right, of course. New York is also fascinating and exciting and full of opportunities and life. I hope the same for Boston. It's a new start for both of us." She wanted for him and herself such opportunities and excitement, just to be alive in our messy, disastrous, frightening, painful, sometimes amazing and wondrous condition.

He changed the topic abruptly. "You might miss it, though. The lake, I mean, if not grandpa and grandma's cabin."

"You're right. I know I will. And I just want to keep it until I have time to think about it some more. I also want you to have a place to come home to," she corrected herself. "I mean, maybe I still need the idea of being able to come home even if I don't actually follow up on it." Just saying the words made her feel like she was losing the concept of home if she hadn't already lost it.

"You don't need to keep the cabin for me. I'll come to wherever you are. Home can be anywhere."

Grace was crying silently, holding it back the best she could. She knew how much her son hated it when she cried, and she did not want to cry either. Her typically steady voice had a pitchy sound to it she was aware of but unable to alter. She breathed deeply before going forward with the conversation.

"Mom, are you okay? You're not crying, right? Mom?"

She pretended to cough. "No. Fine. Fine. I'm just a little nervous about this whole new adventure. Okay, I'm a lot nervous."

"Don't be. You'll do great there. Hey, can you get a place that will let you have Sammy? Is it going to be a problem? I mean, I guess I could take him for—" The thought had just occurred to him, and the first real edge in his voice surfaced.

"Of course, Sammy is going where I go. Any apartment I take will have to have a small yard or at least a park or some grass nearby and an extra bedroom or at least a couch for you." She had no idea at the time how difficult finding a new home was going to be. In the meantime, she had discovered a week-to-week rental that allowed a small pet. The wonders of the Internet. She knew it had to be a disaster, the rental, but then finding her new residence could only get better from there.

"By the way, I'm proud of you," he said.

"I'm proud of you, too." They both meant it, and then they hung up, quickly, before Grace started bawling into the receiver. Instead, though, she felt better than okay. There was simply too much to do.

And, it seemed an instant later, she was packing her bags, Sammy biting the laces on her old running shoes as she tried to stuff them into one of the suitcases. She had to offer him a dog treat just to let go. Grace was pretty sure shoe laces were not particularly digestible although Sammy had proven almost everything in life can be ingested. The packing would be different this time, she thought, realizing how much she would be leaving behind. Perhaps we leave nothing behind really, she reconsidered, suddenly envisioning Tim.

This dealing with history meant she was always looking back in order to figure out the present, let alone the future, whatever that meant or if it existed at all. The pain of the past was not in the least offset by the angst of the nebulous future. Then she was thinking about Faulkner and Sartre and metaphysics, considering ideas about the future not existing, she told Sammy some amalgamation related to it.

Her dog apparently had taken no position on her speculations or those literary and philosophical debates which lay mostly in the dreams of the subconscious if not in scholarly texts. Dogs live in the very conscious and unselfconscious world of present. Yet they always seemed to remember the way home, she thought.

"Sammy, you're going to have to make some big changes," she told him as she ruffled his shiny black coat and rubbed a white spot under one ear. She thought about how dogs are comforting even as they create messes, chew valuables, and establish disorder as the natural order. Cocking his head to the side, he, of course, didn't answer Grace but looked expectant, ready to go.

She brought along her cellphone on their nightly walk, then held it as she moved along the road, calling Holly. "No, I won't be coming back any time soon," she said in answer to Holly's question. "But I promise you a place to stay in Boston whenever you want to visit."

"My second favorite city," Holly said, sounding and acting more like her old self. "Hey, I see you changed your name. I mean, you took your old name back, your maiden name Collier. Does it feel strange? Do you miss your lyrical Storey last name?"

Grace had finally gotten around to changing all her records, waiting for the papers and her license with her maiden name again. "No." she lied. "It's a relief, but what a hassle to change everything. Still, I'm glad I made the decision." How could she not miss the last name Storey?

"I'm thinking of changing mine back, too. Maybe you could help me through the process sometime. It can't be too difficult, right? But since you've already done it, it should be easier for you, you know."

"Of course," Grace said, thinking about how her married name would no longer appear next to anything of hers, but a large part of her felt the sadness of losing such a wonderful name, as much for its lyricism as well as for all the connections to her younger self, to her history with Bill. It was her son's last name, too.

"You're my inspiration, you know." Holly was still struggling, Grace knew, and she was not sure if anything she said could help her friend at the moment. She tried, however.

"You're a great friend, Holly. You need to visit when you can get away; it's not far. Five hours by car."

"Too far for my liking, but I'm happy for you. I suppose I have to be." The slight hint of betrayal followed its way into her tone.

"You said it was your second favorite city. What's your first?"

"This one. Nothing like the old Salt City; I'll miss you, though." Grace detected just a slight edge in her voice. "I'm trying to imagine leaving everything," she said at last. "I can't believe you are doing this," Holly said coughing into the phone, "it's so radical even for you." But Grace could almost see approval on Holly's face. "What am I saying? Of course, I can believe you're doing this."

"Good. It's something I have to do." They both knew Grace had paved the way for working toward a new life within life. If Holly ever decided to follow her friend, Grace had a few connections which wouldn't hurt in the interview process, and Holly was not too proud to ask for her help.

"I'll come visit," Holly said, and Grace knew her friend would because Holly had long talked about trying something new herself. "I might even join you in that city one of these days."

Boston suddenly sounded like paradise although Grace was pretty certain she would find the city's many faults after she arrived and was living there. It was true of any location. "Until then, the invitation is open any time."

"I won't say good-bye. You're not going to make me cry."

"Talk to you later then."

"Miss you."

"I will miss you, too." Then Holly was gone.

Grace had circled back to her cabin and entered. Sammy bounded back toward her, dragging blue yarn she realized came from Jenna's old hooked rug in the entrance. No point in getting upset about it now. One less bulky item she would have to pack. There was more work to be done, but Sammy looked anxious, so they played catch and retrieve, a game the pup never tired of, the motions ridding him of excess energy while she stared through the big lake window, watching the changing waterscape, the dance of refracted light on waves—wondrous. Her dog's muzzle approximated a smile as he returned the ball time and again. How many times had she looked at the lake and not stopped to acknowledge how transformative it was? No, she knew.

It was almost dark when Grace finished packing. She felt with assurance she would miss the place horribly; was not even sure she could manage without letting those waters wash over her thoughts every evening. Outside, buzzing against the windows, a growing number of mosquitoes were swarming. She turned away from the water and land she loved, would always love.

"We're leaving, Sammy," she called out as he jumped up and muddied her jeans. She lit a fire in her little camp for the last time, broke open a bottle of red wine she had been saving for another occasion, and settled Sammy down with a chew toy before returning to labeling box lids.

As she taped boxes while savoring the oaky taste of the wine, she wondered if anyone would trace her footsteps. Grace thought about the absurdity of such musings, as if anyone would ever want to know what she was thinking or where she was going. She knew; however, she was going to be okay with the fact no one would be searching for her. She was no longer looking for Bill to ask her for forgiveness. God, she thought, the realization was at least three years after the day he left. Although she never entirely accepted how or why he had stopped loving her, she had come to some understanding. It was also apparent she had long since stopped loving him. Dealing with death and dying had been too much in her thoughts for Bill to handle. Melancholy takes its toll. She was determined not to dwell in a place that offered only anger and sadness.

Grace had stopped, finally stopped, imagining Bill coming home to tell her how wrong he was to leave. In fact, she could no longer conceive of taking him back; nor would she want to. She had even forgiven him for being happy with Beth and life, for not knowing the ways his ex-wife had changed. Extended grief has a way of altering you down to your cells.

Picturing Susannah looking out over fields from the window of her home with William standing beside her, Grace wondered if her ancestor forever imagined Ezra walking home. No, that was not right. Susa, like

Grace, wanted to fully love and live again. She must have found falling in love with William was a surprise. Susa would likely have wondered if William sensed the old longing still in her. Trying to solve the mystery of why her Ezra never returned, Susannah carried on, reared her children, loved her new husband as well as she could. The children would have come to think of William as their father. It was not disloyalty but more than the need to simply survive, to thrive in our short existence.

Ezra's letters never completely revealed what Grace was asking for from them. Inference, however articulately enumerated, remained in a murky realm. When she began her historical search, she was looking for more than history, outside of what historical records could reveal. Grace realized she was seeking answers in one of the letters or all of them together, as if in reading them over and over, she would finally discover the meaning of it all, some explanation of losses, death, and how we go on, how we survive knowing the certainty of our own terrible losses and death. Of course, the historian was also looking for the less nebulous answers, too: what had happened to Ezra? Why had he never returned? How was Susa able to keep going from a practical standpoint, not an existential one?

Returning to Susa again and again, Grace tried to imagine from Ezra's written responses to his wife what she thought of her husband, and how Susa resolved to live her life knowing her fate was no longer tied to her husband's. Grace must have believed early on those answers were hidden in the letters, subtext rather than text, but those primary documents—although counted, studied, and catalogued for qualitative analysis—remained nearly as mysterious as the first day she opened the box her aunt left behind. If Grace were to have resolution, she would have to provide her own interpretations or accept the unresolved.

"Grace?" It was Bill's now unfamiliar, strained voice on the phone.

"Yes?"

"Bill."

"Yes."

"Jason told me you got a new job in Boston—some little college, he said."

"I did."

"Good. I mean, that's nice. I'm happy for you; you got a job. I mean, you have a new job. Sorry, this is a little awkward. I think the move will be good for you."

"I'm happy for me, too. Thanks."

"I just—I mean I thought—I"

"It's fine, Bill. I'm happy for you and Beth, as well."

He wanted to ask something more but did not. Perhaps he was worried about some new financial burden on him, but she had reassured him on that account long ago.

They hung up. What more was there to say between them? "Goodbye."

Some goodbyes were much harder than others. Pale shades of Tim and Ezra must have made peace with the cruelty of their fates. Although she would never know for certain, Grace felt closer to her ghosts while they passed from one state of being to another, almost as if Ezra had been waiting for her to discover him in order to be fully at peace.

Apparently, she was not done living with ghosts. Grace was almost certain Susannah was the woman she imagined her to be. Susannah had endured. Susa continued living and rearing her children after all of the violence and destruction, a country torn in two, ripped to its core. But the evidence of Susa's determination and triumph was there in Grace's own birth—her ancestry. Long without a partner or even a house to plant her life, Susa started again, had more children, carried on. The fact Susa left none of her own letters to Ezra behind did not stop discovery.

"Drop, Sammy," she yelled, as the pup looked guilty before letting go of the stray sock.

Carefully placing the photo of Ezra Cross into a labeled plastic bin, she knew locking him away would not keep her great-great-grandfather from her thoughts. She had given him three endings—all imagined, but there were other possibilities, like her own ending. Each choice we make changes the next moment. If delving into history only allowed her time to comfort herself rather than fully understand events, then it was still welcome. Snapping the lid shut, Grace could feel Ezra disappearing as she locked him away, knowing full well she, too, would vanish in time, joining him in that invisible realm.

For a fleeting instant, she could see Jason, as a middle-aged man, closing the box on her own life—hopefully, years from the moment she packed to leave the cabin. She wistfully believed her son would do it with some tenderness and fond remembrances of his mother.

All the while she stored artifacts, Grace was certain her footsteps, like Tim's and Susa's and Ezra's, and Jenna's and Richard's, were already falling away, fading despite our all too human efforts to hold onto those we love. If in looking for them, she found entrance into their narratives, found a way to walk with them for at least a little while, then she had revealed her story in the process, acknowledged the written and unwritten pages in the making, those still waiting, as long as someone has the courage to keep looking, to keep writing, to keep living until even history is lost.

TWENTY-NINE

What cant bee cured must be endured

A few months later, Grace was comfortably settled in a studio apartment in Brookline, on the Southwestern edge of Boston, remaking her life just as Susannah did long before her but not in the same way. Her commute to Norton was far worse than she had first imagined, but she also found time in the car to be therapeutic—time to let go of the day and the stresses of teaching in exchange for allowing her imagination to take root even as she navigated traffic. Susannah, it turned out, had been her inspiration, not Ezra. Women had been losing and been abused forever, but she knew she was part of the tribe creating and enduring, too.

As to whether Grace met another history professor with an interest in the Civil War, she briefly thought about moving in with a kind man on the North End where they would begin collecting first edition texts. He might read to her in bed before they made love or not. They went out to dinner nearly every night, and Boston came to be familiar. With the Professor, initially, there was budding friendship and comradery, but gradually, Grace fell in love again. Or not.

It is all speculation from here on out. What is known is she was not the same woman whose husband left her years earlier. Grief had leveled her for a time. Her divorce had nearly wrecked her then made her nearly immune for a while, yet she lived through that, too, and reinvented herself. She discovered she was more than fine alone as well as with someone she might or might not love.

Romance could have happened in a number of other ways: she could possibly have fallen into an intense sexual affair with a younger man, relationship slowly evolving into friendship and, later, love or not. Either one of these professors—because those were the people she met and most often interacted with—might have broken it off at any point in time, but one or the other might not. He, like she, had been divorced once and wanted to make this relationship work. Making relationships work, however, is always fraught because we are human.

*

Then again, maybe Grace considered returning to her cottage on the small lake in Central New York, had another change of heart, packed and unpacked her things, decided to go back to teaching high school English—or maybe history this time—in familiar surroundings, returning to a place she had once loved. Her movements mirrored her emotional state in all of these and other potential futures with each moment of imploding past changing the outcome.

What was certain was the fact she could alter her future each time she changed course, and her state of contentment depended upon her decisions and not those of someone else. She had her grown son and pride in his independence, but she had come to know pride in herself, as well.

Grace did, in all her narratives about what was to come, cease cataloging only losses and began once again considering and embracing the enormous gifts found in living. Interacting with those lives she had discovered, and always searching for the stories of others in the process of continuing to make and re-make her own.

Whatever her weaknesses as an historian, she finally knew she could survive and create another story.

Nancy Avery Dafoe takes on the way we look at history and ourselves as proscribed by historians in this novel about the disappearance of a Civil War soldier and the woman he left at home. *Yet in the Land of the Living* is also very much about our present, the way in which women find resilience and strength even in adversity and sorrow. Resonating throughout this work of fiction is the voice of the author's actual great-great-grandfather Lafayette Cross through his letters home from the battlefields in the Civil War, letters preserved across the ages.

Dafoe is an educator and the author of sixteen books in the genres of fiction, memoir, fable, educational texts, and poetry. Her published work has won national awards for poetry, short stories, memoir, and fiction, including the William Faulkner/William Wisdom Creative Writing Award in poetry; the New Century Writers Award in the short story; the Human Relations Indie Book Award in fiction for *Socrates is Dead Again*; and the Director's Choice for Book of the Year from the Human Relations Indie Book Awards for her memoir *Unstuck in Time*.

Her work appears in numerous journals and anthologies. Dafoe is also the editor or co-editor of several anthologies including the collection *A Domain of Her Own* and *Lost Orchard II*.

She lives in Central New York on Little York Lake with her husband Daniel and their dog Lincoln.

www.ingramcontent.com/pod-product-compliance
Lightning Source LLC
Chambersburg PA
CBHW050440200726
48295CB00024B/743